UNZIPPED

LAUREN BLAKELY

ALSO BY LAUREN BLAKELY

Big Rock Series

Big Rock

Mister O

Well Hung

Full Package

Joy Ride

Hard Wood

One Love Series dual-POV Standalones

The Sexy One

The Only One

The Hot One

Sports Romance

Most Valuable Playboy

Most Likely to Score

Standalones

The Knocked Up Plan

Stud Finder

The V Card

Wanderlust

Come As You Are

Part-Time Lover

The Real Deal

Unbreak My Heart

Far Too Tempting

21 Stolen Kisses

Playing With Her Heart

Out of Bounds

Unzipped

Birthday Suit (2019)

Best Laid Plans (2019)

The Feel Good Factor (2019)

The Heartbreakers Series

Once Upon a Real Good Time

Once Upon a Sure Thing

Once Upon a Wild Fling

The Caught Up in Love Series

Caught Up In Us

Pretending He's Mine

Trophy Husband

Stars In Their Eyes Duet

My Charming Rival

My Sexy Rival

The No Regrets Series

The Thrill of It

The Start of Us

Every Second With You

The Seductive Nights Series

First Night (Julia and Clay, prequel novella)

Night After Night (Julia and Clay, book one)

After This Night (Julia and Clay, book two)

One More Night (Julia and Clay, book three)

A Wildly Seductive Night (Julia and Clay novella, book 3.5)

The Joy Delivered Duet

Nights With Him (A standalone novel about Michelle and Jack)

Forbidden Nights (A standalone novel about Nate and Casey)

The Sinful Nights Series

Sweet Sinful Nights

Sinful Desire

Sinful Longing

Sinful Love

The Fighting Fire Series

Burn For Me (Smith and Jamie)

Melt for Him (Megan and Becker)

Consumed By You (Travis and Cara)

The Jewel Series

A two-book sexy contemporary romance series

The Sapphire Affair

The Sapphire Heist

ABOUT UNZIPPED

Picture this - I'm ready to win back the love of my life, and I'm going big this time. We're talking boom box, sing her name in the rain, let the whole damn neighborhood know I'm good and ready this time around. After all, if you're going to grand gesture the ever-loving hell out of a second chance, you need to pull out all the stops.

There's only one little problem.

My college girlfriend isn't the one who shows up when I play my "I'll do anything to win you back" tune.

The woman who flings open the second-floor window tells me my ex doesn't live here anymore. But she'll help me win her back. Anything for romance, anything for a guy so willing to go big for love. And that's what I want at first. Until I get to know my new "romance coach" and discover she's funny, clever, and keeps me on my toes. And boy, do I ever need that.

Now I don't want to win anyone else's heart. I want the woman who's been helping me all along.

Trouble is - she thinks I'm in love with someone else, and when we take off on a road trip, everything I think I know about women is about to be unzipped and turned inside out.

PROLOGUE

Him

Everything I know about women I learned from an '80s flick.

For instance, eating birthday cake while sitting on a dining room table is always a good idea.

"Ditto" completely works as a way to let a woman know how you feel.

Men and women can be friends, and friends can fall in love, but it's best if they don't fake orgasms.

Finally, learning your soul mate is a fish is not the worst thing that can happen. The worst thing is losing the mermaid you love, so merman-up and be with her under the sea. But if you're stupid enough to let the girl get away, the surefire way to win a woman back is with a grand gesture.

That's what I intend to do.

I've planned every detail of how I'm going to get the girl back.

Music? Check.

Props? Check.

Totally improved self? It took nearly a decade, but finally I can scratch that off the list.

It's *go* time.

1

HER

There are only a few things you truly need to be successful in comedy.

To make people laugh, to make people laugh, and to make people laugh.

See what's in there? No, not the laughter, but the people. You need an audience. Or, really, *I* need an audience. A bigger one.

Make that an exponentially larger one.

I dive into the pool at the gym on a Thursday morning in late May, determined to use my lap time to devise a brand-new, brilliant idea to get that audience for my TV show.

The first order of business—let go of distractions. Thankfully, my phone can't ring in the water.

Well, I suppose it technically can ring while I'm in the water, but I can't hear it since I didn't stuff it inside my swimsuit, and I haven't yet resorted to wearing a waterproof Bluetooth headset. If I did, I'd ask my best friend, Christine, to have me committed for crossing every acceptable social line.

I push through the water, goggles snug against my eyes, doing my best to open my mind to new ideas and fresh concepts. I reach the end of the lap lane, smack my palm against the smooth blue tiles, and flip around, shooting like a dolphin the other way.

Water ripples from the next lane, and when I turn my head to the side, a man in a black Speedo is torpedoing through the chlorinated blue, his flipper-like feet propelling him.

Big feet? Would that work as a bit? Maybe an episode about whether big feet really mean men have . . . the need to wear big shoes.

Nah. Dick jokes are low-hanging fruit.

But what about Speedos?

Speedos are always ripe for comedy. You can double the laughter if the banana holders are in a funny color, and the funniest colors are usually orange, green, and yellow.

As I breaststroke my way down the lane, I ask myself what Seinfeld would do with a Speedo bit. That was a show that defined top-notch laughs. It didn't even rely on romance. It didn't depend on tropes, over-the-top setups, or a quota of jokes based on bodily functions.

Because . . . eww.

All I have to do is connect the Speedo to some sort of social commentary like Seinfeld would do.

What if my heroine is shopping for a new bathing suit for herself? That has potential because bathing suit shopping ranks on the awful list next to root canal and running into an ex while not wearing makeup.

Let's suppose our heroine is at a department store trying on a bikini, and she spots a guy next to her in the dressing room testing out a Speedo, and she can't help herself. She has to comment on it, big mouth that she is. She's trying to be helpful, and she wants to save him from buying the Speedo, but he misunderstands her, thinking she's hitting on him. That's perfect, since the heart of *Mars and Venus* is finding humor in the confusion between men and women about what the other says and what the other truly means.

Satisfied with this direction, I finish my laps and park my elbows on the edge of the pool so I can catch my breath. The scent of chlorine is thick in the air, but so is possibility. I can save my show this season, starting with a bright yellow Speedo.

I climb out of the pool and head to the women's locker room, feeling pretty damn pleased with myself. After a quick shower, I tug on a pair of shorts and a tank top then root around in my bag for my phone.

I cringe when I see the screen cluttered with notifications fighting their way to get to me.

Seven missed calls.

My stomach pitches with worry. It's never good to have seven missed calls as a TV comedy writer. The only thing worse is when your phone mocks you with quiet.

Silence equals no work.

But this many missed calls? It's the universal sign you're about to get served Really Bad News.

Like when a dude in a fedora shows up on your doorstep. *Are you Finley Barker?*

Yes.

You've been served.

Hustling out of the community center and into the bright morning sun of Hope Falls, I drop my rhinestone-studded purple shades on my eyes—because life is too short to wear boring black sunglasses—and race-walk out to the quaint side street, stabbing at the contact information for Bruce Fargo, the VP at LGO, the TV network that carries my show.

I swear he answers before it even rings. "Finley," he barks. "What took you so long? I've been calling you all morning. It's been hours."

I look at my waterproof watch. "I was doing cardio," I say, defending myself as I walk past a vineyard in the heart of our wine country town. Cardio is like a free pass, right? Everyone in the entertainment business knows workouts are sacred. "And I was only away from my phone for thirty—"

"Network brass is breathing down my neck."

"With a twenty-two-episode offer for a second season renewal?" I ask, my voice rising as high as Minnie Mouse on helium.

My show hasn't even been renewed for a second season yet.

He scoffs. "Funny. Why don't you work that kind of dry humor into *Mars and Venus*?"

"Thanks, I'll —" But before I can say *try my best*, he slices into my words with a serrated knife.

"Your show is on the chopping block."

I stop, grabbing the wooden fence post next to a vine of Chardonnay grapes. My legs turn into rubber bands, and my stomach becomes a salad spinner.

"Are you serious?" I ask, the words tasting like dreams dying on my tongue.

"I'm as serious as a pimple on a teenager's face. You think I'd joke about that?"

About pimples? Doubtful. About my show's fate? I wish he were joking, but I know he's not.

Hope leaks out of me like air from a punctured balloon. "How far on the chopping block? Are we talking the executioner has the ax out and my head is already hooded, or am I being walked to the guillotine—"

He has no patience for analogies. "This is how it's going to work. Tad and Chad are demanding a strong storyline," he huffs, naming the top execs at LGO. "Like blow-my-mind-and-make-me-die-laughing-so-fucking-hard-I have-a-hernia storyline."

"I can do that," I say, optimism returning. This is what I do. I write storylines. That's not too far on the chopping block. I breathe a small sigh of relief. "I had all these ideas this morning, and I'm about to start working on a new story arc. The first episode will make them laugh till it hurts."

"Yeah, that's the issue."

My stomach plummets. "What's the issue?" I ask slowly.

"They're asking for that knock-their-socks-off story-line before they even agree to renew it." He pauses, giving weight to his already-heavy words. "For six episodes. That's it, sweetheart."

I press a hand to my stomach as if I could quell the churning. But it's a cyclone inside me as I learn my show is on death's door, and I don't know if CPR is enough to revive it. *Mars and Venus* is my baby. It's my dream. I've worked on it for years. I fought to have it made.

"Six episodes?" I repeat, as if the words will change if I say them again. A six-episode storyline on spec simply to claw your way out of the ratings basement is like Luke, Leia, Han, and Chewie trying to escape the trash compactor.

Meaning it's epically unlikely, except on film.

"Count 'em. You only get a half dozen episodes, and that's *if* you can turn the ship around with a brilliant storyline. Otherwise, there's no green light. It's *Goodnight Moon*."

I furrow my brow. "I don't think that's what *Goodnight Moon* was about," I say quietly.

"The kids' book? Never read it. So let me make this clear in TV writer lingo." He takes a beat, his voice somehow going gruffer. "They'll *sunset* you."

Bruce loves to grab sayings from TV shows and movies, usually ones involving cool and cruel crime bosses issuing directives to underlings. "Got it now?"

I swallow past the lump in my throat. I will not let Bruce hear me cry. "I understand. I know what *sunset*, used as a verb, means." My heart is a limp doll in my chest, torn down the middle.

He sighs, and it borders on sympathetic. "The sooner, the better. And, hey, I believe in your talent. I'll fight for you, kid."

I'm not a kid. I'm twenty-nine. But that's neither here nor there. "Thanks, Bruce."

"Also, it's just going to be you. No other writers for this," he says, since most TV shows have a head writer as well as a team.

"I can write it solo. I write most of the key scenes

anyway." I swallow any remaining morsel of pride. "Any advice on how to proceed with the storyline for these six episodes?"

Bruce is the network VP in charge of my show, so he has a vested interest. The more successful the shows he brings to his higher-ups, the more money he makes.

"Yeah. Go make up some funny stuff, and don't take too long."

"Besides that."

"Fine," he huffs, and I imagine he's tapping a pen on a too-big desk. "How about a bit with a monkey? Monkeys are always funny."

"A monkey?" I ask, incredulous. "A monkey is going to save my show in six episodes?"

"Monkeys are comedy gold." His tone tells me he's dead serious.

"Should this primate be a recurring character or a new series regular?"

"Slap a diaper on him and make him a regular."

That sounds like when you remember a show from your childhood as brilliant, but when you watch it again years later, you ask with abject horror what your younger self was thinking.

"Do you think perhaps a monkey in a diaper is old-school funny?" I ask, trying to let him down gently.

"I'm old-school funny, honey, and you're new school. Your new-school hipster show about men and women just being friends isn't cutting it. So maybe you ought to lean on old-school funny."

Ouch.

I'll have the bruise marks on my ego for days from that gut punch.

"I'll do that, Bruce. I'll work on old-school funny," I say, since I don't have any bargaining chips.

"But listen, Fin. I'm rooting for you. Maybe add a kissing scene too. Some flirting. Dress your lead in fish-nets. You want to run anything past me, you know where to find me."

"Thanks," I say, but he's already hung up.

I stare at the phone as if it's a device from an alien planet.

Maybe I should have tucked it into my bathing suit. Maybe it would have been better waterlogged.

With leaden feet, I walk to my lemon-yellow, two-story rental home on the outskirts of town.

I unlock the door, my mind speeding away from me as I recall the bundle of enthusiasm the network execs wrapped me up in when they picked up the show after years of me pitching, writing, revising, getting rejected. Lather, rinse, repeat.

It's about real life! We love it! Don't make it like everything else on TV. We want something different! Be quirky! Screw the tropes!

That's what I delivered for the first thirteen episodes —a baker's dozen of shows that were critically acclaimed, but disastrously under-watched. The ratings are so low it feels like I could personally email every viewer and ask for tips for new storylines. Hell, I could visit their homes and serve them pancakes for breakfast while shooting the breeze on what they like and don't like about Lane and Amanda, my hero and heroine.

My stomach rumbles as I lock the door, wanting those pancakes.

As I head toward the kitchen, shock still rippling

through me, I wonder if there is un-mined comedy in pancakes. Some hilarious bit about that time Amanda went to a friend's house and her friend served those terrible pancakes from Trader Joe's that taste like soap, and Amanda called them soap cakes, and that becomes a bit on what to do when a host serves awful food?

Best friends and former roomies Amanda and Lane would laugh about it, and it would help them buddy-comedy their way back to living under the same roof.

But as I turn on the coffee maker, I don't know if soap cakes are funny.

As the coffee drips, I don't even know if Speedos are funny. And I should know the answer to that.

Most of all, I don't have a clue how the hell I'm going to pull this off in a mere six episodes.

The ironic thing is that deep down in the squishy, soft part of my heart, I knew this was coming.

But knowing something is coming doesn't make it hurt any less.

With a cup of joe in hand, I flip open my laptop and try to play with all the ways a lime-green Speedo can spawn humor.

2

HIM

This is a foolproof blueprint.

I run through a drill one final time in the driveway of my brother's home in Oakland. Everything goes off without a hitch. When I'm done, I hold my hands out wide, raise my eyebrows, and ask, "Am I ready or am I absolutely, no-questions-asked, one hundred percent good to go?"

"I'd say you're ready, but are you really doing this?" My oldest brother, Ransom, marches up to me, a curious glint in his brown eyes, his infant son attached to his chest, courtesy of a Baby Björn.

"You don't think I should?"

He laughs, shaking his head. "I think it could definitely work. But I also think a phone call could work."

I cut a hand through the air. "No way. Phone calls are for guys who don't make an effort."

"That's clearly not you."

"Damn straight. I am the king of effort." I narrow my

eyes, the same shade as his. "Besides, didn't you win Delia's heart like this?"

He seesaws his hand. "Not entirely like this. But I did propose to her at the office and carried her out of there like Richard Gere did Debra Winger."

"Minus the naval uniform."

"Obviously."

I point to his kid and the home behind them, the reminders that life can work out fantastically if you big-gesture a woman the right way. "So it worked."

He holds up his left hand and wiggles his ring finger. "Damn straight."

"And this will work." I look at his son, talking in a singsong voice. "What do you think, Harlan?"

The three-month-old gurgles.

"Clearly, he agrees with me," I say.

"Then you better hit the road. You need to be there at dusk. Timing is everything."

It's my turn to laugh him off. "I'm an engineer. I'm well aware of the need for precision timing. I built in time for traffic, for unexpected road closures, and for any other unforeseen circumstances."

"You're such a nerd."

I smile proudly, owning it. "I believe I'm what's known as a hot nerd."

He rolls his eyes. "You do know you're not hot, right?"

"We share the same genes so if I'm an ugly bastard, you are too."

"Takes one to know one," he says, clapping my back as we say goodbye in our usual style.

I let go and tap the hood of my Tesla, giving myself a final pep talk. "I'm ready. As ready as I'll ever be."

"I can't believe it's been eight years since you were a sophomore in college. I hope you wind up taking her to Nash's restaurant tonight." Our brother works as a sous chef a few towns over from where I'm headed.

I salute him. "I'll report back later."

I open the door to my car, switch my regular black glasses for prescription shades, and head up the coast.

May was the month when my college girlfriend issued her directive at the end of what was shaping up to be an epic night.

Try again when you get your act together. Show up when you know what you want.

She made it clear what I needed to do, and I've spent the past eight years doing exactly that. I have become the kind of man who deserves a woman like her.

The first few years of college, I was aimless. The consummate slacker, I hardly knew what I wanted. With her sharp, swift kick, I got my act together, focused all my energies for once, pulled my average grades up, completed my engineering degree, earned a master's, and went on to become a designer of thrill rides.

So yeah, I owe her big-time.

And from what I've seen on social media, the girl I once thought of as the best thing I'd ever done is successful, funny, and just as beautiful as she was then. Better yet, even though I haven't friend-requested her and learned the true skinny on her life—I don't want to ruin the surprise—Facebook shows her relationship status as "single." Now that's something worth pulling out a grand gesture for.

Especially since I haven't met anyone since who can hold a candle to her.

Fine, calling her might be easier. Picking up the phone and asking her to dinner could work too.

But why do anything halfway?

You either go big or go home.

No one ever said the big gesture was easy. That's why they work. They show that the hero is busting his ass to win back the woman.

As I exit the highway into the little wine country town, I don't see how she can say no.

Ione Skye couldn't turn down John Cusack, after all.

* * *

The thing you learn as an engineer is to prepare. To plan. And to test scenarios.

Don't go into any situation blind. The more data you have, the better off you'll be.

I looked up my girl on Zillow. I checked property records. Not like a stalker checking out an ex, because that's not cool, and I aim to be cool. Especially since I spent so much of my younger years being thoroughly uncool. Which might explain why I do my damnedest to avoid social media now. I'm not sure I'd know what to say or post, so why bother?

Since I still have Cassie's phone number—a reverse number search tells me she didn't change it from college —the plan is to call her and ask her to come to the window.

But first, since I'm one hour and twenty-seven minutes early, I stop at a coffee shop, grab an iced tea, and review the projects I'm working on, as well as the requests to use my patented safety feature. I check the time, tuck my phone into my jeans, and head to the restroom to brush my teeth. Fresh breath is a prerequisite for any big gesture. I comb my fingers through my thick brown hair then nod at my reflection.

Yep, I look good.

I get back in my car, turn on the GPS, and head to her home, smiling as I set eyes on it. *Yellow.* Her favorite color.

Somehow, seeing she hasn't changed that much makes me feel like this can work. She didn't need to change. I did. I park a block away and do my best to ignore the nerves that are flickering around in my chest.

Tom Cruise wasn't nervous when he was being chased by Guido the Killer Pimp. I don't need to be, and my hero, Lloyd Dobler, certainly wasn't either when he pulled up in his Chevy Malibu.

I grab the clunky boom box from the front seat. Thank God for pawnshops because that's where all boom boxes have gone to die. Or to find second lives. When I picked this out amid the old electric guitars and gaudy jewelry at Twice Around, a pawnshop near where I live in San Francisco, the grizzled, tatted dude at the counter shook his head in amusement. "Never thought I'd move this bad boy," he'd said.

"Maybe it was fate that it was waiting for me," I'd suggested.

"Sure. Fate. How about forty dollars and fate can be yours?"

That was good enough for me. But tracking down a boom box of this size and shape wasn't even the hardest part. The toughest thing to do? Getting her favorite song, "Unzipped," transferred onto cassette tape. Ransom's wife said her parents were pack rats and kept everything, so she found an old mixtape in her folks' garage, and with a Mac and some elbow grease, I managed to jury-rig a solution to transfer "Unzipped" on top of Debbie Gibson, saving me the trouble of waiting for Amazon to ship me a new cassette tape.

Of course, that also means I get to give my brother's wife a hard time about how much she loved the bubblegum singer and her tunes like "Lost in Your Eyes" and "Only in My Dreams."

But then, we're not that different. Even though I was a kid in the '90s and a teen in the first decade of this century, I always felt like I was born in the wrong decade. The '80s are where it's at for me.

Technically, I could stream "Unzipped" on my iPhone and hold that above my head in the driveway.

But I could also design a roller coaster that doesn't get above twenty miles an hour. What's the point of that?

As twilight falls, I walk along the sidewalk. For a moment, I consider the risk I'm taking. Neighbors might get pissed. I could get cited by the cops for disturbing the peace.

Most likely scenario? Since I'm a glass-half-full guy, I'll say it's that the love of my life will hear our song, run out the front door, throw her arms around me, and say, "Kyler, I'd been hoping you'd show up *today*."

When I'm a few houses away, my stomach nose-diving with nerves, I dial her number. It rings, and rings, and rings.

Voicemail.

Nope. Won't go there. Dudes who leave voicemails end up on the never-date list that gets circulated to all women. I hang up.

But I don't fret, because when I reach her home, a light shines by the front window, and another one flickers upstairs. A car is parked in the driveway. A little red Honda.

Excellent.

I walk halfway up the stone path and plant my feet in a wide stance. I hit the play button and hold the silver beast high above my head at full volume, waiting for the opening notes of the ballad.

Briefly, I wonder if Lloyd Dobler felt at all like he was about to make a gigantic fool of himself. But I decide Lloyd Dobler didn't feel that way at all. No matter how dorky or nerdy he was, that dude knew how to get things done.

The tune begins, and my jaw drops.

What the hell?

No. No way. No fucking way.

Scrambling, I kneel, setting the boom box on the grass as I stab the stop button. But I hit fast-forward instead. Crap. I hit play once more, and it's Debbie Gibson, singing about her dreams, and there's no way this is happening.

No way at all.

I cannot serenade my woman with Debbie Gibson.

I can't serenade any woman with Debbie Gibson.

I need the Peter Gabriel soundalike and his rocker cool, taking it slow and easy, melting women.

I hit the fast-forward button again. The player makes

another squealing noise, and I notice a gray-haired lady a few houses down, peering over her porch swing, watching me.

I slap on a play-it-cool smile even as my heart ticks a million miles an hour.

Finally, when I reach the end of the pop princess's "Only in My Dreams," my heart rate starts to settle as "Unzipped" comes on.

Minor snafu.

That's all this is. I check out the house. She's not even at the window yet.

Whew.

I can do this. I can right this ship.

Especially since there's a shadow behind the curtain, almost as if she knew she had to wait for me to cue up the song. She knows I'm not the smoothest guy, and she's okay with that.

I hit play. Take two.

This time, our song begins, and as it echoes around me, so do memories, fantastic ones of her and me dancing, laughing, planning to spend the night together.

As the chorus starts, I see feminine fingers tugging at the white curtains at a window on the second floor.

Yes. Come a little closer.

"I want your love unzip—"

The crooner's voice shorts out and stops.

Just. Stops.

My shoulders sag, and I groan in epic frustration.

Take three.

Hitting buttons over and over again, I try to get the song to play. But no music sounds. Instead, the noise that fills the air is the boom box eating the cassette tape. This is why we went digital.

And this leaves me with only one choice.

I raise the boom box above my head a third time, and I do something I only do in the shower or the car.

Sing a cappella.

I'm no Peter Gabriel. I'm definitely no Debbie Gibson. But this will have to do.

I sing my off-key, no-one-would-even-want-to-hear-me-sing-Happy-Birthday heart out.

And what do you know? It's working. Oh hell yeah, it's working so damn well she yanks back the curtain, flings open the window, and waves.

I blink.

The woman peering back at me is definitely not Cassandra.

3

HER

It is a truth universally acknowledged that any ice cream will do when you're wallowing.

Häagen-Dazs. Ben & Jerry's. Talenti. It doesn't matter.

Mint chip. Chocolate peanut butter cup. Salted caramel. They all fit the bill.

I hold up the pint, talking like a ringmaster to my audience of one—me. "Step right up, ladies and gentlemen, children of all ages, welcome to the big top of . . . *Chunky Monkey*." I let my voice reverberate like it's carrying through the circus tent and I'm surrounded by peanuts and sawdust, a tent and a trapeze.

"Watch as the forlorn TV writer tunnels through a pint of Chunky Monkey. Marvel as she uncovers every single chunk of chocolate and consumes each piece of walnut. Thrill at the way she reaches the bottom of the container in less than thirty minutes."

I let the empty carton drop on the marble counter with a weak thump, grab a bottle of Chardonnay from the counter, and use my imaginary megaphone again. "Prepare to be amazed as she adds alcohol to the party of one."

I find a corkscrew and get to work.

Holy hell.

Did someone say opening wine isn't exercise? Because that person is dead wrong. I can literally feel my triceps growing as I speak. I am totally adding opening wine bottles to the calorie-burning counter on every website ever.

I grunt as I yank the cork higher, then at last, triumphant, I toss the cork to the ground, briefly considering whether I should use a glass.

Only *briefly*.

I down a thirsty gulp straight from the source.

I return to the kitchen counter and my open laptop, where I did indeed bang out a scene today, thank you Speedo very much.

Even when I'm sad, I write.

Because Tina Fey, the goddess of comedy, said it best in *Bossypants* when she wrote, "I'm unstoppable because I don't know how to stop."

I am definitely *not* unstoppable. But if I act like Tina Fey, maybe, just maybe, I can finagle that six-episode renewal.

As I peruse the scenes, the opening notes of a song filter from the front of my townhome. What the hell? Did I leave the streaming app open on my phone? I step away from the counter and head to the front door, looking for my phone, even though I swear I had it with me in the kitchen.

The song grows louder, and it's not coming from my

cell at all. It's coming from outside. I peer through the peephole.

I jerk back.

Rub my eyes.

What the hell?

Am I really seeing what I'm seeing? I don't think I had that much wine. I had one sip.

Fine, fine. One large sip. One very large, very hearty sip. All right, it was a gulp.

But I can't possibly be hallucinating, can I?

I peek again, and holy smokes.

There's a guy on my front lawn going full Lloyd Dobler.

The hair on the back of my neck stands on end, and my paranoid brain leaps three thousand steps ahead. Did he escape from Alcatraz? Is he going to bang down my door? Attack me?

I pivot and grab the baseball bat I keep handy. As the youngest sister of two older brothers, I've learned a few valuable lessons: boys are trouble, pizza is good cold, and always keep a baseball bat near the door and/or bed.

With my bat in hand, I scurry to the kitchen to grab my phone, then fly upstairs to the bedroom, taking the steps two by two.

I race into the bedroom, set the bat at my feet, and keep my phone clutched in my hand, ready to call 911 if need be. I pull back the white curtain a smidge.

And I nearly die laughing.

The song has stopped, and the Dobler wannabe is now kneeling on the ground, furiously hitting buttons on the boom box.

I peer around the curtain's edge, and it's like watching a sideshow act auditioning for my circus.

He hoists the boom box up above him again. A new tune plays. I cock my head, listening, and I cringe when I recognize the tune.

For real? Is he truly playing "Unzipped"? I could never stand that song when it was popular eight years ago. The music sounds like a can opener mating with a trombone. I wish he were playing Peter Gabriel's "In Your Eyes," like Dobler did in the film.

But as I study the bizarre suburban male mating ritual, I decide to award him points for sheer balls. He also deserves bonus points because he chose to go without the super cheesy trench coat that Dobler wore. It worked for Cusack, but on anyone else that attire screams serial killer.

This guy seems harmless.

And admittedly, from my vantage point two stories above, he's kind of handsome with the glasses, the thick, floppy hair, and the jeans that fit nicely. Strong jaw too.

Fine, fine. He's more than kind of handsome. He's 100 percent good-looking, in that hot nerd kind of way.

The song stops playing. I straighten and inch closer. What will he do?

The answer?

Go balls to the wall.

He does it. He sings solo. He belts it out. His voice is scratchy and terrible and off-key in ways I've never even known a song could be.

He's singing about wanting her love, wanting her back. And the look on his face, the hope in his eyes, the commitment to the song, it touches a part of my heart.

The *creative* part of my heart, because I'm witnessing a gift from the muses.

This man is an angel.

I've never seen him before, which means he's surely got the wrong address. He's embarrassing himself for nothing.

And I'm the lucky recipient of the sideshow. This is real life on steroids, and truth is stranger than fiction if a living, breathing man thinks something like this is going to work to win a woman who's not even here.

This is exactly what I need for my TV show.

As the song nears its end, I fling open the window, yank back the curtain, and wave.

He blinks when he sees my face, then falters on the words in one of the last few lines.

I make a keep-rolling gesture. "Go on. I want to hear the end of it."

His brow knits. "Do you enjoy badly sung ballads?"

I nod vigorously. "Seems I do."

He shrugs as if to say *suit yourself*, then does as requested, and when he's done, I cheer. "I love it."

He scratches his jaw. "So, is there any chance Cassandra is hiding back there?"

Ohhhhh.

"You're looking for Cassie Martinez?"

"Yes, that badly sung ballad was intended for her, and it'd make my night if she's crouched behind the curtains, beside herself with happiness."

I try to rein in the laughter. This guy. His heart.

Most of all, these damn numbers on these

townhomes.

I frown on his behalf. "It's just me." I pat the windowpane. "This is my home. 101 Vintage Oaks Lane. But technically, it's 101A, and technically she's 101B. We share a doorway."

His face is crestfallen. Utter devastation slides across his features like a neon sign flashing *all that for nothing*.

Poor guy.

"Don't worry—even the mailman gets confused. Don't get me started with the UPS mix-ups when it comes to Amazon Prime. I got her yoga candles, and she got my—"

I cut myself off. Maybe best not to let on I ordered some underwear from Amazon. But when I saw the black low-rise undies with the words *pants are dumb* on the butt I could not resist.

I point to the window a few feet from me. "Anyway, I suspect that window is the one you wanted. That's her bedroom. But she's not home. She never is. She Airbnbs the place all the time."

The guy shakes his head, hanging it. "Just my luck," he mutters.

"But look on the bright side. Last night, there were two big, burly biker dudes staying there as they rode up the coast. At least you got me tonight." I flash him a cheery grin. "And we need to talk, Lloyd. Don't go." I hold up my hand as a stop sign. "Stay there."

I race downstairs and invite the *Say Anything* imitator out for a cup of coffee. I need to know everything. Every single detail about his antics tonight.

After all, when the muses drop a gift like this into your lap, you don't leave it on the table.

4

HIM

There is planning, then there is damn good planning, and then there is precision-timed planning.

And there are also townhomes listed on Airbnb. The fly in the let's-get-back-together ointment.

Why didn't I think her place might be rented? Cassie's name is on the property record as the sole owner. Plus, the light was on in what I now know is the house *next door*. To top it off, she's posted photos on Facebook in front of the yellow house.

That damn double home.

It's like a trick duplex townhouse.

I prepared for every possibility . . . except this one.

That's why I'm making the quick drive into town, following the pedaling blonde who's most definitely not my college girlfriend at all.

She's the woman I serenaded. Terribly.

And yet she's the woman who invited me out for coffee anyway, but not to the Italian restaurant where I imagined Cassie and I would be laughing, drinking wine, and toasting to my ingenuity and chutzpah.

This has thrown me for a couple of loops, and since I'm not sure what to do next, coffee with the witness to my massive face-palm seems as good an idea as anything.

When we reach the main drag, she hand signals that she's pulling over. Not-Cassie takes off her helmet, secures it to the middle bar, and locks up her bike at a lamppost on the sidewalk while I park along the curb.

"Nice electric bike," I remark when I get out of the car.

"Nice electric car."

"Can't beat the gas mileage."

"Ditto."

She turns to the coffee shop, and its CLOSED sign seems to mock us.

Her shoulders sag. "Shutterbug. I forgot Cup of Joe closes at seven."

I lift one brow. "Did you just say 'shutterbug' to replace a curse word?"

She nods, a little impishly. "It's my language test this week."

"Explain."

"Each week I give myself a new language test." She counts off on her fingers. "Don't swear. Don't use adverbs. Use the subjunctive mood—correctly, I might add—in nearly every conversation."

"And do you grade yourself on your own proficiency?"

Her eyebrows wiggle. "I do." She peers from side to

side. "But honestly, sometimes my teacher is a bit of a slacker."

"Sometimes those are the best teachers to have," I say, still trying to figure out what her deal is and why she's so eager to chat. I want to know partly because she's connected to Cassie but partly because she's oddly interesting.

She points a thumb at the empty coffeehouse. "Also, how is it that no one in this town needs a caffeine hit in the evenings?"

I gesture to the block after block of wine bars and chichi restaurants lining the main street. "I'm guessing it's a town ordinance that any beverages consumed after eight must contain grapes."

She snaps her fingers. "You're right. It's in the bylaws."

My eyes sweep the block, catching sight of an ice cream shop. "Want to follow the bylaws? Or grab a gelato instead?"

She pats her stomach. Her flat, trim stomach that goes along with her flat, trim figure. "There's a warrant out for my arrest if I eat any more ice cream."

I scoff. "Who would ever arrest you for doing that? That's like arresting someone for helping a little old lady cross the street."

"I filed it myself. I had to implement tough love when I noticed my cardboard recycling consisted primarily of Ben & Jerry's containers." She tips her forehead to a wine bar. "Is it wine o'clock?"

"It's after five, so I believe it is."

But she doesn't order wine when we grab a high table at Red, White, and Rosé. She orders an iced tea, and since I'm still discombobulated to be sitting across from this woman rather than Cassie, I follow suit.

"So, um . . ." I gesture to her. "I didn't catch your name."

"I didn't throw it. But that's okay. You didn't exactly hurl yours at me either, Lloyd. I'm Finley."

"I'm Kyler," I say, extending a hand and shaking hers.

She arches an eyebrow, her light-blue eyes sparkling with curiosity. "Did your parents put Tyler and Kyle in a hat and shake it up?"

"Wow. I've never heard that before. Do you want to ask me next if Tyler rammed into Kyle to make my name?"

She cracks up so loudly she snorts.

"You're a snorter," I point out.

"And proud of it," she says between chuckles, then catches her breath. "I bet you're one of those people who always has to say your name twice, aren't you?"

"Every. Single. Time."

She shoots me a coy smile. "For what it's worth, I heard it right the first time."

"You're a rare breed, then."

She narrows her eyes, studying me as if she's a detective. "I am. Also, call me crazy, but I get the feeling you don't like your name."

I tap my nose. "I can't stand it. I don't think you can measure how high my levels of can't-stand-it go. Every school year, I had to explain my name because the teacher thought it had been written wrong on the class roster."

"That's the worst, not being able to blend in."

"It is, and other kids would ask how I got my name. It reached a point where I'd say, just for kicks, that my mom wanted to name me Ky and my dad wanted to name me Lar."

She laughs. "And the reaction to that?"

"At first, it was so absurd the other kids stopped asking. But then someone figured out K-Y was a popular brand name, and that became my nickname in sixth grade."

She cringes. "Oh, that's terrible, John."

"Why are you calling me John?" I ask, laughing as I still process how the hell I'm sitting across from this motormouth rather than Cassie. This adorable blonde motormouth who seems like she's never met a question she wouldn't ask.

"John has to be better than K-Y. From here on, I shall call you John."

"John?" I arch a brow and point in the direction of the bathrooms. "Trust me, kids will mock you for anything."

"True. Scratch John from the potential new name list. So how exactly did you wind up with Kyler? Were your parents going through a let's-give-our-kid-a-unique-name phase?"

"Precisely. My mom wanted an original name. It could be worse. My brothers are Ransom, Nash, and Gannon."

"Like Dannon yogurt."

"I bet Gannon has never heard that comparison before."

"If you don't like your name, why do you keep it?"

I furrow my brow. "It's hard to change a name."

The waiter swoops by with two iced teas, depositing them on the table with a cheery grin. I thank him, and so does Finley. She takes a drink then continues. "It's not that hard. You go to the county and file some papers."

"I don't mean literally hard. It's more socially hard." I take a swallow of the cold beverage. "I'd have to explain to everyone why I changed it. Plus, my brothers would never let me hear the end of it."

She's like a dog with a bone. She won't let go. "What's your middle name?"

"Tom," I say as a smile tugs on my lips.

She shoots me a knowing look like she's caught me red-handed. "You like Tom."

I take a drink. "Tom's a good name."

"You totally wanted to be Tom."

Busted.

I heave a sigh. "Look, Tom is better than Kyler. Tom is solid, Tom is sturdy."

"I had a cat named Tom growing up."

"Is that a compliment?"

She practically slams her glass down for emphasis. "Of course. He was the epitome of cool. He had swagger but not in an in-your-face way. He was a striped tabby. Silver and black. All manly and cool. No one messed around with Tom."

I pick up the thread, liking this direction. "Tom's a builder, a fisherman, a man who works with his hands."

Her eyes gleam. "Tom's the guy you call to get you out of trouble. He's your buddy who always knows his way out of a jam."

"Tom is a man's man."

She points at me. "And the ladies love him because Tom is fantastically easy to "say"—she sweeps her gaze from side to side, then lowers her voice to a whisper —"in bed."

"Maybe you could show me what that sounds like," I say, since why not indulge in a little harmless flirting?

She hums, sliding into a sexy purr. "*Tom.*"

And maybe the flirting isn't so harmless judging from my body's reaction. But she switches gears in a second. "Tom also doesn't need to be trendy," she adds, and I don't think she can shut up, but I don't mind. "Tom doesn't need to be Braxton or Jayden or Dane."

"And Tom doesn't have to be Jax or Ace or Diesel or some other aggressive male name."

She slices a hand through the air dismissively. "Tom doesn't care about any of that. Because Tom is easygoing. Tom gets along with everyone."

"But do you know what Tom likes most of all?"

"What does Tom like best?"

"Tom likes that no one ever asks how his name is spelled, or what it means, or why the hell he was given that name."

"Um," she says, a sheepish expression on her face as she speaks in a confessional tone. "What does Tom mean? I don't actually know."

Laughing, I realize I don't entirely know either. "I think it's from the Bible. Wasn't he an apostle?"

Recognition seems to flicker in her eyes. "Yes, that's it."

"But mostly I think Tom means"—I pause to sketch air quotes—"'the name I really wanted but my parents needed a name to match my brothers.'"

"Tom." She says it like a statement, and I tilt my head in question. Her eyes light up. "Look! You answer to Tom."

"Like a dog?"

"Exactly like a dog." She holds up a finger. "Hey. Idea. What if *I* called you Tom, instead of Kyler?"

"Why would you do that?" This woman is a bit of a nutjob, and yet I'm digging her crazy company.

"You like the name better, and this way you can test it out. You think your brothers would give you a hard time. You worry it's too hard to change. I don't know you from Adam, so you might as well be Tom to me, and then you can see how it feels."

Right now, it feels unexpectedly good. "I'll be Tom to you."

She smiles. "You're Tom to me, and Tom is strong, charismatic, and the ultimate good guy. You can trust Tom."

"Now that we have that out of the way, are we going to change your name too?"

She shakes her head. "I'm good with Finley. Want to hear why it's my name?"

I think she's going to tell me anyway, so I say yes.

"I have two older brothers, and my mom didn't want to get her hopes up by picking a girly girl name, so she chose one that could go either way."

"She must have been happy to finally get her girl."

Finley shrugs. "She probably was at the time, but I promptly began disappointing her, though that's a story for another time. As for the name, it's for the best that I didn't land a Y chromosome because my dad was leaning toward Adler for a boy."

"Adler is uncommon," I say diplomatically.

"Adler sounds like something you take when you're not feeling well." She affects a falsetto voice. "'Honey, can you pick up my Adler? Oh, I need to go to Target and get some Adler. I have a terrible headache, and I'm all out of Adler.'"

I laugh. "You're funny, Finley."

She flicks her hair. "Thanks. I kind of have to be."

I knit my brow. "What do you mean?"

She waves it off, zipping away from my question. "Anyway, so tell me all about Cassie. You decided to big-gesture her, and you got me instead."

"That's my life in a nutshell. I went all out, and I had the wrong house, wrong girl, wrong everything."

"Townhouses with A and B addresses are literally the worst thing that has ever happened to big gestures," she deadpans.

"Fine. It's a first-world problem."

"A first-world *love and romance* problem. But don't worry, the doctor is in." She taps her chest and takes another drink of her iced tea. "And my diagnosis is that your effort was impressive. I've never seen that kind of commitment to a re-enactment. I need to know everything. What inspired you?" Her tone drips with curiosity.

"You want me to tell you everything?"

She swirls the straw dramatically in her drink. "Hello? I'm plying you with iced tea. Doesn't that entitle me to all the deets?"

I can't quite tell her *everything*, but I can tell her enough. "Cassie was my college girlfriend about eight years ago when I was twenty, a sophomore in college," I begin, leaning back in the chair. "I met her freshman year working on a protest—"

"Ooh, what were you protesting?"

"Straws. They're bad for turtles. She wanted them to be banned, and so did I."

"And that was before straw protests became a thing."

"We were on the vanguard."

She holds up a fist for bumping. "Long live the turtles."

I fist-bump her back. "Turtles are cool. Anyway, we became friends, bonding over sea creatures and our amazing ability to drink beverages without needing straws."

She hoists her strawless ice tea glass dramatically, taking a deliberate drink then smiling. "Look, ma, no straw!"

I laugh.

She makes a rolling gesture. "Keep going. This is far more fascinating than going to T.J. Maxx and shopping for toys for my dad's dog."

"Was that on your agenda for tonight?"

"That's tomorrow night, actually. Dog toy shopping is fun, but this is better."

I tell her about the required American History class we took together in the fall semester, how Cassie was pretty and smart and clever, and how she was thoughtful in her answers about the Chinese Exclusion Act and the Vietnam War, never strident or rude.

"She was the real deal," Finley says, seeming to soak up every detail like a sponge.

"I suppose so. She was also pretty."

"What did she look like?"

I tap my nose, remembering Cassie of eight years ago. "Cute little nose. Great hair. Lips like a bow."

"Darn, you did like her," she says, her voice laced with interest, as if she's never heard a better story. Warmth spreads across my chest, as I remember those college days with the first girl I loved. The *only* girl I've loved.

"It was more than like. She was my first real girl-friend. She cared deeply about the world and others. She loved music. She used to wear her hair back in a pony-tail every day. I remember it bounced when she walked, and I somehow thought that was the greatest thing."

She sighs happily. "The bouncing ponytail. It's the best. My hair isn't long enough for a bouncy ponytail, but it's seriously a dream of mine. An unattainable one since my hair can't ever seem to grow past here." She sets her hand against her collarbone.

I do a quick scan of her face. A spray of freckles decorates her nose and beneath her blue eyes. Her hair is curly blonde and shoulder length. "Your hair is fine."

"Fine?"

"What's wrong with fine?"

"Fine is for Switzerland."

"And Switzerland is a fine country. One of my roller coasters is in Switzerland."

"One of your *what*?"

"I designed the Boomerang Flyer."

She blinks, recognition in her eyes. "The Boomerang Flyer? With that crazy vertical loop that launches you from the station at something like five hundred miles per hour?"

I laugh, loving that she's heard of the ride. "Sixty-six

miles per hour, to be precise. I worked on that one for months to hit just the right send-off moment."

She shakes her head, looking amazed. "You're a gold mine. Keep going."

"About the roller coaster?"

She taps the table. "We'll return to the ride. What happened with Cassie?"

"Finally, in our sophomore year, I decided to ask her out. I did the whole prom-posal thing before it became trendy, and it wasn't even prom."

"You did a prom-posal for a regular date?"

I tap my chest. "Big gestures and me are tight."

"Evidently." She parks her chin in her hands, like she's fascinated. "How did you do it?"

"Back then, I didn't really know how to ask a girl out, so I gave it my best shot. When I was home for ski week—my family's in Oakland, and I went to school in Berkeley—I grabbed some of my dad's honey. He's an amateur beekeeper, and Cassie's favorite band was the Honey Sticks. I started to write a note, but since my handwriting is worse than a doctor's and illegible to anyone but me—and even then it's debatable—I asked the woman down the street if she could write a note to go on the lid."

"Why the woman down the street?"

"My mom died when I was thirteen. Cancer."

Her lower lip quivers for a second "I'm so sorry, Tom." She reaches a hand to take mine and squeezes. I stare at her hand momentarily, appreciating the gesture even though the loss was so long ago. She clears her throat, speaking softly. "Mine died a year ago. Complications from diabetes."

Glancing at our hands, I take the lead this time, squeezing back, feeling her pain, along with the memory of mine. "I'm sorry, too, for your loss."

"Yeah, death kind of sucks," she says, but it doesn't come out callous. She says it in a matter-of-fact way that seems to underscore how we all, universally, feel about that particular aspect of the human condition.

"Couldn't say it better myself."

She moves her hand off mine, and I miss the warmth of her touch for a fleeting second. I shake off the feeling and return to the story.

"Anyway, I asked Sadie Mitchell, this kind lady who was friends with my mom and liked to look out for us, if she could write the note. She agreed and wrote, 'It would *bee* so sweet, and such a honeyed treat, if you would say yes to going out with me.'"

She furrows her brow. "So it sort of rhymed, but sort of not."

I laugh. "I suppose that's fair to say. Anyway, I brought the honey back to school, stopped by her dorm, played 'Unzipped,' and handed her the jar. She loved it. She threw her arms around me, said yes. She said she'd been waiting for me to ask her out for a long time. And then we went to see *The Social Network*."

Finley squares her shoulders and goes full Jesse Eisenberg. "*'If you guys were the inventors of Facebook . . . you'd have invented Facebook.'*"

I grin. "That's my favorite line from that movie."

"That's the best line from that movie. It's the ultimate throwdown statement." She leans in closer. "Did she like the film?"

"Loved it."

"I love her. She has good taste."

"Anyway, that started things, and we were together for a few months. She was interested in choreography, and she had choreographed a modern dance thingy."

"A thingy?"

I make a you-know-what-I-mean gesture. "A dance."

She arches a brow. "A dance thingy?"

I try again. "Like a routine? A performance?"

She laughs. "Yeah, I get it. I don't think they're called thingies though, and hopefully you didn't call it a thingy. Hopefully you called it a *concert dance*."

"Yes! That's what it was. A concert dance. And there was a cast party after for all the dancers, and she invited me. We danced at the party."

"To 'Unzipped'?"

"Naturally. Trouble was, the next day she dumped me."

She frowns. "That's terrible. Did she give a reason?"

I sigh heavily and drag a hand through my hair, remembering that last night together. But I don't want to serve up all the details to Finley, or anyone for that matter. Some things are best left unsaid. I focus on the facts as I lived them. "I was kind of a slacker, and she said that's why. Not in so many words, but she said to come back when I got my act together. She was hyper-focused and studious, and I sometimes skipped classes or missed assignments. Especially to hang out with my buddies. Cassie's breakup made me get my act together," I say, then I repeat her words. "*Try again when you get your act together. Show up when you know what you want.*"

"But you were only in college, and besides, you had

to deal with a name you didn't like," she says, and it's adorable that she's defending my younger self.

"Thanks, but honestly, it was what I needed to hear. She obviously didn't want to date a slacker, so I took her directive to heart. It was the kick in the pants I needed. I went on to earn an advanced degree, become an engineer of thrill rides, and invent a new safety feature for roller coasters. And since the Honey Sticks reunited last month, what better sign that it's time to tell her I'm ready?"

She sighs contentedly and sets her hand on her heart. "That is so sweet. I love this story. So much. All the longing and romance, and the roller coaster bit too."

I laugh. "Glad it all works for you."

"It totally works," she says, her eyes a little dreamy, her voice drifting off.

I study her more closely. "Do you know Cassie? I didn't see her after we broke up. She transferred to another school."

"Not really, except I think she mostly lives in Southern California now, and she owns a chain of yoga studios. But I thought her company was based here."

"I think it is, but maybe she's based out of one in Southern California?"

"That must be it. Where do you live?"

I point south. "San Francisco."

"About an hour from here," she says thoughtfully, then adds, "and an hour-long plane trip to Southern California if it all works out with Cassie."

"I like your positive attitude."

"Me too," she says with a wry smile. "I just wish I had more details to share about her."

My shoulders fall. "I was hoping you knew her too."

She laughs sadly, then sits ramrod straight, blinking. She holds up a hand. "Wait. That doesn't matter. You want to win her back, right?" She's all business now, crisp and focused.

"Uh, yeah," I say, in a *duh* tone of voice. "That's sort of why I'm here."

She slaps a palm on the table. "Then I'm going to help you."

"You are?" I ask carefully, making sure I understand her.

She nods vehemently. "Tom, I'm not even going to say 'don't take this the wrong way,' because there is only one way to take this, but everything about tonight on the front lawn was awful."

My eyes bug out. "What?" I sputter.

"Awful. The worst."

I gesture wildly in the general direction of her home. "How can you even say that? That was gold. That's the pinnacle of big gestures. The only other contender is the dude in *Love Actually* who confesses his love on poster boards at Christmas."

She shakes her head. "Never do that one. Please promise me you'll never do a Christmas Eve Mark and Juliet. Never ever, ever."

"Why?" I ask, my curiosity piqued.

She leans forward and whispers, "That scene in *Love Actually* is super creepy and completely stalkery."

I fold my arms across my chest. "And are you saying the boom box above the head is creepy and stalkery?"

"No. My issue is your presentation was a bit lacking."

I hold my hands out wide, conceding. "Fine. I had the wrong girl. But beyond that, what was so bad?"

"Tom," she says gently, "I didn't mean the wrong girl part. I meant because you can't sing."

"I know." I sigh heavily.

"But you *can* design boomerang thunder domes that zip and zing and slide," she says, whipping her hand up and down, imitating, I think, a roller coaster. "Why not play to your strengths?"

"I should design a roller coaster to win her back?"

She shrugs in that it's-not-a-bad-idea way. "That's a better option. You could call it The Cassie. The Loop-the-Loop Cassie. The Screaming Cassie. The Cassie Blaster."

I laugh. "Those are terrible names for coasters. I mean . . . the Cassie Blaster?"

"Not my best idea," she adds, cracking up. "But you get my point. You could turn her name into an anagram. Cassandra." She stares at the ceiling, putting the letters together in reverse, I suspect.

I jump in as she's still spelling them. "The ARDNASSAC Drop."

"Yes! That sounds terrifying, like I'll encounter prehistoric winged dinosaurs at every climb and dip. You could make it a dinosaur-themed coaster."

I file that away. "That's not a bad concept for a roller coaster."

"Listen, the point is this: Dobler's stunt worked because it was a movie, but also because he knew Diane Court's character. If you want to win Cassandra back, you need to understand who she is today, or at least know her a little better. I can help you."

"But you said you don't know Cassie."

She laughs, shaking her head. "I've never met her. That's the crazy thing. Even when we swapped mail, I left it outside her door with a note and vice versa. But I know women, and I want to help you."

My skeptical side steps up to the plate. "Why?"

"I'm a writer. My job is understanding human behavior, and you, Tom, are a fascinating experiment. I'll help you on your quest, and you, in turn, can continue to be one of the most interesting curiosities I've stumbled across."

I laugh, unsure what to make of her compliment, or *un*-compliment. "I'm a curiosity?"

She nods. "Curiosity, noun: one that arouses interest due to uncommon or unusual characteristics."

"Such as singing bad ballads?"

"To a girl you loved before." She raises a glass. "A girl you clearly have your heart set on. It's sweet. It's romantic, and I want to help you win her back. Devise a plan, a blueprint, then follow it. Are you game?"

I study her face, considering her offer. Practically, it's doable. "I'm in town for a few days for meetings. Then I'm cruising down the coast, visiting some parks."

"We can hatch a plan, then. Work out the kinks and make it airtight," she says, and the idea is appealing. I have some free time in front of me to focus on a reboot of my attempt to win Cassandra's heart. I'm nothing if not persistent, and I'm all for triangulating a problem to find the solution. We quickly exchange numbers, but there's also something I want to know.

"What's in it for you? You like observing curious human behavior that much?"

She stretches her hand closer, her eyes intense. "I don't like it. I *love* it."

I lift my glass, considering her offer. Every great '80s hero had a great sidekick. After all, where would Ferris Bueller be without Cameron Frye?

He wouldn't have spent the day in a Ferrari, that's for sure.

"Yes."

It seems like the only fitting answer to give the woman who's just renamed me.

5

FINLEY

I am not spying.

How could this be spying? I'm simply positioning the ladder just so against the back of my home to clean my windows. I'm not actually trying to peer into Cassie's home early the next morning.

At the crack of dawn on a Friday.

When no one's around.

I'm just climbing the ladder with this bucket of soapy water, and I'm a-scrub-a-dub-dubbing my windows.

Who doesn't clean their windows at six in the morning?

I scrub religiously, and maybe if I get this corner right here, at the very edge, where I have to lean, I might happen to see inside her home.

Not that I need to.

But it can't hurt, right?

All I know about Cassie is that she bought the town-home adjacent to mine about two months ago and has rented it to a steady stream of Airbnb-ers the entire time.

Surely I'm entitled to a little peekaboo. After all, I'm practically Cassie's unpaid concierge.

First, there was the couple from New Zealand who had recently retired from their sheep farm and wanted to tour wine country. I pointed them in the direction of the best wineries, and in turn, they showed me a video of their sheepdog back home, hard at work herding sheep.

I mean, really. Videos of dogs at work are stupendously awesome. Fair trade.

Next up came a newly married couple from Dallas, and I don't believe they made it to any wineries. The wife did ask me for directions to the nearest pharmacy that sold lube . . . so I have a good idea of what kept them occupied on their honeymoon.

Also, I wore headphones for most of their stay.

A few weeks ago, a mélange of Manhattan society gals rented the pad for a girls' weekend, tottering in and out on their skyscraper heels. I suspect the half dozen of them were sober for a grand total of five minutes. I helped them order a Lyft on their way to the Two Cows Vineyard and then pre-ordered their return trip too.

And Cassie rented it recently to a lovely gay couple from San Francisco who were so damn cute they invited me over for a barbecue on the back porch. Since I don't eat meat, I declined, but I gave them the name of the best butcher in town.

See, I'm such a Good Samaritan that it's only reasonable I get to peek at Cassie's life, right? She never even introduced herself to me the one time she was here. Fine, fine. I was in Los Angeles visiting the network when she finalized the sale, and she did leave me a lovely gift bag with a package of gummy bears inside. Points for her—they were the gelatin-free variety.

Which reminds me. I do know something about her. She must be a vegetarian. I don't know anyone else who buys gelatin-free gummy bears except vegetarians.

But I get nothing else on her from staring in her window.

I can't see any books, so I can't report back to Tom that her shelves are teeming with titles like *The Joy of Deep Throating* or *101 Ways to Tie Up a Woman and Make Her Meow*.

Besides, those are on my bookshelves, and by book-shelves, I mean e-reader. I'm no dummy. I don't leave that kind of self-help material out for anyone to see.

From my vantage point, Cassie Martinez appears to be 100 percent minimalist—her home looks like it's been staged by a real estate firm.

I will say this though. She treats her renters right in the towel department. She had some linens from Restoration Hardware shipped here a month ago and brought in by the cleaners. I was tempted, vaguely tempted, to snag that box. I've always wanted Restoration Hardware towels.

But that's all I know, and really, I suppose that's all I should know about the woman who doesn't live next door.

Helping Tom should be less about Cassie and more about women in general. Like, learning you don't ever say *fine* in reference to a woman's hair. What was that man thinking with that comment last night? My hair is fluffy. So what?

I lower the bucket, climb down the ladder, and congratulate myself for having the cleanest window I've ever had in my life.

"Well done, self," I say then head inside and dump the bucket in the sink.

The notification light on my phone blinks at me, and I slide my thumb across the screen. I'm greeted by an email from my father, titled, as nearly all his emails are, "Daily Doggie." He lives a few towns over, and every morning on the dog walk, he sends me a picture of his shepherd-beagle-dachshund-mix, and every day I respond, noting the canine's cuteness as we correspond about what we're up to.

It's part of his efforts to be happy, to rise above the depression he's been battling since my mom died.

My heartbeat spikes as I open the note, hoping it's not bad news. It's been bad news, and that's one of the reasons he keeps emailing me daily. To bring positivity into his life. Something his shrink advised him to do several months ago, along with the suggestion to adopt a dog.

Today's missive asks how my show is going.

I wince, hating to disappoint him, especially since he was the only one who believed in me for so long. He was so proud when the network picked up my show. *You'll be on your way to an Emmy in no time*, he'd said.

I'd laughed him off, telling him there was no way that would happen.

I believe in you. I always have.

I write back now: *It's great! I have a fantastic new idea*

for a storyline. I'm busy tap, tap, tapping away on the keyboard. How are you? How's Mister Dog? What's for lunch? Back soon —need to go hit the daily mileage quota!

Our emails aren't *War and Peace*, but the focus on the mundane details seems to help him stay positive, so there's no need for me to share my negatives.

I pull on a pair of running shorts and sneakers and head for the nearby trails to run with my bestie, Christine. We're training for a triathlon, so I FaceTime her as I hit the path.

"Question," I say, diving straight into the thick of it, as we usually do.

"Answer . . . maybe," she says, already pounding the pavement in Golden Gate Park. Since we live an hour apart, we train together through FaceTime. This sometimes makes me feel like I'm thirteen, talking to my best friend via an app while I work out—yet my bills very much remind me I'm not a teenager.

I fire off my question. "Is it considered spying on someone if I'm sharing information gleaned simply by noticing the things around me?"

She laughs, her freckled face and big brown eyes bouncing around on the screen as she jogs. "You realize that's the kind of question that if you're asking it, the answer is probably yes? Now, fess up. Who are you spying on and what dirt have you dug up?"

"I had a feeling that was what you were going to say. But in my defense, it was sort of a fruitless mission. I learned nada."

"As you should when spying. What's this mission all about though?"

As we run, I tell her about the angel that the muses dropped on my front lawn last night.

"He sounds like one determined camper, and if he'd have come to me beforehand, I'd have said maybe call the woman first," she says, the therapist in her doling out advice from afar. I love her therapist advice and the fact that she gives it to me for free instead of one hundred dollars an hour. Like when she helped me come to terms over how my relationship with my ex-boyfriend Anthony ended. That was a bit of a bummer since, well, I was madly in love, and he was . . . not.

"I know, but she must be something special for him to go all out like this. I want to help him."

She lifts a brow. "Be honest. You're going to use him as inspiration for your show. This is a two-way street kind of thing?"

I gasp. "Use him? How could you think such a thing?"

She laughs, rolling her eyes. "Because you are like a sponge. Anything remotely funny, interesting, quirky, bizarre, or unusual that someone says, you file it away and break it out later on an episode. Like that time you were writing for the late-night comedy show, and David was dipping carrots in hummus and moaning in pleasure, and you asked if he wanted to marry the hummus, and he said, 'I just want to fill a bathtub with it.' And there was a bathtub full of hummus in your next sketch."

I point at her. "And the bathtub hummus line was a huge hit with the audience."

"I found it amusing too," she admits. "So you're

going to mentally record every funny moment while taking on this guy's romance rehab?"

I smile as I round a switchback, my breath coming faster. "Exactly. Seems like a fair trade. I think I can help him in the love department."

She nods. "You've always been good at relationship advice. Like that time you told me to surprise David at dinner wearing a trench coat, heels, and La Perla."

I laugh, remembering when she surprised the hell out of her then fiancé. "Was that relationship advice or sex advice?"

"Sometimes they're one and the same," she quips.

"True that."

"Are you giving this guy sex advice?"

I scoff. That would be the height of irony since I'm no expert in that field, despite my avid reading interest in it. "No way. But honestly, he's so clueless it's endearing. Sort of like how David was when you first met him."

"The sheer woman-hours needed to deprogram a man after attending an all-boys school can be exhausting." Christine met her husband their senior year of college, and she said you can always tell the guys who went to an all-boys school because they don't know how to act around women. They are all sex talk, sports comments, and grunts.

"But you liked it," I point out as I run past a morning warrior, a woman practically sprinting along the trail. She shoots me a look of disdain, which I suspect is due to my use of a cell phone while exercising. What can I say? Running is Capital D Dull if you don't have someone to talk to or a great album to sing along with. Since I can't hit a single note, the running warrior ought to be grateful I'm gabbing instead.

"He was my lovable buffoon. And he still is. So what's the deal with your Dobler?"

"He's kind of making me think about new directions for my show. Maybe a touch of romance isn't such a bad idea. It worked on *Kiss and Tell*," I say, mentioning the online series I wrote for a few years ago—it was one of those limited-run shows with an ensemble cast where the viewer is left guessing till the last episode as to who winds up with who.

"I loved *Kiss and Tell*. But then again, I'm a devotee of all things kissing, especially 'Times They Should Have Kissed.'"

"You're such a romantic," I say, laughing when she mentions her favorite Tumblr feed, detailing fictional on-screen and literary couples that fans think should be together.

"Seriously, Watson and Holmes should absolutely kiss and so should Harry and Hermione."

I shake my head. "Nope. Ginny is perfect for Harry."

"But you do agree Watson is perfect for Holmes?"

I smile, conceding that point. "You won't get any argument from me on that."

As Christine jogs beside a field of flowers, her expression turns more thoughtful. "But I do think it's a good direction for your show. After all, people generally are looking for love. That's kind of why I have a job."

I arch a brow at her small-screen face. "I figured you had a job because people have mommy issues, like me."

"You do have mommy issues, but your mom was

wrong. Also, don't forget about daddy issues. Those are a big thing too."

We chat more as we run, virtual-training together till we're done. "Have fun with your science experiment," she says as we say goodbye.

"Have fun fixing all those mommy and daddy issues."

When I return home, I down a glass of water and jot out some notes for my next scene after the Speedo bit.

I picture a glasses-wearing hottie showing up at a girl's door and trying to win her heart.

Carrying poster boards.

On them, he confesses his love.

Wait.

That doesn't feel quite right.

Because my character isn't a creepy stalker. Yet, there are fan fiction sites dedicated to Mark and Juliet from *Love Actually*. *What if they were together? What if they kissed more deeply on Christmas? What if she left her husband?* I hop on over to Christine's favorite Tumblr page where fan fiction enthusiasts have imagined their favorite silver- and small-screen couples lip-locking.

I peer at the images. Scully and Mulder. Duckie and Andie. Jack and Liz. I cringe at the last one, a reminder that some shows don't need romance to work.

But my show isn't working as is.

What if Tom and Cassie were together? What if I wrote them in as characters?

I imagine Cassie, the yoga queen, serenely turning her body into a warrior, holding that pose when Tom shows up with his placards.

He's about to profess his true heart. But before he

launches into his re-enactment of *Love Actually*, his trusty gal pal grabs him by the hem of his shirt and reminds him that the guy holding the placards always loses.

"You're right. Of course you're right," he says.

He throws away the cards, strides into the yoga studio, takes off his shoes, and does the best yoga pose Cassie's ever seen.

"Your downward dog is so good," she says.

"I've been practicing for years," he says huskily.

"Yoga?"

"No, to ask you to have dinner with me."

Hearts flutter, but she doesn't say yes to dinner. That would be too easy.

Hours later, I close the laptop and get ready to see the source of my inspiration.

6

TOM

My phone buzzes with a text.

Ransom: Give me all the deets.

Me: In a nutshell: Wrong Girl.

Ransom: NOOOOOO. But holy shit. That's awful and awesome at the same time. I need more details. Please tell me Wrong Girl caught everything on video.

Me: If there's a God, she did not.

Ransom: I pray there's no God, then. So what happened with Wrong Girl? Was she so moved by your awesome grand gesturing that she decided to take up with you for the rest of her life?

Me: She bought me an iced tea.

Ransom: Huh.

Me: Huh, what?

Ransom: Huh. I have no clue what that means, and I'm usually good at understanding women.

Me: Same here.

* * *

It seemed like a good idea at the time.

But do I need that much help? I'm not some hapless twit who has no clue about women, like Finley suggested. I've had my fair share. I've made sure I never have to worry about someone pulling a Sally-at-the-diner on me.

Plus, I get along great with the ladies—of all ages.

Take the hyper-serious Midge Waterson. She's known for rarely cracking a smile, but she's smiling in our meeting as we review the recent sandbag trials I ran for the Space Blaster. That's when we test rides with sandbags instead of people.

"And all sandbags were tall enough to ride the ride," I say to Midge, my new contact at the standards organization that oversees thrill rides. She's grinning now, so clearly I know something about how to interact with the fairer sex. Fine, this is work-related, but the lessons still apply.

"Were they all well-behaved?"

"I'm happy to report they screamed their lungs out—or would have, if they had any."

"Screaming is a sign of a top-notch ride. Good screaming, that is." She peers down her sharp, straight nose at the report, reviewing final details of how the ride fared with sandbag thrill seekers. After nodding her satisfaction, she looks up at me with curious gray eyes. "You're awfully young to be doing this. Were you a roller-coaster kid? The kind who dragged his parents to all the rides?"

I scoff playfully. "Roller Coaster Tycoon, right here. As soon as I turned on the Xbox, I was determined to build the best park."

She laughs. "That video game brought more people into the business than anything else. Everyone thinks they can do anything once they play a video game. If that were the case, I'd be in the NBA, thanks to NBA 2K18. But you actually *can* build fantastic rides."

"Thank you. And I'm sure your jump shot is fantastic, Midge."

"You're sweet to say that." She rises and offers a hand to shake across the conference room table. "By the way, I have a daughter about your age. She's a math teacher. Lovely young lady."

"You must be proud of her."

"Very much so." She tucks a strand of hair behind her ear and clears her throat. "It must be so tough to meet like-minded people. Do you find that to be the case?"

I scratch my jaw. "Not really. I meet engineers all the time."

"I meant female ones," she says with an apologetic smile. "Especially smart, pretty, and single ones."

I wave off her concerns about the field. "Nah. Engineering isn't a boys' club like when I was in school. Even in the last few years, there are so many more women coming into it."

Her brow knits, and she takes a beat. "And you find meeting women is easy?"

I shrug happily. I'm not entirely sure why she's asking, but her concern is sweet. "Sure. I met a new woman just last night."

Too bad Finley's not the one I went looking for, but I'm confident the Cassandra Quest simply swerved down a detour last night, and I'll find the way back to her soon. I did some more digging last night, made a few calls to her various yoga studios, and found out she's leading a retreat for her studio somewhere in San Diego. That must mean she's unplugged for a few days, which gives me time to recalibrate and devise a new plan.

I say goodbye to Midge and hop into my car to return to Hope Falls where I'm staying for a few days to tend to meetings. As I turn on the engine, I noodle again on what went wrong last night, like it's a math problem I can solve if I find the right formula.

Did I go too big?

Did I plan poorly?

Or were there too many holes in the plan?

Is it possible I don't truly know Cassie? Sure, it's been eight years since I knew her, but we were tight in college, even before we dated. We went to the food trucks in Berkeley, hung out at the school's basketball games, and kissed for the first time after *The Social Network*, which released my sophomore year. We went out for late-night sushi, and after edamame and hamachi rolls, Cassie and I ventured to the crepe dealer where we shared a cinnamon sugar crepe. We stopped in front of a T-shirt shop on the edge of campus, sharing a cinnamon sugar kiss.

We shared more the night of her dance performance.

First love, first girlfriend, and first time. She was clever and kind, always had a thoughtful word for others, and laughed at my jokes.

Hell, maybe I should simply call Cassie. I've spent the last several years bettering myself, fixing the areas where I failed, and shoring things up elsewhere too, just in case.

A few weeks ago, I stumbled across an online ad for the Honey Sticks, her favorite band. They'd broken up, ironically, shortly after we had. But they'd reunited and had gone on tour. The tour was leaving California, but the seed was planted. If the band could get back together, surely we could too. That's why I decided to go for it again with her, with a nod of sorts to the way I asked her out in the first place.

But maybe I should go simpler. Do the whole standard reconnection thing, like you hear couples talk about when they share how they met. *Oh, my college boyfriend reached out to me out of the blue, and naturally we hit it off again, just like old times.*

It isn't my first choice for contacting her, but I guess this is the one option I have now. I open her Facebook profile and tap out a message.

Hey Cassie! Remember me? I haven't forgotten you either. We had the best time back in the day, and I took your advice to

heart. I'm ready now to try again, just like the Honey Sticks.
Want to get a bite to eat sometime soon and listen to
"Unzipped"? I'll find a place that has great cinnamon sugar
crepes near you. :)

I read it again, pleased with myself. Hell, that's a damn good note. Except for that stupid smiley face. I'll delete that right now.

Done.

I re-read it, picturing the reunion playing out. I'll drive down the coast and meet her for a bite to eat. But as I stare at the draft, something nags at me. This note is a tree that falls in the forest.

Does it make a sound or not?

See, I won't know, because it's a one-way deal. I want to see her in person, talk to her, have a real-time conversation. I don't want to fire off a shot in the dark and wonder if she read it, laughed at it, deleted it.

Or worse. What if I send this and my note lands in her spam folder? She'll never know my intentions, and I'll never know hers.

That's an echo in the dark.

I delete the draft.

I back away from the curb and hit play on a new episode of a podcast on the greatest heists of the century, my eyes nearly popping when the host details a daring escape where the thieves made off with ten million dollars in diamonds.

I make my way back to the hotel, and as I drive, my gaze snaps to the side of the road. I yank my car over immediately, checking out the view across the front yards, lined with junk sculptures.

Farmers drive tractors. A rabbit races. A man rides a cow. A mermaid rises from the sea, and a surfer hangs ten.

That is some seriously cool shit. I never know when inspiration might strike for a new ride concept, so I'm always on the lookout. I open the door and wander down the block, where every single yard on the street boasts some sort of life-size cartoonish sculpture made from what looks like recycled junkyard metal.

As I snap photos, I wonder if Finley knows about this block.

Crazy, wacky Finley who likes curiosities. I slide open the screen on my phone.

Tom: Did you know there's a wicked witch with a muffler for a nose and hair that looks like it's from an old box spring flying across a front lawn in Hope Falls?

Finley: She's creepy and beautiful, and she lives next door to the Batmobile. Also, you can sit on any of the sculptures and no one cares.

Tom: Is that so?

Finley: Pinky swear you won't be arrested.

Tom: Did you feel that? It's my leg being pulled.

Finley: Okay, maybe not arrested. You'll just be yelled

at. Make that, yelled at loudly. Correction—yelled at loudly and possibly run off the property.

Tom: With rakes, hoes, and other gardening tools shaken at me angrily?

Finley: Shovels too. Don't forget shovels. They're particularly fearsome when shaken angrily.

Tom: But not when shaken gently, kindly, or lovingly?

Finley: No one knows. No one has ever tried to shake a shovel gently, kindly, or lovingly.

Tom: So that was your warning not to climb the yard art?

Finley: I'm thoughtful like that.

Tom: Definitely appreciate the tip, since I was tempted to climb all over this yellow school bus driven by a curly-haired guy who looks like Buzz Lightyear.

Finley: The bus is so cute! It's one mile from my house. Stay there.

Tom: Are we meeting now?

Finley: You're busy looking at art in yards. I crushed my page count for the day. Seems we ought to gawk at junk together. Agree/disagree?

I stare at my phone as I stroll past the bus, not entirely sure what to make of this woman and her eagerness. Finley doesn't even know Cassandra, so I'm not sure how much help she can be in my quest.

My phone buzzes, and I figure it's another text from her, but it's from my brother.

Ransom: Kyler, this is Delia, texting you from Ransom's phone. Don't worry! I have faith you'll find Cassandra! Trust the new girl.

Me: Did you take my brother's phone?

Ransom: Of course. He's so ridiculous, but I can't let him give you a hard time. Also, keep it up. You're such a romantic at heart.

Me: Yeah?

Ransom: I swear! You should show up at her place of work next and carry her off. It worked for me. I swear it'll work for you!

See? I am good at romance. My brother's wife thinks so. Obviously, Finley is wrong. She said women don't like big gestures. Or wait. Is that what she said? I flash back to last night, snapping my fingers. Ah, she said my grand gesture sucked, for many reasons. But now I wonder—did it? Do I have to be a good singer to pull off the boom-box move? My brother is no Richard Gere, but his big gesture worked like a charm.

Wait.

Wait just a hot minute.

How did I not see it sooner? I bet Finley wants to sleep with me. Yes, that's it. She totally wants to bang me. Finley doesn't really want to help me win Cassandra.

She wants to seduce me.

I let that prospect roll around in my head for a few seconds, picturing Finley with come-hither eyes, pouty lips, a flip of her hair. The image is both incongruous with the woman I met and weirdly appealing too. It seems my brain thinks Finley's hot in an adorable sort of oddball way.

Trouble is, I can't be thinking of New Girl as hot. She's Wrong Girl, and I'm a man on a mission to win back Right Girl.

Me: Thanks for the advice, Delia!

Ransom: Bro, that was epic punking. You do know that was me pretending to be Delia, right?

I groan and drag my hand over my face. He's such an asshole, and I'm such an idiot for falling for his tricks.

Me: This is me ignoring your texts.

Then I think about Finley again, doing that come-hither thing, and I like the image more than I should.

I shake my head to clear it while texting her to find out where she wants to meet.

7

TOM

Ten minutes later, her mint-green bike appears on the crest of a hill as I stare at a rusty fire engine assembled from what looks to be old motorcycle parts and manned by three cartoonish metal dudes that were once water pipes. As I stare at it, I calculate the weight, the angles, the amount of pressure the structure can hold. This is the part of the answer I didn't share with Midge—I went into roller-coaster design because math and I were best friends growing up, and nothing intrigued me more than figuring out how structures of all sorts of shapes and sizes worked.

But I shove formulas out of my head when Finley's a few feet away. She stops, hops off the bike, kicks the kickstand, and wiggles an eyebrow. At least I think she's wiggling an eyebrow. Hard to see beneath these crazy sunglasses she wears. They're gold and covered with plastic flowers that look like the kind on a decorated cake.

"It's hard to take you seriously with those sunglasses on," I say, pointing at her freckled face.

"Who said anything about taking me seriously?"

"Well, now that we're on the same page . . ."

"Please don't take me seriously at all. Unless I'm telling you what to do. Then take me very seriously," she says, stopping in front of me. I'm not sure if I should hug her or shake her hand or something else entirely.

I point to the glasses instead. "What's the story with the kooky shades? Are they part of a costume?"

She whips them off. "I don't have a desk job."

My brow knits. "And that means?"

"If you don't have a desk job, that means you can and should regularly go pantless." She counts off on one finger. "Write in a bikini on the porch." She adds another finger, and the image of her in a bikini conveniently pops in front of my eyes. "And wear fun sunglasses."

"What color bikini?" I ask, because I'd like to fill in the paint by numbers image precisely.

"A polka-dot one, of course," she says with a wink, then parks the shades over my glasses, steps back, and appraises her handiwork. "I say we need to get you some crazy shades too."

She reaches for her phone, snaps a picture, and sends it to me.

I take off the shades, since it's hard to see through two layers. "Is this where we do the sunglass-shopping montage scene?"

She laughs, pushing the glasses on top of her head.

"Are we living in *Pretty Woman* now? Don't tell me you want me to take you shopping on Rodeo Drive?"

"Of all the elements of *Pretty Woman*, that's the one you key in on?"

"Instead, should I hire you to be my boy toy?"

I part my lips to speak, but I don't know how to answer her. Or *that*. She rocks back and forth on her heels like she's waiting for me to say something, and I realize I don't know what I'm doing with her. I don't understand her.

Is this her ruse to get me in bed? Calling me a boy toy?

Truth is, I wouldn't mind getting naked with her because, hello, hot chick, but I need to keep my eye on the prize, so I'm going to have to cut this seduction strategy of hers off at the knees. "I want to level with you. I'm not interested in you that way."

She blinks, coughs, and then laughs. For several seconds. Okay, more like half a minute. "I'm sorry. Say that again." She gestures for me to keep going.

"I'm interested in Cassandra."

She points at her chest. "And not me, right? I just want to make sure I understand. It's a touch confusing, and I don't want to miss a beat."

I frown, totally confused now, because isn't it self-evident? "That's what I said."

She shakes her head, amused. "Tom, I need you to know something."

"Yes?"

She brings her hand to her chest. "I solemnly swear I have not once thought of you naked. I absolutely haven't dirty-dreamed of you. And I'm definitely not harboring delusions about stripping you down to nothing and having my wild, wicked way with you."

Wild, wicked way.

What does Finley think is wild and wicked?

My brain spins, crafting scenarios that involve her bent over the Batmobile, or daring me to climb the fire engine sculpture and test its strength for a wild, wicked screw. I have no fucking clue why my mind finds these images permissible for assembly, so I shove a hand roughly through my hair, trying to clear my head.

"And I'm not thinking of stripping you down to nothing and having my wild, wicked way with you either," I say.

She dusts one hand against the other. "Good thing neither one of us is remotely attracted to the other."

"Yeah, not at all," I say flippantly. But wait? She's not? "You're not?" My voice ticks up. Why does her statement bother me?

"Did you want me to be remotely attracted to you?"

I shake my head, unsure what to do or say next.

"Because I thought this was about figuring out women, and Cassie in particular," she adds.

I hook onto something she hinted at last night. "I'm not terrible with women. I don't know why you think I am."

And that came out defensively.

"I didn't say you were terrible with women," she says gently. "I said I'd help you with *one* woman."

"I've had plenty of women, you know," I add, since I can't seem to stop defending my track record. It's one I embarked on post-Cassandra. After all, she dumped me after we slept together once. Only once. How would I know whether that had anything to do with it? I decided if there was an iota of a chance that I was bad in bed, I'd work my ass off to become good in bed. Suffice it to say, I know I'm the latter now.

She crosses her arms. "Tell me more about all the women you've slept with. Was Cassie your first or your tenth?"

"First. Same for her. We were each other's firsts. The night of the cast party."

"And now you're a stud. So tell me all about your sexual prowess. You're a good-looking guy. I'm sure women flock to you. Do you have to beat them off with a stick? Maybe some brooms? Sweep them away?"

"All I'm saying is I don't think I'm a terrible case. The women I've been with have been pleased, thank you very much. And I get along well with women I work with too." I point in the direction of the meeting I had earlier. "Just today, a woman at the standards organization laughed at my jokes before she asked me a bunch of questions about female engineers."

Finley tilts her head. "What about them?"

"If there were many in my field. Because her daughter is in a related field. So I told her I meet lots of women."

She raises one inquisitive brow. "Did she tell you anything about her daughter, by chance?"

"Like what?"

Twirling a finger around a strand of hair, she tosses out, "Oh, I don't know. Maybe did she say her daughter is smart, pretty, and lives nearby?"

"I think so. Do you know her?"

Finley chuckles, clapping a hand on my shoulder,

doubling over in laughter. "Did it ever cross your mind she was trying to set you up with her daughter?"

My jaw comes unhinged. I start to speak, but I sputter. "Seriously?"

"I suspect so."

I replay the conversation with Midge in my head. "I honestly thought she was making conversation about the field."

"I suspect she was trying to glean whether you were single so she could play matchmaker."

I scratch my head. "Really?"

She pats my cheek. "You're adorable. You truly didn't realize that?"

Maybe she's right. Maybe I'm not picking up on all the signs. I cycle back to earlier in the day. *I meant female ones. Especially smart, pretty, and single ones.* Smacking my forehead, I blow out a long stream of air. "I'm oblivious?"

Finley laughs. "I think you might have high levels of obliviousness flowing in your blood. Do you want me to test you?"

"Like a pinprick? Won't hurt, will it?" I hold out a finger, glad we've slid back to familiar ground—teasing, joking, playing around.

She shakes her head. "I'll be gentle." She tugs my finger then pretends to stick it with a needle.

"Ouch." I yank back my hand like it's burned.

She shoots me a chiding look then declares, "You're off the charts. Just like I suspected. Which explains why you thought it was okay to tell a woman her hair is *fine*."

Ah, the plot thickens. I might have been oblivious to Midge's ulterior motives, but Finley is putting her cards on the table. "This is about your hair and the fact that I don't want to sleep with you?"

That's a lie. I'd totally sleep with her. I mean, I would if Cassie wasn't in the picture.

Rolling her eyes, Finley flicks her hair off her shoulder. "I don't care if you like my hair or not. I don't care if you think I'm hideous. I care that you don't scare off Cassandra."

But that's what I don't understand. What's in this for her? "Why do you want to help me? Why do you care? Are you a hopeless romantic?"

"Hopeless isn't the adjective I'd use."

"Then what is your preferred adjective?"

She taps her finger against her chin. "Practical. I'm a practical romantic."

"What does that even mean?"

She glances down the street one direction, then the other, then speaks like she's revealing a secret. "Look, even though I don't think you should Lloyd Dobler your way through life, I did like *Say Anything*. And I can't help but root for you to win this woman back. You love her. You're looking for her. I want to help you. And yes, selfishly, I'm curious how it all pans out," she says.

"Because you're a writer? Do you hang out with everyone you find curious?"

Sadness streaks across her blue eyes. "Here's the deal. I have this TV show. It's kind of struggling. Well, more than kind of. And I'm casting about for any inspiration. For ideas to make it fresh. It helps to get away from the screen and talk to interesting people, to hear about their lives. You're interesting, and spending time with you is"—she pauses, licks her lips—"creatively stimulating."

"You do know that sounds vaguely dirty?"

"You can't say *stimulating* without sounding dirty."

"Some words are naughty by nature," I say as the iron mermaid catches my eye, reminding me why I stopped on this street in the first place. *Inspiration.* I need it for my rides, Finley needs it for her show. "What's your show?"

"*Mars and Venus.* I'm the creator and writer."

"Are you kidding me?"

"No," she says, laughing lightly.

I grab her shoulders, grinning. "That show is awesome."

She smiles shyly. "Stop it. You've never seen it."

I mime hitting a buzzer. "*Wrong.* I've seen every single episode. Every single one."

"No way. I have maybe ten viewers."

"Want me to prove it to you?"

"Yes." Her eyes are sparkling with excitement.

"Fine. How about the one where Lane is convinced his shrink gives everyone the same advice, so Amanda makes an appointment and pretends to have all the same issues."

The total delight on her face is beautiful. And I want to put it there again.

"But the shrink was onto the gambit, so she played them by giving them contradictory advice."

"And they didn't even realize it at first," she says, completing the thought.

"What about the time Amanda becomes obsessed with what the T.J. Maxx salesman wore every time she went to the store on Friday night, and whether he only owned one pair of pants?"

She bounces on her toes. "They clearly had to get to the bottom of the mystery."

"So she and Lane stake out the T.J. Maxx, and it turns out"—I stop for dramatic effect—"he organizes his outfits by day of the week!"

She clasps her hand to her mouth, shaking her head. "I can't believe you really watch it."

"Correction—really *love* it." My brain catches on something she said last night. "Wait. You said something about shopping at T.J. Maxx last night. Was that storyline inspired from real life?"

She nods excitedly. "I used to go to T.J. Maxx every Friday night to pick up a new dog toy for my dad's dog, and after a few visits, I realized the manager was wearing the same green jeans every Friday, so I went back on a Tuesday night just to test my theory."

"And he was wearing something else? Please say yes because I don't understand why anyone would own green jeans."

"Yes. He wore khakis on Tuesday."

"Thank God. Also, that's awesome." I rub my palms together. "All right. Let's do it. You can be my dating doctor, and you can diagnose everything I need to fix so I can win back Cassandra. How about we grab something to eat and formulate our plan?"

She grabs her phone, checking the time. "I need to go see my dad and write. Do you want to meet tomorrow night for dinner?"

We set a time and I suggest a place—one of Nash's recommendations for favorite restaurants in Hope Falls

—and, as she heads to her bike, it occurs to me I should probably say I'm sorry for some of the things I said earlier, like the comments about her hair, and not wanting to sleep with her.

But I don't always seem to get the right words out with her. Or with Midge either, it seems. And I definitely didn't get the right words out with Cassandra.

And that needs to change. I need to improve my skills in that area so I can win back Cassie.

She's the endgame, and I need to focus on the girl I came looking for.

8

FINLEY

"And this is the Sonoma Suite. If you choose this option, Mister Dog will get a peanut-butter-filled Kong every night, as well as a bedtime story."

The crinkly-haired woman who's giving my dad, the mutt, and me a tour of the newly opened Wagabond Hotel gestures to a king-size bed where my dad's pooch would be lucky enough to lounge in the lap of luxury when my dad takes a trip next month.

I gawk at the plush accommodations for the canine. "Can I please stay here?" I flash my best smile and hold up my hands like they're paws.

My father pats my head. "Have you been a good girl?"

"I've done all my obedience training."

"Then I'll consider it."

"He likes you so much better than me," I say to Mister Dog, who wags his tail and generally shows off how completely cute he is.

Crinkly-haired woman suggests letting him try the accommodations.

"Go to the bed," my dad says, pointing to the mattress.

The pup bounds over to the bed then curls up on it. Spoiler alert—Mister Dog is a pampered prince.

"I want to come back in my next life as your dog, Dad."

My gray-haired father laughs then tells the woman he'll make a reservation. We head to the front desk, and as she enters his info into the system, I pet Mister Dog's silky head and ask my dad if he's ready for his trip. He's always wanted to tour famous ballparks, and he's finally doing it later this summer. I found him a group of other seniors to go with to visit Camden Yards, Yankee Stadium, Fenway Park, and others. "Are you looking forward to your trip?"

"Definitely. Are you sure you don't want to go along?"

I wave a hand. "Nah. You know all those Viagra-popping septuagenarian dudes would hit on me."

"Then it's best I keep you away from those old geezers," he says with a smile, and I pump a fist quietly since he's happy today.

I convinced him to take the trip, and I even paid for it as a birthday gift. I told him, too, I would keep Mister Dog with me for the ten days of his extravaganza, but he said he didn't want to cramp my style. Honestly, beyond "pajama couture," I don't have a style to cramp, so I wasn't worried, but in the end, he's choosing a peanut-butter-Kong lifestyle for his pooch over kibble at my house. I'd do the same.

After he books the room, he sighs heavily as we leave the dog hotel.

"What's wrong?" I brace myself for today's Sad Moment brought to you courtesy of our sponsor, the Suckitude of Death.

"The wildflowers bloomed this morning," he says, resignation in his tone.

I draw a deep breath. "She would have liked seeing them."

"I took a picture. I wanted to send it to her. How ridiculous is that? There's no place to send it." His voice falters.

I squeeze his shoulder. "It's not silly, Dad."

He swipes an unseen tear away as we walk to his car, Mister Dog gamely trotting by his side. "I keep thinking of her every day. Missing her so much still. When will the missing stop? Shouldn't it have stopped by now?"

"It's grief. It comes and goes on its own time frame." A pang of guilt stabs at me. My grief for her loss is mostly gone.

He inhales deeply and nods, then shifts his focus. "Tell me how the show is going. I can't wait to see the next season."

My chest squeezes. "Great. So great. Everything is ticking along."

His smile is as wide as the sky. "And the network still loves you?"

"Absolutely," I lie.

I don't want to tell him the truth. He's always believed in me. Always rooted for me. He's the only one who did.

My mother never wanted me to go into comedy. An

accountant, she wanted me to write research reports or tech journals or some other drudgery that I would never have been any good at. *When are you going to get a real job?* was her war cry, especially since my brothers are both tax attorneys, in practice together. A few days before she passed, she clucked her tongue and told me it was time to get serious about steady work. How could I be renting still? I was in my late twenties and it was time to buy a home and settle down.

When my show was picked up after her death, my dad said, "Your mother would have been so proud."

I bit back the words I wanted to say. *No, she wouldn't.*

In the afternoon, we work on a jigsaw puzzle at his home, and when I tell him I have to go, he asks what I'm doing that night.

"I met a muse."

He arches a brow. "Tell me more."

"He a-muses me."

He laughs, and the warm, rich sound is my favorite sound in the universe. Better than music. Laughter is my music.

9

FINLEY

Dinner in wine country is like going to a show.

When you're seated and the curtain goes up, the waiter and the rest of the ensemble cast of host, busboy, and sommelier set the stage for the star. Then it's a lively opening number, a medley of delish appetizers, and a showstopper of a main course.

Right now, we're off to a promising Saturday night start, thanks to the tongue-tickling flavors of white grapefruit and pear in this sauvignon blanc, and I offer a toast to Tom's newest successful roller-coaster test, and he offers one to my show.

He clinks his glass to mine. His chocolate-brown eyes light up when he tastes the wine. "Good choice."

"Thank you. I might have picked up a thing or two about grapes from living here. Also, nice touch asking me to choose the wine. I bet Cassandra would like that too."

Tom flashes me a grin, and I sit up straighter. Because . . . those teeth. Those straight white teeth, and that magical smile that I didn't expect—it reaches his warm eyes that seem to twinkle with delight. A butterfly sensation zips through my chest.

And maybe because I've been hard on him, or maybe because I've learned, too, that positivity goes a long way, I say, "Let me preface this by saying I'm not coming on to you, but you have a fantastic smile, and you ought to unleash that grin on Cassandra. *A lot.*"

"You think so?" One corner of his lips curves up, and dear God, now it's a lopsided grin. Why do crooked grins have to be so sexy? Especially on hot nerds like him. Hot grin plus sexy nerd equals unicorn.

Whoa.

I don't think Tom is hot.

I don't think he's a sexy unicorn either.

And I definitely didn't feel a little buzz of pleasure when he smiled.

Nope, that was pride. Because he's a good student. I'm simply pleased he suggested I pick the wine, so I'm giving props for that. But so I don't get caught up in his grinning superpower and its kryptonite effect on me, I lift the glass to my lips and indulge in a sip, shifting my focus to the wine and away from those soulful eyes, that hint of stubble on his jaw, and his dark brown hair that swoops across his forehead in thick waves.

I am immune to good-looking men, I tell myself. It's a mantra I devised when my last relationship imploded on account of my handsome, brilliant ex-boyfriend, Anthony, ditching me for the woman he dated right before me. I was his rebound girl, and he used me to springboard right back to her. Really, when I think about it, that was his one flaw. He was an all-around good guy, and we were a great match in every other way, barring his still being secretly in love with someone else.

Sigh.

I have no interest in tumbling down that rabbit hole again or developing even an iota of a feeling for someone who has his heart set on another.

I set down the wine and recalibrate. "Project Cassandra begins now. I did a little research on her after I saw my dad."

He arches a brow curiously.

"Facebook is an amazing thing," I say, since I poked around her page today, learned more about her transition from choreography to yoga, and even read a few older posts from friends, complimenting her on a blog she kept a few years ago. But there was no trace of the blog, so she must not write it anymore. Still, I gleaned plenty from her yoga studio's site, as well as her Facebook page. "I assume you looked under the rug a little bit online?"

"Definitely. I went to her yoga studio's site. It's very . . ." He stares at the ceiling like he's thinking of just the right words. "Yoga-y."

I laugh. "Yes, that's a good thing for a yoga studio site to be."

"It was all about mindfulness and embracing your whole self and being one with the universe. Ergo, it was yoga-y."

"Yes, but that's part and parcel of who she is now. Her favorite quote is from Laura Ingalls Wilder: 'It is the sweet, simple things of life which are the real ones after all.' That's why I think we have to eschew big gestures with her."

He quirks his lips. "Eschew? Is that your new language test?"

"Of course. It flips on Fridays. The new one is 'insert an unusual synonym into everyday conversation.'" I run my finger along the wineglass stem. "Do you agree?"

He pouts. "I agree that your plan sucks all the *merriment* out of the pursuit."

"Ooh. Well played."

"But seriously, why are big gestures forbidden?"

"Big gestures are fine, but only once you know a woman is into you."

He wiggles his eyebrows. "She'll be into me."

"Cocky bastard."

"I'm an irresistible bastard too. Just ask Midge."

I lower my voice to a stage whisper. "I think we've established the Midge Misread is why we're here right now. While we're at it, let's also agree to no placards at the door, no boom box, and definitely no chasing her down at the airport."

"But don't you writers love all that stuff?"

I sketch air quotes. "'All that stuff' is for the end of the story. The story should begin with a meet-cute. And when it's a second-chance romance, like yours could be, you don't need a meet-cute. Especially since Cassie seems to value a more simplified approach. My vote is you be earnest and honest and show up humbly and ask for a second chance."

Reaching under the table, he takes out his phone and taps on the screen. "Just writing this down," he mutters, and then shows me a note he's sending himself.

Earnest, honest, ask for a chance.

Wow. The man is actually taking notes, and I'm impressed. Also, it's a little adorable that he thinks he can't remember otherwise. He looks up and clears his throat. "I was thinking of showing up at a restaurant where she's dining, standing on the table, and confessing my undying love for her. Would that be earnest and honest?" He tilts his head, his eyes wide, totally playing me.

I shake a finger. "You will do no such thing. Just keep it simple. Knock on her door. Send her a note. Heck, send her flowers and ask her if she'd like to go out."

"Flowers? That seems like something any guy could do."

"But in this case, you want to be *any* guy. You want her to see you in the same light she'd see anyone she's thinking of dating."

"I'd actually like it to be a better light."

I roll my eyes. "You know what I'm saying. Cassie is a woman who values the heart. Speak from the heart, not a script."

Before he can weigh in, the waiter arrives, ready to take our orders. Tom holds up a hand, speaking confidently. "I've got this."

I furrow my brow. "Got what?"

"The ordering. I'll handle it."

"Why would you handle it?"

"Returning the favor and all, for the wine. I checked out the menu online before I arrived."

He turns to the waiter, and I'm about to cut in, but then I decide to watch the show, like it's a nature documentary. *Watch the modern male as he navigates the wild of restaurants.* Tom orders roasted corn ravioli for himself, saying he's been dying to try it, then the pan-fried sea bass for me, wiggling his eyebrows, adding for my benefit, "It's wild-caught, that's the best. I bet the fish was happy."

"The happiest," I echo as I wait, just wait, for him to realize his mistake. But he doesn't, and I'm not going to let on yet. As they say, this is a teachable moment.

When the waiter leaves, Tom flashes those pearly whites. "Okay, give me more stuff. I need all the details. If I'm on a date with Cassandra, what else shouldn't I do?"

The thing he just did, which I'm not going to let on right now. I sidestep to other issues. "Besides discuss religion and politics?"

"Everyone loves to discuss who they voted for and the existence of God, right?"

"Absolutely. Those are great topics."

He grabs his phone and taps out another note, then shows the note to me. *Discuss gun control and church attendance.*

"Boom. You're good to go. Wait. One more topic. On the first date, you definitely shouldn't talk *a lot* about sex, favorite positions, and size too."

He blinks. "Wait. Why can't we talk about sex?"

I stare at him. "You're seriously asking?"

"Why wouldn't we talk about sex and favorite positions on the first date?"

I can't quite believe he doesn't have a clue, so I keep it simple for him. "She might think you're only into her for sex, and clearly that's not the case, since you have a big thing for her."

"It is a big thing," he says, deadpan.

I give him an oh-no-you-didn't look.

He holds up his hands in surrender. "Got it. No sex talk because she'll think I'm well-endowed and she doesn't want a well-endowed man."

I reach across the table to poke his shoulder. "You do know women are not as obsessed with size as you think?"

He scratches his head. "They're not?"

"It's all a matter of what you can do with it."

He leans closer, drops his chin in his hands. "It's how you use it?"

"Yes. Of course."

"Can we talk about how I like to use it? How I'd want to make a woman feel so fucking good with it?"

A spark shimmies down my spine, and my cheeks go up in flames. I press my finger to my lips. "Shh."

His lips curve up. "You're embarrassed."

Glancing around the tiny dining room, I whisper, "You're just loud."

His eyes glint mischievously. "And you're completely embarrassed by sex talk."

I straighten my spine. "I'm not embarrassed by it at all," which isn't a lie.

What I'm embarrassed about is how his "so fucking good" comment turned me on.

He holds up a thumb and forefinger. "A little? You're a little embarrassed?"

"Are you trying to embarrass me?"

He laughs. "Honestly, I kind of am. You're hilarious when your goat is gotten."

I stare at him with narrowed eyes. "You did not get my goat."

"I kind of did. Just admit it. Admit I got your goat."

I cross my arms. "No way."

He leans back in the chair, parking his hands behind his head. "Then let's just talk about your favorite positions instead. Or maybe how you like to feel *so fucking good.*"

Tingles have the audacity to zip down my body once more.

I hold my hands out wide. "Fine. You. Got. My. Goat. Happy?"

"So satisfied," he says in a sexy rasp, and my traitorous body grows warmer.

Must abort this conversation, stat. I sit up straighter. "If you were on a date with Cassandra, I bet this would be a good time to talk about likes and dislikes, her job, your job. Why don't we talk about roller coasters?"

"I can do that all day. Do you like roller coasters?"

I breathe a deep sigh of relief as we move to a safer topic. "Love them," I say, and that's the God's honest truth. "There's nothing better than fear and thrill mingling together. Tell me more about the ones you've designed. What's the secret to creating a great ride?"

His face is animated as he talks. "You want it to make a rider's stomach flip upside down, yet you don't want them to vomit. We try to discourage rides that lead to loss of lunch," he says, and I laugh. "What about you? What's the key to writing a great character and getting a laugh? Besides going to T.J. Maxx."

"Comedy is timing. It's the jokes, but it's also all about knowing the right pace for the joke." I take another drink of my wine.

"Which makes comedy a lot like delivering an orgasm?"

I nearly spit out my sauvignon blanc. "You're still doing sex talk."

He shakes his head, smiling impishly. "That's analogy talk."

I wiggle my eyebrows, playing along. "Fine, then. If you stimulate the funny bone just so, I suppose comedy is a lot like delivering pleasure."

He snickers, lowering his gaze. "Like you said, you can't say *stimulate* without it sounding dirty."

"It's an analogy!" I insist.

"An analogy you chose because you're thinking about sex."

I slap a hand on the table. "I'm not thinking about sex."

He points at me, a self-satisfied grin on his face. "But you are thinking about the big finish? The peak? The summit?"

The blush? It returns. Full force. Beet red.

"I'm not thinking about orgasms."

I am. It's like when someone says don't think about cookies and then all you can think about are cookies. And right now I can't think about anything but how toe-curlingly good a cookie would be. That's why I need to wrest control of this conversation. "If you think about it, we're both in the same business. A good ride should hit the right peak, and a good joke should too."

He strokes his chin as if in deep thought. "True. You need to make sure you deliver the right amount of joke prep. A word here, the right delivery there. Then the joke rises, strengthens, insists on being noticed. And then you have to make sure the joke recipient is ready, primed, right on the cusp of hearing the great joke."

I toss a napkin at him.

"And then when she's there, hovering on the edge, you deliver the punchline." He makes a moaning sound.

I drop my head into my hands, whispering, "You did *not* just do that."

"Sally did it in the movie."

I raise my face. "You think everything's okay because you saw it in the movies?"

"No?" He mimes making a check mark. "No acting out the famous scene from *When Harry Met Sally*, and no discussion of orgasms. Not on any level, right? I mean, can we discuss the timing of orgasms? Minutes to climax? Those sorts of things?"

I blush more. I can feel the color spread from my cheeks down my skin. "You're trying to make me blush."

He smiles again, clearly pleased with himself. "Honestly, it's adorable when you blush. I've never seen someone turn that shade of tomato before. Wait, no, it's fire-engine red. Hold on, you've moved into beet territory."

That's because we can't seem to stop talking about sex. And there are some parts of sex that I'm bad at. So I try to cover it up by making jokes. But I can't tell him that. I can't tell him that I suck at X and Y but not Z.

"Why are you blushing so much?" he presses. "Do you have something against orgasms?"

"No," I insist.

"Do you dislike them?"

"God, no."

"You do like them, then?"

"Of course I like them. Everyone likes them."

"Are you sure?"

"*Tom.*" He's pushing all my buttons, and I don't know how to get him to stop. Nor do I understand how this train left the station and sped away from me.

"I embarrassed you again," he says, his voice soft and gentle.

"Yes, because this isn't what we're supposed to talk about."

Because it's making me squirm. Because I'm thinking about sex with you and I'm not supposed to.

"Let's talk about work. Do you want to hear more about how a thrill ride works?"

"Yes," I say, relieved.

He leans forward. "Angle. It's all about angle."

I wave the napkin. "I surrender."

* * *

When dinner arrives, I'm practically bouncing in my seat. I can't wait to throw him this curveball and see if he can hit it.

"Your sea bass, madam," the waiter says, sliding the plate in front of me.

He sets the ravioli in front of Tom, who raises his fork, ready to go. He gestures to my fish as the waiter leaves. "It's the happiest fish, right?"

I exhale heavily. "Hold on." He lifts a brow in question. "Let's say you're on a date."

"Like we're pretending to be."

"And the food arrives." I gesture to the plates.

"Like it has, and it looks good."

I raise a finger. "But there's one thing you forgot to do."

He tilts his head, clearly perplexed.

I drop my voice, imitating a man. "Oh hey, Cassandra, I forgot to ask before I ordered, but you're not going to break out in hives from the fish, are you? Or wait. Are you, by chance, a vegetarian?"

He groans an *oh hell* groan. "Is it door number one or door number two for my faux pas?"

"It's the 'I don't eat anything with a face' door. I think Cassie might be a vegetarian too."

He puts down his fork, holds up his hands, and winks. "Don't worry. I got this." In a flash, he switches plates, sliding his dish across the table and taking mine. "How about them apples?"

A smile stretches across my face. "Well done, Good Will Hunting."

"What can I say? I'm a problem solver."

"I'm seriously impressed with your quick save."

He blows on his fingertips. "Yeah, I'm not so terrible at this dating thing. Now, where were we?" he asks, as my fork dives into the ravioli and I take a bite. "Oh right, you were about to enjoy the best roasted corn ravioli in wine country, and I'm going to eat some happy fish." He slices into his food, chews, and makes a Food Network host–style sound of appreciation. "Definitely the happiest fish ever."

"Also, this is amazing," I say once I finish a mouthful.

"See? I totally meant to do that." He takes a drink of

his wine, then slides his knife across the fish again. "Have you always been a vegetarian?"

I shake my head. "I started in high school. My mom had a terrible diet."

"And you stopped eating meat because of that?"

"I wanted to be healthier. And yes, I do indulge in ice cream and wine, but I figure if I keep the bulk of my meals on the lighter side, I'll be better off. I'm not saying being a vegetarian is a hedge against health problems, and obviously I'm indulging in corn ravioli tonight, but in general, I try to eat differently than she did. She kept eating processed meat and pastries and drinking Frappuccinos right up until the end."

"Were you close to her?"

I make a seesaw gesture. "In some ways, yes. In other ways, no. She never really understood my desire to write comedy. She wanted me to do something more practical. To write technical manuals or press releases. She worried that I'd never have a stable job."

"Do you think that's true?"

"Oh, it's fairly accurate, but at the same time that's the risk in my field, and I was willing to take it."

He nods thoughtfully as he chews. "Would you consider yourself a risk-taker?"

I let that question rattle around before I answer. "I always wear a helmet when riding my bike, I don't text and drive, and I try to limit my vices. But"—I lean closer —"I did go skydiving last year."

His eyes widen. "What was that like? I've always wanted to go but never have."

My eyes float shut briefly as I recall the summer day

when Christine and I leaped from a plane. It was her birthday, and it had been on her bucket list. Her husband had refused to go, but she'd convinced me rather easily, not only luring me with the sheer thrill of it, but also with its creative powers—she said she'd bet it would inspire me to write a hilarious scene about skydiving.

She was right. Falling from the sky was a total rush, and I wrote a skydiving scene into my show.

I open my eyes. "Pure exhilaration."

"And a little bit of fear?"

"Absolutely. That moment when you look out the door and the wind rushes by, and you can barely hear anything but the whoosh of your life roaring past you, and you ask yourself if you're going to back down? That's terrifying."

He pops a piece of fish in his mouth and chews. "And how do you get past that?"

I shrug happily. "You give fear the middle finger."

He laughs. "And that, ladies and gentlemen, is how you skydive."

"And when you're falling, it's the craziest, wildest, most thrilling thing you've ever done."

He sets down his fork with a flourish. "Now I have no choice. I have to go skydiving."

"You do. I dare you," I say, challenging him.

"All you have to say to a guy is 'I dare you,' and we're pretty much doing it. What about you? Does 'I dare you' work on you?"

"Try me."

He raises an eyebrow, pointing to his fish. "This is fantastic. I dare you to take a bite."

I chuckle. "You can't dare me into eating fish. Again, I don't eat anything that has a face."

He smirks. "I like to eat certain things that have faces."

My jaw drops. "You did not just make a joke about oral sex."

"It wasn't a joke. I'm very serious," he says, completely deadpan.

And I'm completely off my game once more. He's knocking me off-kilter, and I'm a fidgeting mess. I keep trying to reroute the night away from all the sex talk, because sex talk is the start of flirting, and flirting is the start of liking. That's the real trouble.

I'm not attracted to him, he's not attracted to me, and he's interested in someone else.

But one of those things is a lie.

I am attracted to him.

But his heart belongs to someone else. After my last boyfriend ditched me because he was still in love with his ex, there's no way I'm veering down that road again.

"Tell me what your high school was like," I say, then pop in a piece of the ravioli.

"The guys there were cool. We totally bonded."

Something clicks in my brain. "Did you go to an all-boys school?"

"Yes." His eyes gleam with excitement. "How did you know?"

"My friend Christine. Her husband went to one, and she said you can tell guys who did because they resort to sex talk all the time. It's like they were raised by wolves."

He points his fork at me. "You started the sex talk.

Did you go to an all-girls school?'

But I won't let him distract me. I'm on a mission, and the puzzle pieces are clicking—he has three brothers, his mom died young, he attended an all-boys school. He hasn't had a lot of female influences in his life. It truly is like he was raised by wolves. Since men are, well, wolfish.

"Listen, have you had a serious girlfriend?"

He looks down at his food like he doesn't want to answer. "Here and there."

For a moment, I think he sounds embarrassed. "It's no big deal if you haven't," I say gently.

He raises his face, shrugging it off. "I've had a few somewhat serious girlfriends. Nothing to write home about though, and I'm cool with it. I've been pretty busy with work. I've dated though."

"But not that much?"

He sets down his fork. "Look, even though my first time was in college with Cassie, I do know what women want. I know how to make a woman happy in bed."

I hold up my hands, the sign for backing off. "My first time was in college too. But, Tom, I wasn't talking about horizontally."

"Then why are you asking?"

"I'm saying you might need practice. Not at sex, but at how to be a boyfriend."

He scoffs. "I don't need practice."

"You spent most of the meal trying to get me to blush. And, trust me, I like sex."

"You do?" he asks, and his gaze darkens.

"I do, but I also don't want to talk about sex on a first date."

He licks his lips, glances away, then turns back to me. "I promise no more sex talk. We can even practice that starting now."

We spend the rest of the meal talking about where we grew up—we are both California natives and therefore addicted to sunshine and avocados; favorite books —I devour celebrity memoirs, and he adores how-stuff-works stories; and the all-time best flavors for ice cream —we both adore anything with coconut.

"Thanks for the practice, Finley. Let's do it again," he says as we leave.

"I'm up for a round two."

Out on the main street, I say hello to Sandy Davidson, who owns Tren-day, a cute clothing shop next to the restaurant. "Hey, Sandy. How's business?"

The Jane Lynch look-alike smiles and waves. "Can't complain. I'm outfitting all the coolest cats in wine country." She glances at Tom. "If you ever need anything stylish, come see me. I have a shop here and one in our sister town of Lucky Falls. That one has even more of the hippest duds."

"I'll be there," he says.

She turns down the street and walks the other way, and I look at Tom, my pulse skittering as our eyes seem to lock for the briefest of moments. "So . . ."

"So . . ."

"That was fun," I say.

"It was a lot of fun," he adds, then drops a kiss to my cheek. It's a chaste kiss. A mere brush of lips to skin. But there's nothing chaste about my body's reaction to it.

I force myself to focus on the goal—to help him win

back the girl, and in doing so, to help myself. To save my show. "More practice tomorrow?"

He smiles in the lopsided way that threatens to weaken my knees again. "Tomorrow sounds good. Glad you liked the ravioli. I had a feeling you would."

I laugh as I ride my bike home.

* * *

What tastes even better, though, is what I write into the episode that night.

With a little help from his lady friend, the hero preps to meet the yoga queen. He says he wants to sing a song to her, but his lady friend promptly nixes that idea over dinner. At said meal, the hero tries to order for both of them.

"Ordering for someone else is a deal breaker."

"It's called chivalry."

"It's called steamrolling."

"Steamrolling sounds vaguely dirty."

"Steamrolling sounds horrifically filthy."

They agree to never use the word *steamrolling* again. He segues to sex talk that sounds deliciously naughty, and they wind up talking about a million other things, like music and risks and friends. That feels dangerous to his lady friend—every path the conversation takes.

I send the draft of the first episode to Bruce and cross my fingers that he'll like it, then find a message on my phone from Tom.

Seeing his name makes me feel giddy, so I tell my feelings to settle the hell down while I slide open the text.

10

FINLEY

Tom: Since timing is everything, what time should I pick you up for tomorrow's practice date?

Finley: Seven is a perfect date time for dinner. But we're not doing dinner. So five, please.

Tom: Should I bring a snorkel?

Finley: Why on earth would you bring a snorkel?

Tom: You never know what risks we might be taking. It's good to be prepared.

Finley: I assure you, there is no risk of snorkeling in or around Hope Falls.

Tom: Maybe a blowtorch, then? A bowling ball? A badminton racket?

Finley: Do you think we're going to weld, join a league, or engage in lawn sports?

Tom: Fine, fine. Just surprise me. But just so you know, my badminton game is on fire.

Finley: *makes note to challenge you to badminton soon* Also, you're such a weirdo. :) P.S. Dress casually.

Tom: I can do that. Also, I think it's cool that you love roller coasters.

Finley: I think it's cool that you design them.

Tom: You should ride one of mine sometime.

Finley: Is this you trying to trick me into naughty talk again?

Tom: No. I mean, maybe. That is going to be pretty hard for me to resist doing. But I'm serious. I'm ridiculously proud of my work, and seeing a thrill-seeker like yourself ride one would be a total high.

Finley: I would love to ride your rides. And no, don't go there!

Tom: *engage resistance to sex talk mode*

Finley: Do you have that mode?

Tom: I do. I absolutely do. Also, I was thinking about

what you said about timing and chasing laughs. Makes me realize we're both pursuing the same prize in our jobs—that moment of elation.

Finley: I like that description.

Tom: It's a good gig, isn't it? Loving what you do?

I smile as I settle onto the couch, enjoying the direction our texts have taken.

Finley: Yes. I'm lucky I get to do this. I only hope I can keep doing it.

Tom: Keep up the timing and you will. You make me laugh.

Finley: I guess that's helpful, since you don't want to sleep with me.

Tom: Your laughter keeps me totally focused on not sleeping with you.

I want to tell him it's the same for me. But that'd be a lie.

11

TOM

"You're doing it wrong."

I flip Nash the bird as I shave. "If I'm doing it wrong, it's because you taught me wrong."

My brother points at me from his perch on the corner of my hotel bed, surrounded by bags of produce he picked up at the Sunday farmers market this morning for his restaurant, a few towns over from Hope Falls. "What have I told you? You need to shave in the opposite direction of the hair."

"Oh right. Of course. How did I ever forget that key detail?"

"Just like I taught you." His tone is notably evil, as it often is.

I rinse off the stubble and shaving cream then bring the razor back to my jaw. "I know, jackass. You tried to trick me into shaving the wrong way when I was fifteen."

Nash cackles, a familiar sound I've heard my whole life. "It worked though. You totally fell for it." He runs a hand over his shiny skull. He says he's bald by choice, and since he shaves his head nearly every day, I have no clue if his hair would grow in if he let it. But he likes the look and claims the ladies do too.

"I was fifteen! I trusted you guys! And you were eighteen then."

He waves a hand dismissively as he roots around in his bags. "And look at your handsome face. Not a single nick. You'll look so pretty when you see our cousin," he says, since I'm grabbing a bite with our cousin Gabe before a quick meeting with a contractor. "Also, you didn't actually get hurt the first time you shaved backward, so don't cry wolf."

My lips curve up in a grin, thinking of Finley's "raised by wolves" comment last night about guys who went to all-boys schools. The way she said it was cute—she shook her head, sort of bemused, her wild, curly hair moving back and forth, her lips looking all mischievous. If only she knew how close she was to the truth.

While I work the razor over my jaw in the hotel mirror, he finds a cauliflower head and holds it up, Simba-style. "How beautiful is this cauliflower?"

"As beautiful as your bald head is not."

"Bald by choice is beautiful."

I smirk at him, running a hand over my hair. My *thick* hair. "I wouldn't know."

"Enjoy the rug while you have it." He points in the direction of my face. "But you do know you hardly had any facial hair when you were fifteen? It was like a layer of peach fuzz. When you came to us and said you wanted to shave, we had no choice. We had to fuck with you."

"Yes, you had no other option but to fuck with me at all times. No other options existed."

He shrugs. "Dad was busy with work, so it fell to us to raise you as our own. We had to toughen you up to prepare you for the world," Nash remarks as he tucks the cauliflower back into his bag. Our father's management consulting business grew exponentially larger when we were teens, which meant he traveled more, so my brothers did more of the heavy lifting with me than my dad did.

"Like wolves," I say, testing the idea, since all four of us went to the same all-boys school.

Nash lifts his face skyward and howls. "We were the wolves. We were wolves raising wolves."

"I'd say that's an apt description. When I was learning to drive, you told me the windshield wipers needed to be on all the time. It's a wonder you didn't try to convince me to put on a condom backward."

Nash scoffs. "No way. Can't mess with that stuff. I've spent thirty-one years trying to prevent that accident, and you seem to take after me rather than Gannon and Ransom, those seed-spreaders."

I correct him as I swipe the razor down. "Thirty-one years? I hope you haven't been practicing safe sex since you were born."

"Fine. I've been practicing it since I was fourteen."

I give him a look. "I remember you sneaking out to date, but were you really only fourteen when you started?"

He puffs out his chest. "When you got it, you got it. I can't help that the ladies wanted a piece of me."

"You seemed older than that, but maybe it's just because you were older than me."

"You were a late bloomer, Kyler." He wiggles his eyebrows. "But not me. The ladies have always thought I was hot."

His use of my real name snags on my ears. I haven't heard it used much in the last few days, and it makes me wonder if I could pull off a name change. "Hey, Nash?"

"Yeah?"

"What do you think about the name Tom?"

"Your middle name, you mean?"

"That's the one. You like it?"

"Is this your way of telling me you want me to call you by your middle name? If I did the same, then I'd be Larry, and that's boring as fuck. Can you even imagine?" He affects a higher-pitched voice, on the cusp of pleasure. "Oh, Larry. Give it to me, Larry. Right there . . . Larry." He shudders.

"That wasn't entirely my purpose, but yes, point well taken."

He rises, setting all his bags on the bed. "The way I see it is this—Nash has served me well, but if you don't like Kyler, change it."

"It's that simple?"

He smiles, the genuine way, not the I'm-going-to-give-you-shit way. "Yeah, change it. I'll still give you hell, but it's your name. Do what you want."

Okay, so maybe it was a bit of the I'm-going-to-give-you-shit kind of grin. "Thanks, man."

"I do reserve the right to give you a hard time about

absolutely anything else. Like Cassie. Any luck with the girl who knocked your heart on its ass in college?"

"Working on it. I met this cool new girl who's been helping me."

"Is she hot?"

I meditate on the question for a few seconds as I wet the razor, prepping to finish the last ribbon of skin.

"That's a no," Nash answers. "If you have to think about it, a woman is not hot."

But he's wrong. We don't have the same taste in women. Nash likes Barbies. I like women more like . . . Finley.

I mean Cassie.

I like Cassie.

And that also means this—a great body is all well and fine, but I'd rather be able to talk to a woman. To have a deep conversation. To laugh. That's what drew me to pursue a second chance with Cassie, truth be told.

My twenties have been good to me, and I've enjoyed the company I've kept at night. But I haven't met many women who stimulated my mind. I've had a few girl-friends, but nothing that lasted incredibly long. Plus, between finishing college and getting a master's, I was consumed with studies till I was twenty-four. I've also never met someone who interested me enough to want to text them for hours on end or talk till we lose track of time.

I don't know if I'd ever admit this to Nash, but I'm bored sleeping around. I want someone I can connect with. The last time I experienced that was with Cassie, and that's why I'm determined to find a way to her again.

And that way back to her goes through Finley.

I slide the blade over my skin. "She's fine," I tell Nash, since I don't want to let on with him that I think Finley is more than hot.

"What if Cassie doesn't want you back though?" he asks as he shows me some radishes plucked from a canvas bag. "Are these a perfect shade of red or what?"

"Um, yeah," I say since I know fuck-all about radishes. "But to your question—how is that even a possibility?"

"True. The Sutcliffe men are known for being impossible to turn down. But still, every now and then, it happens. I'll be here for you if it does," he says, and he sounds earnest.

But I don't know if he's fucking with me.

We've spent so much of our lives fucking with each other that it's hard to know at times when we're not. "Thanks, Nash," I say, keeping it simple.

"By the way," he says, then grins knowingly, "*'I don't understand. All my life, I've been waiting for someone.'*"

A smile takes over my face as he rattles off one of his favorite movie quotes. I pick up the thread, continuing, "*'And when I find her, she's . . . she's a fish.'*" I smile at the memory of *Splash* then shoot him an inquisitive look. "Don't tell me you're still using that line."

He shrugs happily. "It worked with Cindy Wilkins in high school."

"With or without the fish bit?"

"With the fish bit."

Shaking my head, I laugh. "That's not the most

romantic thing to say to a woman, but hey, if the shoe fits, wear it."

"Oh, the shoe definitely fit with her. You should write it down. Use it. Have I ever led you astray?"

"Besides the shaving and the driving?"

"With women, dickhead. Have I ever led you astray with women?"

Truth be told, he hasn't. "No, asshole," I say, "but I don't need to write that line down. I know it well too. Especially what comes next."

Together we say, "*'Nobody said love's perfect.'*"

"It was Mom's favorite flick." There's a faraway sound in his voice.

I tap my temple. "I know how she felt about that movie."

"She loved them all, but that was tops for her." Our mom loved the silver screen—with a special joy reserved for films from the '80s—and passed that passion on to her kids. It's a piece of her we try to carry on.

"I remember," I say, even though I don't remember her terribly well anymore. I recall bits and pieces, and most of my memories come from the last year of her life. "Also, I have something really important to tell you."

"What is it?"

I point at the canvas bag. "No one likes radishes."

"You're wrong, *Tom*," he says, pronouncing the name like it has five syllables. He tries again, like he's testing them out. "Tom Tom. Tommy Boy. Tom Cat."

I laugh. "And even so, I still like all those nicknames better."

"And I like radishes, so to each his own."

He takes off, and when he's gone, I pat a towel on my face and leave the bathroom to pull on a shirt. I get dressed so I can pop over to neighboring Lucky Falls to grab lunch with my cousin Gabe.

I find him parked in a chair at a table outside a burger joint.

"What's shaking, Kyler?"

"You can call me 'Tom,'" I say, trying it on for size.

"You're kidding me," says the fireman, lowering his shades and staring hard with his blue eyes. "You changed your name?"

Grabbing a menu, I shrug. "Yeah. I always hated Kyler, so now I'm Tom."

"This is going to take some getting used to, but I'm up to the task. Do tell though, Tom. Why the hell did you change your name at the ripe old age of twenty-eight?"

"A girl suggested I do it."

He arches a brow then nods. "Girls have a way of making us do things, don't they? There's this woman who I've been dying to get to know better. But I have to take my time. Want to know why?"

"Why?" I ask, since Gabe's always been good with women.

He laughs. "Because women have all the power."

"That they do."

We order, then he asks me what brings me to town.

"Work, and my ex." I give him the gist of things with Project Cassie.

"Why do you want her back?"

That's easy. "I just do."

After lunch, I head over to the office park for a quick

meeting with one of my contracts, then return to the hotel and power through some projects before I see Finley.

Five hours later, I've worked on some of the rudimentary concepts to present to a client in Singapore, a real estate investor named Keith who's determined to have the fastest coaster ever, and I wonder briefly why he wants the fastest ride. For the claim to fame, of course. But fastest isn't always the most fun. Keith is set in his ways though, and I've tried to steer him in a new direction, but he wants what he wants.

Then again, I'm the same way.

I want Cassie.

Plain and simple.

I brush my teeth, grab my wallet, and let the hotel door fall shut behind me, ready to tackle more Cassandra prep. As I leave, I reflect on Gabe's question from earlier.

Why do I want her back?

I just do.

Now, I ask myself again why I want her so badly.

The answer comes easily.

Because we could talk to each other.

But there's a nagging voice asking me if I only want Cassie so she'll give me another chance at sex? So I can prove that I'm good at something I didn't know if I was good at then?

But who's good at sex at twenty?

Except I hope I was.

When I step out of my car and check my reflection in the window once more, my hope shifts. It's no longer about Cassie. It's about Finley, since I want her to like how I look.

But then I remind myself that her opinion doesn't matter since I'm not into her that way.

That's why it's weird to feel a burst of excitement when I see her.

12

TOM

I point to the moon, already visible in the late afternoon sky. "The moon is full."

"It's five," Finley says, giving me a look like I'm crazy. Perhaps I am. I can't seem to stop thinking how cute she looks in a blue sleeveless argyle sweater and shorts, with emerald-green shades perched atop her head. She's preppy sexy, if that's even a thing. If it's not, it should be.

I return to my routine, hoping it works as well as it did the last time I used it. "Did you see the moon last night?" I ask as we walk through olive trees that are planted alongside grape vines at the Tavendish Ranch, home to wine and olive tastings. In the distance, a huge barrel looms, and a few dark-haired women are stomping grapes in it.

Finley tilts her head, looking skyward, contemplating. "I don't recall."

"I've never seen the moon so big before or since."

She spins around, staring at me as we stand beside a fragrant tree. "Wait. Are you doing *Moonstruck*?"

"Well, it's romantic, isn't it?" I ask. Plus, she liked my *Good Will Hunting* quote yesterday. Hell, she started it with the *Social Network* bit the night I met her.

"Let me guess. That's something you and Cassandra did in college?"

I puff out my chest. "I did it a little more than she did, but she did appreciate *Moonstruck*."

"It's a good flick. I love it. You know I love movie quotes. But . . . just one, teensy, tiny little piece of advice."

I rub my fingertips, the sign for *give it to me*. "I'm ready, dating doctor. Give me your best professional advice."

"Call me crazy. But maybe make sure she likes them as much as you do."

"Are you saying you grow out of movie quotes?"

She purses her lips and exhales. The pale pink gloss she wears reminds me of candy and makes me wonder if she'd taste as sweet. I grit my teeth, trying to ward off these inappropriate thoughts about Finley and her lips and her damn sweater. Why the hell do I think her sweater is cute? What is wrong with me?

"It might be something she liked then, or even did for you then, but doesn't like now," Finley suggests.

"But you like them now?"

"I like them now, but does she?"

"How could she not?"

She laughs. "I'd encourage you to recall the sea bass incident."

"So now I have to get approval first before I send

music or quote films?" I grab my phone and tap out another note. *Make sure the woman still likes music and movies and hasn't become a stick in the mud.*

I show her the phone, and she grabs it and shoves it back at me. "No! That's not what I mean."

"It's too late. You basically said I'm not cool. And I thought Tinder was the biggest change since I was in college, but apparently it's that I'm not cool anymore."

She laughs. "News flash. I'm not cool either."

"Then what the hell am I doing here with you?" I ask, chuckling too. "Now you admit you're terrible at this too."

"I'm just saying movie quotes are an acquired—"

I clasp my hands together, banging them against my chest like I'm stabbing a dagger. "Don't say it. You've already driven a stake through my heart."

"You know what? Do them. They're you. You're having fun with them."

I shake my head like a toddler. "Nope. I'm retiring from movie quotes. I'm terrible with women. I'm bad at dating. There's no hope for me. You can never make me do quotes again."

Silence reigns over us until she breaks it.

"*'I'm going to make him an offer he can't refuse,'*" she intones, imitating Brando.

I shake my head. "Can't make me."

"*'But this one goes to eleven,'*" she says in clipped British, quoting *Spinal Tap*.

I hold up my hand like a stop sign. "I'm immune. They no longer work on me."

She grabs my shoulders, staring fiercely at me, then goes full Cher. "*'Snap out of it.'*"

My gaze meets hers. Her eyes link with mine. For a moment, I don't move. I want to kiss her. So fucking badly. "You just quoted *Moonstruck*," I whisper.

Her voice goes soft and gentle. "I had to. I had to get you back to yourself."

"Are you going to slap me now?"

She studies my face, her eyes curious. "Do you want me to?"

I do. But I don't. I mean, *fuck no, I don't want to be slapped*. The trouble is I'm not sure what I want from her at all, except to make her laugh. That, I enjoy without question. But still my thoughts are spiraling away, and I can't stop thinking about kissing her.

That's a big problem since she's not the one I'm supposed to want.

I clear my throat, segueing back to the matter at hand as we resume strolling along the sunny path over the rolling hills. "You're saying Cassandra has probably changed, so I need to make sure she still likes the same things?"

She shakes her head. "No, I'm saying this—you do you."

"But I thought you said I was the problem?"

"Only if you're ordering fish for a vegetarian or talking too much about sex."

"I don't know. She might want the Tom two-point-oh model. I might need to let her know I've been upgraded."

Finley laughs, grabbing my arm. But her laughter fizzles away. "Tom, you're a character, you know that?"

"Why, thank you."

"No, I mean . . ." She takes a beat, like she has a

confession to make, as she looks me in the eyes. "I've said before that you're kind of an inspiration for my show. It's more than kind of. I'm basing a character on you."

My lips quirk up in a grin. "You are?"

"Is that okay?"

Noodling on this new piece of intel, I go quiet for a spell as we walk through the olive trees toward the tasting room. "You're really basing a character on me?"

"I am, but it's more than basing a character, truth be told."

"How much more?"

She fiddles with her rhinestone-studded sunglasses, moving them on and off her head, her expression tight with nerves. "It's actually the whole storyline. I sent it to my network rep this morning, and the good news is he did a quick read and likes it so far," she says then twists her fingers together. "He has to show it to the higher-ups, and I hope they like it too."

"That's great that he likes it. What's the storyline?"

"Your character is trying to win back the woman of his dreams."

I stop for a second, as a smile overtakes my face, and hell, practically my whole body. That might be the coolest thing that ever happened to me, so I blurt out the first thing that comes to mind.

"I bet Cassandra will enjoy that." But even as I voice those words, I know they're all wrong. What I truly mean is . . . *I* enjoy it. I like that Finley's finding her story.

I also like being her muse.

A whole hell of a lot.

As she wanders ahead of me, I ruminate on whether I even know what Cassandra would enjoy. What does my college girlfriend like these days? What is *she* like? I had a perfect image of her in my head, but is it truly the real woman? Or only my idea of her?

Lately, the woman I'm thinking about is the real one in front of me.

And that's a confusing twist in the script. I don't know what John Cusack, Nicolas Cage, or any of my movie heroes would do if they were me.

Except they'd be way cooler when perplexed. That's for sure.

* * *

"Try this one."

She hands me an olive, and I pop it in my mouth. "It's salty and tangy. Also, how is this date prep? Seems more like taste bud training."

"Many dates involve going to tastings. Chocolate. Wine. Olives. You have gone on dates, right?"

"Sure," I grumble. "But not an olive-tasting one."

She eyes me curiously at the counter in the tasting room. "Where have you been taking women on dates?"

"The movies," I say, raising my chin proudly.

"The. Movies?" Her eyebrow arches into another hemisphere.

"Dinner too. Is this where you give me a hard time like you did about movie quotes?"

"I relented on that. But this? I'm not so sure."

I groan. "What am I doing wrong now?"

"You've never taken a woman to a wine tasting? Or

to an art gallery? Or bowling? Or to the Ice Cream Museum?"

I scoff. "That ridiculous place in the city that exists solely for the purpose of Instagram pictures?" One of my clients went there and showed me shots of her kid perched on a unicorn statue, wandering through a room full of oversize gumdrops like some Willy Wonka dreamscape, and another of her kid eating a coconut popsicle in a mirrored room that looks like a pink '50s diner. They made zero sense.

"People like to take pictures in crazy places."

I shake my head. "Can't do it. Won't give in to the Instagram madness."

"You're so crotchety. You're probably going to tell me you're not even on social media."

"Not much. That's one of the reasons I didn't friend Cassie. I don't post much on Facebook, and I have maybe fifty friends, so I didn't want to look like a loser."

"Fine, you don't need to be on Facebook to date effectively. But we need to shake it up. Get you out of the dinner-and-a-movie rut." She hands me a small olive from the tasting tray.

"Dinner and movies are a rut?"

"Dinner and the movies are fine, but that's what old married couples do."

"I'm not old."

"Nor are you married. That's why we're eating olives." She pops one in her mouth and moans. "If I could survive on ice cream, wine, and olives I would." She sighs happily.

"Have you ever tried?"

"No. But I'm willing to make an attempt. Want to try

with me?"

"Definitely. Should we pack a cooler with a few dozen flavors, a bunch of bottles, and some olives?"

She drops her voice. "Meet me at dawn by the docks, and we'll escape on the first boat out of town."

"It's a plan." I reach for a sage-green olive, biting into the meat then dropping the pit in the white dish. "Have you always lived here? It's odd to live in wine country. Just like you think it's odd to go to the movies as a date. Sheesh."

"I don't think movies are odd, but you don't get to know someone at the movies. Oh, but wait. You were never that interested in getting to know anyone."

I hold up my hands. "In my defense, I honestly never met anyone who blew my mind."

"Oh, your mind? I'd have thought it was something else you wanted blown . . ."

As her voice trails off, I have no choice but to slow-clap. For several beats. "Well done."

She stands up and takes a well-deserved curtsy. "Thank you very much. Please make ample use of the tip jar on your way out." Sitting down, she answers, "My dad was a business manager at a bunch of different wineries, so it was kind of here or no place else."

"And your mom?"

Her expression shifts when she mentions her mom, a hardness in her features. "She was an accountant."

"Did you mean it when you said you disappointed her?"

She taps her chest, her voice cold. "Finley Barker. Disappointing mothers since 1989."

"How does that happen? You're awesome. How did

she not think you're kick-ass?"

She shrugs. "My brothers were the superstars of the family. They were both jocks. In fact, they weren't only jocks. They were student-athletes. And they were student council. They could do no wrong."

"And you? Were you a troublemaker?"

"No. I was a solid B-plus student. But it didn't matter. They earned straight As. So my decent enough grades were meaningless. Every single B-plus I brought home, she wanted to know why it wasn't an A."

"Ouch," I say, cringing. "What did you tell her? I can't imagine because I never had the pressure. My mom was gone at that point, and my dad was so worn out raising four boys on his own that he was thrilled if our socks matched."

"Did they match?"

"Rarely, but enough to make him happy."

She smiles sympathetically. "Nothing pleased my mom. She wanted to know why I didn't earn As, and I never had an answer that was satisfying for her. I told her I had tried hard enough. I told her that was the best I could do. I told her what I was really good at was making people laugh. So that's what I did. I became . . ." She rubs her fingers together as if trying to recall something. "What's that name for the kid who always makes jokes?"

A dash of excitement shimmies through me. "Holy shit. You were the class clown?"

"You've never met a female class clown before?"

I have to hand it to her. She's right. "Not that women aren't funny, but it's something that guys do— assume the class clown role."

"It was the *only* thing I could do better than my brothers. The dry humor. The little asides. The deadpan comments. I was never going to be faster, smarter, or more popular, so I picked my weapon."

"And you chose the sword of humor," I say as if I'm holding a weapon and anointing her like a knight.

"And I wielded it. I did talent shows at school. I would do open mics. And yet, it wasn't what a daughter of hers should be doing."

"Did you want her to be proud of you?"

Finley fiddles with the napkin, looking down as she licks her lips. She raises her face, nodding. "Yeah, I did. I wanted that for a long time." She sighs, and that one sad sound seems to say *but it wasn't meant to be.* "Look, she wasn't awful. She cared about me. I'm sure in her own way she did love me. But I never felt like I was good enough for her. I was the third child. I was the girl, which you'd think would bond us, but it seemed to do just the opposite. And I was the one who didn't fit in her neat, orderly box. That's probably why I'm so much closer to my dad. He gets me. He supports me. He's in love with my *Mars and Venus.*"

"He has good taste, then."

"But he loves it *so* much, and that's why I haven't told him it's failing. Maybe Mom was right. My show is pretty much on death's door." She makes a sound like a plane sputtering as it heads to the ground, about to crash land.

I bang a fist on the table. "We can't let that happen. What can I do to help you with your show?"

"Set up a computer program so it looks like my show was watched by five million people?"

I tap my temple. "Will add that to my to-do list. In the meantime, how about I keep being your inspiration for the guy trying to find his dream girl?"

"That works too." She shoots me a wide smile. "Just keep being you."

"I'll do my best. And you know what I think?"

"What?"

"Sometimes we don't really understand other people and what they want from us. Maybe your mother *was* happy with you, but maybe she couldn't show it. Or maybe she was unhappy with herself."

"You think so?"

"Was she funny?"

"Not really."

"Maybe you were a threat to her in some weird way. Maybe you threatened her idea of womanhood."

She tucks some curls behind her ear. "I never thought of it that way."

"Maybe she wanted a daughter who was pink and princess-y. Who liked ruffles and did cheers. Maybe when she had a girl who liked argyle and Joan Rivers, Wanda Sykes, and Lily Tomlin—"

Her blue eyes twinkle. "How did you know they were my heroines?"

"Good guess?" I say hopefully.

"Very good guess."

"And now, I bet it's Amy Poehler and Tina Fey."

She points a finger at me, nodding. "And Ali Wong. Do not forget the rising queen."

"She's hilarious. Baby Cobra is the best."

Her phone trills. She reaches for the device and shoots daggers at the screen.

"Mortal enemy?" I ask.

"Spam." She shows me the red "Spam Likely" screen then hits ignore with a flourish. "Is the spam notification on phones the best or the absolute best thing ever?"

"The best, of course."

"I used to answer it, just in case it was someone offering me candy or money, but it was never free candy or free money, so now I hit ignore freely."

I laugh. "I haven't received free candy or free money via email either. Took me a while to accept that too."

"And now look at us. We've achieved nirvana over spam," she says with a happy sigh. Her eyes sparkle in a way that makes my chest feel funny. Not ha-ha funny. A whole different kind. A kind I haven't felt in a long time. "Also, you're good at talking on dates. It's among your strengths. You just haven't done it enough. But what about you? Would your mother be proud of you and your work?"

I nod confidently. "She loved thrill rides. She took me to all the amusement parks when I was a kid. She adored them."

"That part of you—that massive part of you—came from her?"

"Definitely. I was always good at math and engineering and structural stuff. But the love of the thrill? She instilled that. She was fearless about everything. She took us on all the rides from the time we were tall enough to ride them."

"Were you ever scared of them?"

"Maybe for a hot minute, but there was no real room to be scared. Not with three older brothers and a daring mother. My first memory is of being five and staring at a tall roller coaster and feeling complete terror, but also knowing I had to move past it."

"And you did?"

"I got on it with her and flew. I was never scared again." I hold up a finger and modify that. "Correction— I felt fear, but I drop-kicked its ass. I never let it get the better of me, and I got that from her. When she got sick, the day she told us, she made us go wig shopping. She said, 'This is finally my chance to wear crazy wigs.' She bought pink, purple, electric blue. A few months before she died, she put on a banana-yellow wig and took us all to Great Adventure."

Finley swallows hard, like she's choking back a tear. "She would be so proud of you, Tom. She would be over the moon." She stretches her hand across the table, grabbing mine. "If she could ride the Boomerang Flyer —can you even imagine?"

I smile because it's all I can do. "She would've loved it. And then she'd have found some eighties flick retrospective and taken off with my dad to go see *Some Kind of Wonderful* for the twentieth time."

Finley's blue eyes flicker with a new kind of awareness. "That's where your love of movies comes from. I thought it was your brothers. But it's from your mom?"

"They kept it going, but it started with her. Watching her favorites, it felt like we were honoring her memory and following her advice."

She cocks her head. "Her advice?"

"She said the great rom-coms had all the answers to the heart."

"Oh, this explains so much of you."

"It does?"

"It's like you've been taking advice from the movies, but it's really your way of trying to connect with her."

I nod slowly, digesting that. It feels true. It sounds about right. "I suppose so."

She nibbles on her lips like she's thinking. "I wonder though. Did she mean for you to take them literally, or did she want you to listen to them because so many are all about love? Pursuing it. Going for it. Like you're doing."

Is that what I'm doing? Going after love? It felt that way a few days ago.

Now?

I don't know what I'm pursuing. Or what I want to pursue.

Or who, for that matter.

* * *

We leave the tasting room and wander through the vineyard. Finley stares into the distance, perhaps noticing the grape stompers for the first time. She gives them the side-eye.

I nudge her. "Admit it. You're taking me to make wine right now."

"Oh yeah. I'm a huge wine stomper."

"You really don't like it?"

Her nose crinkles. "People step on grapes. Why would I want to drink that?"

"I think the wine fermentation process actually gets rid of any bacteria and whatnot."

"I'm sure it does. But I'm also sure I don't want to drink anything that has been touched by feet."

"You do know that it's not about drinking something you made with your feet, right?"

"What's it about, then?"

"It's the *fun* of making it with your feet. It's all squishy. I bet it feels great between your toes. You should do it. I dare you to."

She parks her hands on her hips, looking all sassy and sexy. "You did not just dare me."

"I so did." I smile a satisfied grin. "Just like you dared me to skydive."

She gestures theatrically to the vast expanse of blue above us. "I don't see you skydiving."

"But I will. Since you dared me. And now I'm daring you to stomp on grapes. You have to do it."

She tosses her head back and snorts, and it's magnificent. A deep, throaty snort that seems to resonate through the entire vineyard. "I do? I *have* to prove it?"

"You do. Also, that was your best snort ever."

"Are you cataloging my snorts?"

"Maybe I am. They're amusing. But don't distract me. You have a dare to do, and you're a daring woman." I go for a throwdown. "In fact, I double-dog dare you."

"Do you really think I'm going to fall for the banana in the tailpipe?"

My eyes bug out. I'm a cartoon character with pupils bouncing on springs. "Dear God, you might be perfect. You went from *Moonstruck* to *Beverly Hills Cop* on one date. Are you going to make me a mixtape next?"

"Yes, and it'll have Debbie Gibson on it."

"If I listen to it, will you stomp on grapes?"

She screws up the corner of her lips, tapping her chin. "Wait. You might be onto something."

"Oh yeah?"

Her eyes glint with mischief. "I have a date proposition for you."

* * *

A little later, we're stomping on grapes, and the squishy juice spreads through my toes. Finley is laughing so hard, it's like a brand-new soundtrack. If I thought her snort was fantastic, it's nothing compared to the way she cracks up as she stomps on grapes in a barrel, the squishing and squirting sound rocketing through the early evening sweet summer air.

When we're done, she says, "Your turn."

And I'm ready.

* * *

We head to her house and grab her bike, hoisting it onto the bike rack on my car, then go downtown. I park outside Red, White, and Rosé. She stations herself curbside and salutes me.

I turn on my phone, hit play, and hop on Finley's bike, then I pedal down Main Street on a Sunday night, belting out Debbie Gibson's "Only in My Dreams."

A dare for a dare.

Finley stands on the sidewalk, dancing and cheering me on. It's worth it. Riding down the street, missing every single note, and seeing her have the time of her life.

It's worth singing Debbie Gibson horrifically off-key.

Because Finley's cute when stomping.

And when talking.

And when watching me.

And all the time, it seems.

When I circle back to her, I hop off the bike.

She can't seem to stop smiling. "That was a certifiably awesome date."

"Yeah, it was."

"I mean, practice date," she says, correcting herself.

"Yes, it was."

Silence falls over us, grappling at me. I'm not sure what to do or say. Maybe she's not either.

She shuffles a foot on the sidewalk. "I guess I should go home."

"Sure," I say, my chest cratering because I wish she didn't need to leave. "I'll text you to make plans for tomorrow."

"Great." She points to the wine bar. "I'll just pop into the little girls' room first."

As the door swings shut behind her, something hits me.

That didn't feel like a practice date. That felt like the real deal all by itself, and it had nothing to do with Cassandra.

My heart thumps harder, my nerves kick in, and I don't know what the hell to do with these out-of-control feelings. I need to get away from her, or I'll say something. I'll tell her it felt real. I'll tell her I want her instead.

When I see a note on my phone from my client in Singapore, that's the only excuse I need to leave.

13

FINLEY

What in the ever-loving handbasket?

On the sidewalk outside the wine bar, I jerk my gaze right, then left, searching for the guy who had been standing right here when I went in. "Tom?"

No one answers.

I peer in the doorway of the wine bar in case he went in after me, but I don't see him, nor do I spot his car.

Instead, the real estate his Tesla occupied a few minutes ago is now temptingly available for other cars. I pace up and down the block. Did Tom move his car for some reason? But there aren't any No PARKING signs anywhere. And his ride is gone, gone, gone.

Did he dart down an alley? Receive a call from the Bat Cave? Or just leave without saying goodbye?

Scratching my head, I return to my bike and drop a hand to the seat, smacking it hard. Why would he leave without saying goodbye? Who does that?

I check my phone, but my text app mocks me with its emptiness.

I'm tempted to stomp my foot. To pull on my hair. But I do none of those things because I'm all stomped out.

I exhale heavily, shaking my head in frustration.

My phone trills, and since I'm sure it's Tom—wait, he's Kyler to me now because Tom is a good guy and no Tom would ever ditch his date—I don't even look at the name.

I'm a dragon, breathing fire. "You better tell me a giant eagle captured you in his talons and carried you away, because that's the only reason I can figure why you'd leave without saying goodbye."

Tom isn't the one who speaks though. Christine coughs, then says, "And how was the play, Mrs. Lincoln?"

All the air leaks out of me. "Oh. Hi. Sorry."

"Things are going well tonight, I take it?"

"It wasn't a date," I say, even though five minutes ago, it felt like a tremendous one.

Christine is silent for a moment. "I didn't ask if it was a date," she says gently, and I pace down the street, sidestepping a young couple making googly, I'm-going-to-get-you-naked-any-second eyes at each other.

"Sorry. I thought you asked how my date was. Anyway, he left. He just freaking left."

"The guy you're helping? Your muse? Your project? You're dating him now?"

I shake my head, breathing hard. Seething. I stop in front of a boutique selling fifty-dollar aprons with sayings like *Is it wine-o-clock?* "We were at Tavendish Ranch," I explain.

"I love that place. David and I went there for an anniversary trip. It's so romantic."

"It wasn't romantic," I insist. "I'm just giving him . . ." But I trail off because whatever I'm going to say next feels personal. I'm giving him advice? Tips? Strategies?

I've morphed from hanging out with the man the angels dropped on my lawn to coaching him on how to woo women. Only, it didn't feel like coaching tonight. It felt like talking, like a real conversation between just the two of us. It didn't feel like I was the dating doctor or he was the patient. We were simply two people having fun together.

"You're starting to like him, aren't you?" Christine asks.

I sigh heavily, close my eyes, and let my forehead fall against the window of the shop. "Yes, but that's foolish, Christine. He's madly in love with his college girlfriend." A stabbing pain shoots through my chest.

"That stinks big-time," she says.

"And you know how it goes. After Anthony and the torch he carried for Melinda, I can't let myself crush on this guy." I scoff at my own dumb self. "Crush on him more than I already am," I correct.

"That was pretty awful how it turned out with Anthony."

He didn't even cheat on me, that's the thing. His affection for his ex was a long, persistent soundtrack underscoring our relationship. I ignored it for far too long, the little comments he'd make about her, the name-dropping in conversations.

Oh, she's just his reference point, I'd tell myself. *She's simply his last relationship, so it'd be normal to mention that she also enjoyed Trevor Noah's memoir when I raved about how much I dug it. Besides, he liked the book too, and we even discussed it over dinner.*

But in retrospect, was he discussing it with me, or with the woman he wished I were?

Eventually, the Melinda echo became a calling he couldn't ignore. *I'm going to try again with Melinda. Have a go with her. I'm sorry to hurt you, but I have to do this for me.*

"But the good thing is this," Christine continues, putting on her therapist cap. "We can't control our feelings, but we can control what we do about them. There are plenty of good men out there, and if you're feeling emotions for this guy who's unavailable, maybe don't spend so much time with him."

I recoil, snapping my head up and opening my eyes. That idea sounds abhorrent. Even after tonight. Even after he left for no reason. I *like* spending time with Tom. But I also need him. I need this crazy quest he's on, desperately—it's feeding my scenes, and Bruce liked my early drafts, so much he wants to show the first two episodes to network brass ASAP. ASAP being his word.

"I think the key is to separate these silly emotions from the task at hand. Who needs emotions anyway? Besides, I don't have time for them. I have a show to save." I'm marching back to my bike, determined to get to the bottom of what happened tonight, when a new notification blinks at me.

It's a text.

From Tom.

"Hey, I should go," I tell Christine. "Everything okay?"

"Definitely. I was just calling to tell you I'd be in

town in a couple of days for a conference. We can train for our triathlon in person then."

I laugh. "And have lunch."

"That too."

I smile. "Can't wait."

We hang up, but before I can click on his text, I bump into a gal I know from the next town, Arden, who runs my favorite bookstore in Lucky Falls.

"Hey, you. Are you okay?" She's always been keenly observant.

"Just. *Blurgh.* Yes. Fine," I spit out, like words are new to me.

She arches a brow. "That doesn't sound fine."

I sigh heavily. "It's just . . . ugh . . . men. Right? What are we supposed to do with men?"

Laughing, she answers. "That's what books are for."

"Are they better in books?"

"Men are almost always better in books. But the real thing can be good too. Sometimes they just need to be put in their place and told what to do."

"Yes," I say with certainty. "You're right."

"Good luck, and be sure to come by to pick up the new Tiffany Haddish. I'm holding an autographed copy for you."

"She's one of my favorite comedians. It's a pickup date," I say as she leaves, and I pounce on Tom's message, bracing myself for bad news and hoping for good.

Tom: I had to take off. Work call in Singapore. Thanks for a great night.

. . .

I raise the phone over my head, tempted to chuck it to the sidewalk and smash it to smithereens.

Because this tells me nothing. This is the most perplexing message in the history of text messages. But I'm not going to stand on the street wondering about it. He asked me for dating advice, and he's going to get a piece of my mind.

I hop on my bike, snap on my helmet, and pedal like hell through town. I really ought to be huffing and puffing to match my furious mood, but electric bikes do the work for you, so by the time I reach his hotel a mile away, I haven't even broken a sweat. I lock up my bike and realize I don't know what room he's in. I don't bother with texting. I call him.

"Hello?" He sounds wary.

"What's your room number?"

"One-twelve. Why?"

I hang up, march across the hilly property of the inn, and bang the hell out of the door.

He opens it.

Shirtless.

He's stinking shirtless.

My stomach swoops in excitement, zipping down and up like a flying pirate ship at an amusement park. Those abs are traceable with my tongue. The grooves, dear God, the grooves. My fingers itch to explore them.

"Put a shirt on," I snap.

"Why? It's hot."

I flap my hand toward his room. "You have the AC on."

"Fine." He grabs a T-shirt and tugs it over his head, and I instantly regret my request and mourn the loss of the delicious view.

He scratches his jaw. "Are you okay?"

Standing on the porch of his cabin-like room, I grab my phone from my pocket and shake it. "Is your phone broken?"

"No."

"Is your brain broken, then?"

"No," he says, scoffing.

"Were you raised by wolves?"

"No!"

"You. Left. Me. In the bathroom," I add, my eyes widening as if to make my point.

He shrugs. "But we weren't going home together, so what's the problem? I had a call to make. To Singapore."

"Oh, well. Since it's to Singapore, that's totally fine. Let's not have the Singaporians wait for you. Just let your friend wonder if you were freaking dead."

"But I'm not dead," he says, staring at me with intense eyes. "So what's the problem?"

"The problem is," I say, practically flapping my hands in frustration, "you are such a guy!"

"I am a guy!"

"I know, but you don't have to act like one all the time." I cross my arms so I don't huff and puff and blow him down. Or really, push his chest and then thrill at the spark between us.

Except there's no spark between us. The spark is between me and my imagination, and I will not let my burgeoning and unrequited feelings get the better of me. Besides, this isn't about me. I signed up to help him. And the man fucked up tonight. I imagine Cassandra, and I soften. "You don't take off when a date ends."

"You said you were heading home," he says, sounding genuinely confused. "I don't get it, Finley. It's like I'm doing everything wrong with you."

I grab his arm, feeling bad now. "You're not doing it wrong."

"It seems like it."

I try to explain as gently as possible. "You have to wait for your date. You don't just walk away."

"I'm sorry. It was getting . . . confusing. And I didn't know how to end the date."

"How was it confusing?" I ask, confused too.

He shakes his head. "Doesn't matter. Just tell me how you want me to end a date."

"How do you think a date should end?"

He moves closer to me. "Obviously, the answer is . . . not how I did it tonight. So how do *you* want me to end it?"

"You end it with a goodbye. A proper one. Sometimes, when it's a great date, you end it with a great goodbye."

He shuffles closer, moving into my space now, dangerously close. I should back up, stand against the railing or walk along the porch and gaze at the night sky. Instead, I stay in place, letting him come nearer.

"So tell me, since you're the expert. What's a great goodbye?" His eyes darken.

I square my shoulders, trying to ignore my rising temperature. "You kiss," I say, and it comes out way more vulnerable than I intended. "When you have a great, amazing date, that's when you kiss the girl."

"Is that so?" He steps even closer.

Crickets chirp. Stars twinkle. The night air is charged, and it feels complicit.

"Yes, that's so." The words come out choppy. Inside, I'm shaking. I don't know what's happening, or why he's so damn near to me.

He flicks a strand of my hair off my shoulder. "Let me see if I can do this right."

He slides his hand around my neck. My body sings hallelujah. When did I become so easy? But his touch *is* easy. It's gentle and firm, it's tender and hungry, and then it's more than his hand. His body slides closer, erasing the last bit of distance between us.

His head dips to mine, and I have several seconds to say stop, to say no, to say this isn't how we practice.

But I don't say any of that.

A soft breath betrays me, escaping my lips like an inviting sigh. His hand is firm, cupping my neck, and already this almost-kiss is a slow-motion extravaganza. My heart beats rocket-fast, thundering in my chest. My skin tingles as he raises his other hand, gliding his thumb over my lower lip. It's erotic and sweet at the same damn time. A hint, a tease. Sparks of pleasure tango across my skin as my eyes float closed.

He slides his lips to mine, and I melt into the most dizzying sensation.

He brushes ever so gently against my mouth, and I gasp, a sound that says *do it again, do it more, come closer*.

He heeds the call, moving against me and kissing more firmly. A hint of his tongue. A nibble on the corner of my mouth. He slants his face, dusting his delicious lips against mine.

It's the most wondrous kiss, but a few seconds in, I become painfully aware that my arms are hanging limply at my sides.

I don't know what to do with my hands.

I mean, I do. I want to lift them, thread them through his hair, learn how soft it is. Would that turn him on, light him up? Would he like fingers in his hair as much as I'd enjoy dragging mine through it?

He doesn't seem to suffer from the same uncertainty. His hand curls firmly around my neck. A pulse beats harder in my body, zipping down my chest, settling between my legs.

This kiss could last all night, for all I care. I could live in this slow, luxurious dance.

But there's that matter of my hands.

If I rope them in his hair, it'll look like I don't understand the boundaries. I can't fall under his spell while I'm tutoring him. This kiss can't go anywhere. And I'm dangerously close to letting on how much I want this goodnight kiss lesson to continue. How much I crave an all-night-long make-out session with this man.

I end the kiss.

He swipes the back of his hand over his mouth. His eyes look dazed. Was he as affected by that practice kiss as I was? Did it turn him on to no end? I'm dying to cast my eyes downward, but I won't cross that line of propriety.

Swallowing, he steps away, his back hitting the wall of his hotel room. He breathes out hard, a heavy sigh. "Did I do that wrong too?" His tone is honest, and he seems to truly want to know.

"No."

"So I did it right?" The start of a satisfied grin forms on his face, and I'm instantly jealous. That grin is for Cassie. He wants to know if he has the right moves for *her*.

"You know you did."

"Do I?"

"You said you were good in bed, and I'm sure Cassandra will love it when you kiss her again."

His eyes narrow, and he nods. "I want to make sure these practice sessions are working."

"They will when you learn to end a date properly." My voice wobbles, and I speak from the heart. "Don't leave a girl in the bathroom. Even if it was a practice date, it made me feel stupid. It made me feel like you didn't care about me. It made me feel like everything we'd talked about was unimportant to you."

"That's not true. I loved talking to you, and everything you said was important." He drags a hand roughly through his hair. "I don't think I realized the effect it would have—me taking off. Cassie never mentioned it after I had to leave at the end of her cast party."

I snap my gaze back toward him, keying in on what he just said. "What did you say? You left her at the end of her party?"

"She was changing. My buddy was coming to town. His flight was early. I had to go." He scratches his jaw. "So I texted her."

The sky splits, and the gong clangs. "After you slept with her?" I ask because I need to be certain.

"Yeah."

"And you guys were both virgins," I say, like I need to remind him, because evidently, I do.

"Do you want to keep rubbing that in my face?"

"I don't give a flying fig if you were a virgin till your sophomore year of college. It wouldn't bother me if you were still one. But you were one then, and so was she and . . ." I stare at him, waiting for understanding to flash across his eyes.

"What's going on?" His eyes search my face, confusion in them.

I purse my lips, feeling Cassie's mortification, her devastation. This man has no clue. He is that oblivious. He seems spot-on at understanding women half the time, and woefully bad the rest of it. "Tom, she didn't break up with you because she thought you were a slacker. She broke up with you because you broke her heart."

"No." He whips his head back and forth, taps his chest with his finger. "She broke mine."

"It might have felt that way, but I'm pretty sure you sliced hers in two first."

14

TOM

It's a little hard for me to think about Cassandra with Finley in my hotel room. The crazy-haired blonde with the delicious lips instantly makes herself at home, plunking her little purse on the table and flopping down on the love seat. I sit across from her because if I'm next to her, I won't be able to think about anything but kissing her again.

That kiss fried circuits in my brain. I've never had a kiss like that before.

Not with anyone. Definitely not with Cassandra.

And I'm honestly not thinking about Cassandra anymore because Finley's all I can think about.

Except now I *need* to think about Cassie because Finley won't let it go. And what if she's right?

"Why didn't you mention that teeny little detail?" she presses.

I search for an answer, but honestly, it's simple. "It didn't seem like a big deal. She didn't say a thing about me texting her goodbye when she dumped me."

As Cassie's name drifts over my lips, it feels weirder to say. Since I can't stop staring at Finley's lips and remembering the way they felt. I want to taste her sweet mouth again, to feel her melt against me like she did on the porch, like she'd never been kissed in that kind of heart-stopping way. But judging from the horrified look on her face, Finley's not thinking about me that way.

I try to erase that hot-as-hell moment from my mind as she stares at me with the widest eyes. "You didn't think it was a big deal? That was absolutely why she broke up with you!"

I recoil. "No, that's not it. She said it was because I was a slacker."

"You were a slacker in not saying goodbye properly to her."

I repeat Cassie's breakup words. They were clear and simple. A blueprint for what I needed to do. *Try again when you get your act together. Show up when you know what you want.*

Finley lets out a long, frustrated groan, shoveling her hands through her hair, messing it up even more. My eyes drift toward her hair, and now I want to get my hands in it and mess it up too.

"You took off after sex, Tom," Finley says, exasperation thick in her tone.

"My buddy was coming into town. His flight had landed early. I had to pick him up."

Her face contorts like she's going to explode with word bombs, aimed straight at me. She takes a deep breath. "Let me get this straight," she says like a detective recapping the events of a crime. "After you were done sticking your dick in her, you put on your clothes?"

I laugh, rolling my eyes. "If you must put it that way . . . yes."

"And presumably she did the same?"

"Well, she went into the bathroom to get dressed."

Finley holds up a finger. "Correction—she went into the bathroom to do the Mrs. Obama."

"What?" I ask, incredulous.

"It's this Amy Schumer bit. She says all the greatest women have to deal with the same issue after sex, even Mrs. Obama. Picture that. She has to walk to the bathroom carefully, all *squish, squish, squish*, to clean up after sex."

I blink, trying to both see and unsee that image right now.

"So you and Cassie make the beast with two backs, and after, natch, Cassie has to do the Mrs. Obama, and you're like, *Oh hey, I'll just pull up my Tommy Hilfiger briefs and jet.*"

"Okay." I'm completely flabbergasted.

"Am I right? Are they Tommy Hilfigers?"

I glance down at my cargo shorts, tug them away from my waist, and confirm the name on the band. "Yes, but in my defense, I don't remember if I wore this brand in college."

She waves a hand. "Hilfiger. Calvin Klein. Hanes."

I cringe. "I did not wear Hanes."

"So Cassie's in the ladies' room cleaning up your unused children."

"We used a condom."

"Work with me. You're tugging up your Hanes, and

that's when you get the oh-so-urgent text from your friend?"

Her eyes are bullets, aimed at me. I take cover from her fire. "He'd just flown across the country from school in North Carolina, and I was near the Oakland airport."

She stares intently, like she can't quite believe I'm saying this. I can't entirely believe it either. My actions made sense at the time. But now, hearing Finley's cross-examination, it's crystal clear I didn't make the smoothest exit.

"I told her I had a great time, and I had to go," I offer, quietly searching for some kind of exoneration. "It was a really nice text."

She sighs for the whole world and slumps back in the chair, her expression shifting. Gone is the exasperation and in its place is gentleness.

"You needed to stop, pause, breathe, and say goodbye to your girlfriend. Give her some TLC." She leans forward and cups my knees. "Tom Sutcliffe, you are hilarious and thoughtful in a roundabout way, and you're sweet, and you're fun . . . and you're also completely unaware, at times, of how you come across. In a way, it's not entirely your fault. You grew up with three boys, you went to an all-boys school, your mom was gone, and sweet Sadie Mitchell could only do so much."

She remembers the name of the lady down the street. My God, this woman is too much, too wise, too insightful.

"But at the same time," Finley continues in that gentle tone, "she gave you her virginity, and you gave her a few words sent the way that convenience stores send promo codes for hot dogs and coffee."

I close my eyes, a cold heaviness settling into my bones as understanding flares. A pit forms in my stomach, gnawing at me. "After all this time, it was my . . ." I drop my head into my hands, my mind a swirl of conflicting emotions. "It was my fault. I completely messed up."

When I look up, she asks softly, "But why didn't you tell your brothers at the time and ask for advice? Give them the details and ask what went wrong?"

I don't see much point in holding back now. Finley will get the truth out of me regardless, so I relent, even if it makes me look bad. Or worse. "I didn't want to tell them the details of what I said and what she said. I was embarrassed. I was worried they'd mock me. Say I was a two-pump chump or something."

She smiles softly. "Tom, I'm going to tell you something. My last boyfriend left me to be with his ex. Another boyfriend dumped me because he said I sucked at blow jobs. And still another said I talked too much." She raises her chin, exhales triumphantly. "See, I ripped the Band-Aid off."

I stare at her, slack-jawed, understanding what she just did. She stripped herself naked for me. She bared all. It's my turn. "First of all, don't think I'm going to let the bad at blow jobs comment slide. I bet you're not bad at them at all. But we'll return to that."

She laughs and mouths, *So bad.*

I respond with *Doubt it*, then I turn serious. "But I know where you're coming from. Not about being bad at blow jobs, but wondering if I was doing it wrong, you know?"

She nods. "I know."

"I thought maybe she didn't think I was good in bed. That she didn't enjoy it."

"You were twenty. You weren't supposed to be good in bed."

"It was supposed to be good for her."

"News flash. It's never good when you lose your virginity. Except maybe for my friend Clara."

"Who's Clara?"

She waves a hand in the air. "My friend in high school went to Mexico for spring break. Met a guy there. Lost her virginity and had an orgasm, the lucky bitch. She's basically the exception to every rule. But no one else, not a single woman, has had the Clara experience. Honestly, most of the time we're just hoping it won't hurt and we won't bleed the first time. And then we want the guy to whisper sweet nothings."

The cruel light shines brighter. "And I didn't whisper sweet nothings . . . and Cassie broke up with me . . . and I deserved it?"

She shrugs as if to say she won't quite go there. But I can lead myself to the right answer at last. "I wanted it to be good for her. I had three older brothers who bragged about sex, who talked about sex. I didn't want to be the weak link in the chain."

Another sad smile tugs at her lips. "You think you're supposed to know all these tips and tricks and make a woman meow. It takes time to make a woman meow."

"Meow," I offer half-heartedly.

She pats my knee. "She didn't walk away because of

meows. Maybe it was somewhat about her wanting you to focus more on school. But honestly, I think she left you because you hurt her."

I don't necessarily regret my response to the breakup. I busted my butt to take her advice to heart— to focus on goals and motivations. To become disciplined in school and work. And to become a good lover.

But I have to wonder if I became a better man. Or if I missed that critical step entirely.

I meet her eyes. "I kind of feel like my entire view of the world has been tossed upside down and turned inside out."

"I felt that way, honestly, when Bruce said my show wasn't working. I thought I was funny. I thought I was good at what I did. But maybe I wasn't any of those things," she says, vulnerability clear in her tone. "Sometimes we think something is one way, and it's entirely another. And that stops us in our tracks."

"Cassie left me because I was a jerk that night, rather than because I was a slacker in general?"

"I think she left you because she was devastated." Finley stops speaking and her mouth parts slowly, then she talks at a million miles an hour. "I'm willing to bet something . . . Give me your laptop."

"Sure. What for?"

"I need to try to find something." She flaps her hands, shooing me away. "Go read a book for twenty minutes."

I hand her my laptop and click open my e-reader app on my phone.

She peers over the top. "What are you reading?"

"One Hundred One Ways to Act Like a Complete Idiot with Women."

She laughs. "I thought you'd have it memorized by now."

I wink. "Silly thing. I wrote it."

"Of course you did."

I tap the screen. "It's actually the *Updated Standards and Training Manual for Mechanical Engineers*."

She rolls her eyes. "You're such a nerd."

"A hot nerd," I add, adjusting my glasses.

"Be quiet, hot nerd," she says, and I smile at the last two words, taking some solace in the sorta-compliment amidst this mess I'd made of my first real relationship.

I read, peering over my glasses occasionally as Finley hunts.

And pecks.

And gasps and nods.

Several minutes later, she says, "Ta-da!"

I toss my phone onto the table. "What is it?"

"Did you know she kept a blog a long time ago?"

"No."

"It was around five years ago, shortly after she graduated and started getting more into yoga. I poked around Blogger and found it with a lot of other abandoned blogs. It's so old it doesn't show up in a regular search, but I went back to Facebook and saw what she called herself several years ago. *PretzelGirl*."

"Should I read it?"

She sighs, clutching the screen. "Listen. I'm not trying to make you feel bad. I just want you to understand that I do think she was more affected than you originally thought."

"Why do you say that?" I ask, a sick sensation swooping down on me like a bat in a cave.

She turns the laptop around, hands it to me, and sure enough, there it is—Cassie's old blog, and it's open to the *About Me* section.

Finley speaks like a mourner at a funeral. "I'm sorry, Tom."

I prepare to read words I'm sure I don't want to hear.

"Hi there! I'm so glad you found my blog, and I hope you know you're not alone. You are wonderful, beautiful, and good enough. Don't ever let a relationship breakup define your self-worth. Trust me. I know. I'm building a successful business on the ashes of heartbreak that took me a few years to move on from."

I look up from the screen, raising a skeptical brow. "Years? She didn't seem like she missed me that much."

"Just read."

I swallow hard and read on. *"After a beautiful first love that ended terribly in college when he left me unexpectedly, even though I gave him my heart, mind, and body, I fell into a terrible slump and depression. I discovered yoga, committed myself to self-care, and realized I was good enough. Now, my passion is helping other women discover the same thing, and that's what my practice will focus on—how to see your inner beauty and strength. Namaste."*

I'm an ant. I'm a worm. I'm one-inch tall.

I shut the laptop, a new shame seeping into my bones.

What if after all this time, I'm the bad guy in my story? What if I'm the asshole? I thought all along I was the hurt party, but now I'm learning something else entirely.

I was the hurter in one careless, thoughtless moment.

I didn't think. I didn't consider. I just *did*.

"This is me?" I ask, my voice leaden. "This was all because I didn't say goodbye?"

Finley simply nods.

My chest is a storm, a churning sea of awful emotions. "I don't want to be this guy. I don't want to be him at all."

I stand up, pace around, try to process this new twist. I don't like that version of me. I can't have that part of me hanging out there, not when I'm trying to be a good person.

I stop and look at Finley, and the answer arrives with blazing clarity.

I want to be a better man for me, and I want to be a better man for her. For this woman in front of me. The woman who stomped on grapes and tasted olives and did movie quotes with me. Who told me to *snap out of it*.

But I'm the one who needs to snap out of it.

Because *she's* the woman I want. *She's* the woman I'm falling for. And yet I made the same stupid mistake. I left her at the end of a date. Fine, we hadn't had sex. But that doesn't matter.

The difference, though, is she gave me another chance. She came here and told me I needed to shape up, and hell if that doesn't make me want her even more. I've been looking for a connection, for someone I can talk to. I erroneously thought that person was Cassie. But that person is *not* Cassie. That person is this crazy, nutty button-pusher who *gets* me. This fantastic, unexpected someone who appeared in the window next door to my ex-girlfriend's house.

Cassie is my past. I changed my direction because of her last words to me. I changed it for the better, and I don't regret that. But if I don't let go of the notion that she's the one and only, I'll have many regrets.

Cassie's not the one. She hasn't been in years.

I don't know a damn thing about who she is.

I don't know what she likes, what she loves, who she is.

I'm not hung up on Cassie Martinez, and I haven't been in a long, long time.

I am hung up on Finley Barker.

She's real, kind, and funny, and she somehow finds me entertaining. Maybe it's for her TV show, but maybe I can convince her I could be more than amusing or a muse.

Finley's the twist in my story.

But you don't get the girl until you deserve the girl.

If I'm going to be the kind of man who deserves a woman like Finley, I need to repair the past.

If I'm going to be the man I want to be, I need to make amends.

And if I'm going to be the person my mother would be proud of in every way, there's one thing and one thing only to do.

I move closer to Finley, kneel in front of her, and grab her hand. "I have to go to her."

Finley's face falls, sadness etched in her eyes. "*Tom.*"

"Not to win her over," I explain. "I don't want her back anymore."

"What?" She sounds like I just said I wanted to dye my hair pink.

It will take time to convince her I do want to dye my hair pink. Figuratively, I mean.

I have to convince Finley I don't want Cassie. But that's what I have to do—embark on a brand-new quest, one to win the woman in front of me.

"I don't want her back. But I need to go find her and to apologize for what I did. Will you come with me?"

She doesn't answer immediately. Her blue eyes are big and clouded with vulnerability. "I honestly don't know."

15

FINLEY

My big plans at two a.m. that morning? Reread the scenes I just finished writing from episode two. Lying on the couch, with my feet kicked up in the air, I scroll through the pages on my laptop.

* * *

"Have you ever gone hang gliding?" the heroine asks.

"Generally, I try to avoid activities with a high degree of imminent death," the hero scoffs.

"It's not *that* dangerous. How about downhill skate-boarding?"

"One, I'm not thirteen. Two"—he pats his skull—"I like my head too much."

His lady friend rolls her eyes. "How about being a stick in the mud? Oh wait, you've mastered that."

"Why do you want me to try *insane* sports?"

"Extreme, not insane. And I want you to try because

they'll prepare you for the crazy risk of trying to win back your old girlfriend."

"You don't think I can woo her without learning how to bungee jump first?"

Her eyes light up. "Ooh, let's do that one!"

He arches a brow. "Voluntarily fling myself off a bridge and risk bodily harm?"

"That's kind of what love is. Love is bungee jumping. Don't you think?"

He laughs. "I think you just like to push my buttons."

She's quiet for a moment, clearly thinking, perhaps preparing her closing argument. "I dare you to," she says, singsong and taunting.

He gives her a look, one that says he knows he's been bested.

Cut to . . .

He stands on the edge of the bridge, stares at the water, and jumps. The look on his face as he falls is sheer exhilaration.

She's waiting on the bank, and once his jump is over, he finds her, triumph and joy in his eyes. He thrusts his arms into the air, and she does a victory dance. But when he reaches her, he stumbles. He doesn't have his land legs yet. He topples to his butt.

It's hilarious when people fall on their butts.

His lady friend laughs, offers a hand, and tugs him up. They have a moment. They gaze at their linked hands, they look into each other's eyes. But it's too soon for a kiss. Throats clear, hands unlink, and the hero acts awkward.

He turns the other way and walks along the river. He's silent on the ride back.

Later, outside his house, she asks why he's been so quiet.

"Didn't you like bungee jumping?"

"Of course I liked it."

"Do you want to do it again?"

He stares at her. His eyes search her face, then scroll down her body. The audience knows what he's thinking. What he wants isn't to bungee jump again. It's something else entirely.

"Of course I want to do it again," he whispers. He steps closer, but you can't give into kisses that soon, so their next almost-kiss is interrupted by a phone call.

It's his boss, asking him, "Can you take a trip down the coast?"

The hero turns to his trusty lady friend. She waits for him to ask her to join him, and hopes that he will.

Tune in next week . . .

* * *

It's now or never. Taking a deep breath, I click open an email to Bruce and attach the script. My finger hovers over the send button. Am I doing this? Going in the complete opposite direction of what the network hired me for originally? But I have to. Bruce made it clear. Knock their socks off, and do it with some flirting, maybe a kissing scene, possibly a monkey in a diaper.

There's definitely no monkey in a diaper here, but flirting? Yes. Romantic tension? For sure.

Nerves swell inside me, butterflies flapping higher, harder. I hope the network likes this. I hope they love it. Not just because I desperately want my show to stay alive, but because I'm liking it more.

Maybe even more than I did before.

I swallow my nerves, hit send, and shut my laptop. Trudging upstairs, I pass a photo of my family and stop in front of it. It's a shot of the five of us—my two brothers, my dad, my mom, and me—on the Fourth of July when I was a junior in high school and my brothers were home from college. We're on the deck, having just eaten barbecue. I had grilled corn and carrots, and my mom had kept clucking her tongue, rolling her eyes when she thought I wasn't looking. "How can she eat that for a meal? It's not a meal."

She didn't even understand my decision to stop eating meat. How was she ever going to respect my career choice?

She wasn't. She didn't.

I stare at the image, wondering what my brothers are up to lately. I don't talk to them much. They're so busy with their own lives, their jobs, their families. It's not that we're different, though we are. It's that we're not connected.

I look at the two-dimensional version of my mom, faded over the years, her brunette hair arranged in a neat bun, her arm around my oldest brother. "I'm trying," I whisper, not to her, but to my dad, the one who had his arm around me in the picture.

But I realize I'm not just talking to him either. I'm

talking to that seventeen-year-old girl next to him, the one who believed with her whole heart she could do it.

That she might be the next Tina Fey.

I want to succeed for my dad, but I want to succeed for that girl too. The one who believed it was all possible.

* * *

Underwater the next morning, I weigh the pros and cons of a road trip with Tom.

On the one hand, he's inspiring.

On the other hand, he's tempting.

On the pro side, he's fun.

On the con side, he's dangerously attractive to me.

In the yes column, I have a blast with him.

In the no column, he could blast my heart in two.

Unrequited lust hurts like a charley horse.

I emerge from the chlorinated water still undecided, grab a towel, and dry off. Heading to the locker room, I shower, change, and fish for my phone.

One missed call.

A bubble of excitement rises in me when I slide open the screen. I squeal when I see the name, cross my fingers, and hightail it out of the gym, dropping my purple shades over my eyes.

I return the call.

"They love it. They love both the scripts you sent me, Peaches," Bruce barks when he answers the phone.

"I'm Peaches now?" I ask, but I'm smiling.

"Toots, be glad you have a nickname."

"Why?"

"A nickname means I like you. And I like you a hell of a lot more when you have a better chance at renewal."

"I might have a stay of execution?" I squeak out.

"You get me four more episodes like this, and we'll have more than a snowball's chance. Also, that 'love is bungee jumping' line is spot on. There's nothing scarier than love, Sweet Cheeks. One more thing. Audiences like sexual tension. Draw this out. Don't let them kiss for a long, long time."

Oops. Too bad I broke that rule in real life.

"But what if they had a pretend kiss?" I suggest.

"I like the idea of that. I like it a lot. Do it more than soon. Do it next. Find a way to work a pretend kiss into the storyline. Something that messes with her head," he says, then cackles. "That'll be a hoot. That's rom-com gold, Peaches."

Sweet Cheeks, Toots, Peaches.

Do three nicknames mean he likes me three times better? "I'll see what I can do."

"You do more than see, Finley. You do. Oh, and how about you get me another script by Friday?" he asks, and today is Monday, so that's a tight turnaround. "The faster we blow their minds, the more likely we can get you a renewal."

I gulp—that's another pro in the say-yes-to-the-road-trip column. Tom is like a writing aphrodisiac. Spending time with him has improved my storyline, my pace, my output . . . Whatever scent of inspiration I'm inhaling from him is rubbing off on the show, and the network execs are loving the new aroma.

"I'll do that," I tell Bruce, even though I don't know

if my heart can handle being around Tom for three more days.

Bungee jumping sounds easier. The real kind, not the kind that's a metaphor for falling for someone so hard it hurts.

16
_____

FINLEY

"What would you do?"

I stare into big brown eyes as Mister Dog lounges on a deck chair, sunning himself. He cocks an ear, listening to me. "Yeah, it's crazy. Will Dad say it's crazy?"

The mutt thumps his tail.

"What will I say is crazy?" My father's voice booms across the yard as he slides open the door to the deck that afternoon.

I sit ramrod straight, caught in the act of using his pooch as my psychiatrist. I'm seriously the worst at abusing shrink privileges from both my best friend and man's best friend.

"I was asking Mister Dog if I should start feeding him a vegetarian diet."

My dad sneers. "If dogs were meant to be herbivores, they wouldn't have those teeth."

I rub the dog's head. "Just kidding. I'd never do something so cruel to Mister Dog. He does like avocados though. Last time I was here, he jumped up and ate half of one off the counter, including the shell."

"And I paid for that the next day."

I laugh. "I bet Mister Dog paid for it too. And I promise I won't turn him into a lettuce muncher."

My dad sets down a yellow salad bowl with lettuce, tomatoes, chickpeas, green beans, and beautiful carrots. My mouth waters. "Yum."

"I don't know how you do it, kid. But I admire it."

Smiling, I grab the fork and dive into the salad while he stabs his fork into a tomato. "You're doing it too," I point out.

"But I did gnaw through an entire rotisserie chicken before you came over for lunch," he whispers.

I narrow my eyes. "You, you, you . . . carnivore."

He laughs. "And proud of it." He crunches through another bite then sets down his fork. "So what will I really think is crazy?"

Busted.

"Skipping Marlins Park on your ballpark tour?" I offer, as I spear a yummy-looking green bean.

"Not a chance, young lady," he says, and there's something in his voice that's been missing for a while. Something strong. Something fatherly. I don't detect the hitch in it today, the pang of longing for my mother.

He's simply a dad today. He's not a man who lost a woman. My heart thumps faster. This might be a sign he's on the other side.

"The guy, the one I mentioned to you?" I'm not a secret keeper. I don't want to hide what I'm up to.

"The one you've been hanging out with for the last few days?"

The midday sun slips behind a wisp of a cloud momentarily as I answer him. "Yes. He's going on a road trip. He invited me to go with him."

My dad furrows his brow. "Where to?"

"San Diego is the final destination. He wants to visit some roller coasters along the way, and he asked me to join him."

"Like a date?"

I shake my head. "Like friends. We get along well. We've become . . ." I pause, searching for just the right words, and they're easy to find. "Fast friends."

"Is that so?"

"Yes. I'm trying to decide if I should go."

"Do you want to go?"

I think over the question. I do, desperately. Terribly. Even though it will probably hurt in the end. I like this guy so much, which is crazy in its own way since he's such a work in progress. But then again, so am I. I don't mind that Tom's a little rough around the edges. I *understand* his roughness, just as he seems to understand all my imperfections too—my insecurities, my chattiness, my fascinations with words and people and experiences. "I can write as we go. I think it could be fun. I think it could be inspiring. He's funny, and I laugh a lot when I'm with him."

My dad smiles then ruffles my hair. "I remember taking you to the movies when you were a kid. When something on the screen tickled your funny bone, your laugh burst across the whole theater, and then it'd be followed by a snort."

"He likes my snorts too."

"I just might like him, then." My dad assumes a more serious expression. "Is it safe though?"

"You're such a dad."

"I *am* a dad!"

"I'm twenty-nine. He has a Tesla. It's totally safe."

"His car makes it safe?"

"He's not barreling down the highway on a Harley."

"I don't think the make and model of his car signals safety."

"He's very interested in safety though. He invented a safety feature for thrill rides. And he wore my helmet when he rode my bike the other night."

"It sounds like your heart's already set on this. Just be careful, okay? Guard that heart." He points to my sternum. "If he so much as hurts you, I will—"

I grab his wrist and hold it tight. "I'll be fine, Dad. I promise."

He leans across the table and drops a kiss to my forehead. "Keep me posted, kid."

"I will."

When we clean up, he asks about the show. "I need to write more today. It's going great. The network is loving it," I say as I rinse off the plates and serve up a half truth.

I wince, because evidently I *am* indeed a secret keeper. I should tell him the whole truth, that the show is hanging on by a frayed thread. I should ask what to do. But for the first time in ages, the man isn't on the verge of tears, so I figure it's safe to keep this secret to myself.

Besides, I want him to be happy. The other thing that makes him happy is when I shower love on his dog.

"What do you say I take Mister Dog for an extra walk? I need to pop over to Lucky Falls anyway for a new book."

He hands me the dog's leash with a smile.

* * *

My dad lives on the outskirts of town, which means he's only a half mile from our sister town. With the dog speed-walking by my side, we head into the town square and pop into Arden's store to pick up the Tiffany Haddish book. She flicks her blonde hair off her shoulder, hands it to me, rubs Mister Dog's head, then asks if I need anything else.

In my best sarcastic throwaway voice, I say, "I need a book on how not to get hurt by feelings, emotions, and/or falling for someone. Got any in stock?"

She smiles sympathetically. "Oh sure, it's called a cartoon."

That actually sounds like a good idea. "Maybe I should grab a *Get Fuzzy* book," I say, naming my favorite comic strip growing up.

"Let me get you my favorite collection of *Get Fuzzy* strips."

As she heads to the shelves, a handsome man with sky-blue eyes strolls in and says her name. "Hey, Arden. I'm still waiting for you to build on my 'kiss.'"

She swivels around, her eyes wide. "You are?"

"In Words with Friends, woman."

She laughs, but judging from her reaction and his question, I'm going to need to conduct some serious recon with her next time we talk.

For now, she returns to the counter with the *Get*

Fuzzy collection, and I pay for that and the Haddish then tell her we'll catch up next time.

"We will."

I lower my voice, because I can't resist a little inspiration. "And maybe you'll tell me what's going on with you and the hottie."

She blushes. "You love your stories."

"I do. So you'll tell me?"

"If there's something to tell."

"Fair enough." I need to make trip preps, so Mister Dog and I take off.

* * *

Later that Monday afternoon, I call Christine. "I might not be able to see you when you're in town."

"Oh? Why's that?"

I gulp, steeling myself. "I'm going on a road trip."

"You are?"

My chest prickles with something other than nerves. Something I can't quite name. But it feels like guilt. Or maybe it's that feeling of knowing you're going against a friend's wishes. You're willingly flinging yourself into danger.

I tell her about the trip, but as I speak, I hear how it must sound to Christine. Like I'm chasing him. But I'm chasing inspiration, I tell myself. "I'm going to write. The network liked the first two episodes."

"That's great, but what about his ex?"

I lick my lips, wishing this didn't sound like justification as I say, "He's not into her anymore, but he also realizes he made a mistake and wants to apologize to her."

Christine hums. "Did he cheat on her?"

I cut that idea off at the knees. "No. But he was . . . careless with her heart," I say carefully, because Tom's story isn't mine to share. It belongs to him and Cassie, and I'm only a bystander.

"And he's going on a road trip to apologize?"

"She was hurt by how he handled something, and he didn't realize it at the time. She never told him exactly why she pushed him away, and he never asked anyone else to help him understand the situation. I think he's trying to turn over a new leaf."

"Interesting," she says, taking her time with the word, stretching it out.

"Why is that interesting?"

"It's interesting when someone truly tries to make amends. To apologize for a past hurt. As a therapist I wholeheartedly commend it. It can be incredibly healing and freeing, and can help a person move on."

"Why do I hear a 'but' in there?"

She sighs. "But I do worry about what it means for *you*."

"Why?" I ask, as my stomach craters.

"I don't want you to be his rebound girl."

"Maybe his feelings for her from a few days ago were never real in the first place," I offer, clinging to that hope. That foolish hope.

"Are you making excuses because you're falling for him?"

"I'm not falling for him," I insist.

But that's another lie.

I am falling.

More than I should.

A sane girl would say no. A wise girl would stay home.

I'm neither. I'm desperate, and I'm needy.

But I'm also wildly curious. I want to know what comes next. I want to turn the pages deep into the night.

"I know he doesn't feel the same, and I know it's dangerous, but I won't let myself get burned again," I tell Christine.

"Be careful."

I tell her I will, but I honestly don't know how to follow her advice. I don't know how to resist talking with him the way I like to, flirting with him the way we both seem to enjoy, and spending time with him.

I don't know how not to fall. I'll just hope it won't hurt too bad.

17

TOM

The best text ever lands on my phone early that evening.

Finley: What time do we leave?

Tom: 9 a.m. sharp. Also, ARE YOU SERIOUS? You're going with me?

Finley: As serious as a table saw.

Tom: Nuff said.

Finley: Also, what should I pack? Do I need scuba gear, a faux fur cape, or cowboy boots? Because if the answer is yes, I'm out.

Tom: Just a bikini, and you already told me you have plenty of those.

Finley: I'm not sitting in the passenger seat in a bikini.

Tom: Does that mean you'd drive while wearing one?

Finley: Hmmm . . . Fair question, but that's going to be a hard limit too.

Tom: Got it. One final bikini question—would you wear one on the Rapids ride in Wild Days Park?

Finley: Are we going to tour amusement parks?

Tom: If I stop at one each day, I can write off the trip.

Finley: You're such a guy.

Tom: I am a guy.

Finley: What if I didn't like amusement parks?

Tom: But you do, ergo . . .

Finley: Ergo, what?

Tom: Oh wait. This is a teachable moment, right?

Finley: You're getting warmer. Now, let's see what you've learned. :)

Tom: Finley, would you like to visit a few amusement parks with me? I think it would be inspiring for your work, and we all know that you chase inspiration like a bunny chasing the carrot.

Finley: Lukewarm . . .

Tom: *clears throat* *prepares to show off new skills* We could visit some parks, and you could write. Work on that show of yours that we're going to save.

Finley: The thermometer is rising.

Tom: Allow me to keep making my case, then . . . Also, it would be fun, and I'm excellent at road trips, and you're an excellent companion at, well, everything. I have a great time with you. So I thought, hey, why not make this a fun road trip, ride some rides, see some sights, have a good time. It's all on me. Plus, snacks.

Finley: Mercury increasing. Because . . . snacks.

Tom: Let's go for the closing pitch, then. Ready?

Finley: Or not!

Tom: Your hair is pretty.

Finley: Hot!

Tom: P.S. *Fine* was always intended as a compliment about your hair.

Finley: But *pretty* is a better compliment.

Tom: Yes, I've learned that.

As I close the thread and return to work, I let the next few days play out in my head. The way I see them, the real benefit isn't the tax write-off. It's more time with Finley. And time gives me the chance to apply my newfound skills. *Listening.* Paying attention. Asking, when I don't have a flying fig of an idea what a woman wants.

But this new toolset doesn't only work on women.

Since I never told my brothers what happened that night in college, I should do the opposite now. Be up-front.

I open a new group message to the three of them and heave a sigh. In some ways, this is even harder than figuring out what women want.

Me: Hey, dickheads.

Wait. Scratch that. As much as I enjoy calling them names, and the same could be said for them, that might not be the best way to start a more serious note.

Me: Hey, guys. There's something I want to say.

I squeeze the phone in frustration, since they're going to think I'm sick or dying with that kind of opening line.

Delete, delete, delete.

Me: I'm heading out on a road trip for a few days. I'm going with a woman. She's not Cassie. Her name is Finley, and I like her a lot. The whole Cassie thing is over, and I'll tell you sometime, but the details don't matter now. What matters is I don't want to make another stupid mistake with this girl. So I might reach out to one of you guys, and if I do, I need you to be honest with me. Okay? I love you, dickheads.

I hit send. What can I say? I can't resist calling them names.

The replies pour in.

Nash: Dickhead, that's great! Happy to help with anything. Let me know if you need instructions on putting condoms on correctly.

Ransom: Hell, yeah! I won't even let Delia try to mess with you again, Dickhead.

Gannon: Cassie had horrible taste in music, Dickhead. And yeah, sure. I'll help. That's what we do.

Me: Thanks. And mostly I'm impressed you all capitalized Dickhead.

Ransom: Well, it is your name.

* * *

On Tuesday morning I shave, pack my bags, and put on a new shirt. I know as much about fashion as I do about how to give a poodle a haircut, but I'm taking my new "assume nothing" approach to heart. I went shopping yesterday on the main drag in Lucky Falls and bought this shirt at Tren-day. After all, the store does have the hippest duds.

I asked Sandy, the owner, what ladies like, and she picked it out for me.

It's not really my style, but if she says the fairer sex digs Tommy Bahamas these days, so be it.

Then I met Gabe for coffee, and he proceeded to tell me the shirt was weirdly awesome. He seems to have a way with the ladies, so I trust him.

I arrive at Finley's home ten minutes early, cut the engine, and listen to a section from a podcast on the evolution of life.

At one minute till nine, I walk to the front door, smooth a hand over my shirt, adjust my glasses, and tell my crazy nerves to settle the fuck down. I press the doorbell, and I imagine the loud ding-dong heralds the start of a brand-new chance . . .

This time with Finley. Or so I hope.

"Coming!"

Finley's voice reverberates from within. I've never

been inside her house, and I kind of want to check it out, to pick up knickknacks and ask her questions, to see what's on her bookshelf and learn what makes her tick.

Seconds later, she yanks open the door, tugging it so hard I'm surprised it doesn't fly off its hinges. Thoughts of bookshelves and bric-a-brac fall from my head as soon as my eyes land on her. She wears shorts, a blue tank top, flip-flops, neon-pink shades parked atop her curly hair, and pale pink lip gloss.

"Hi," I say, and the one-syllable word feels different on my tongue. Softer almost, or maybe it's more hopeful, like how I'd say it if I were picking her up for a date. *A three-day date.* I want to pump my fist again, congratulating myself on convincing her to spend three days with me. Now all I have to do is convince her—without making it totally obvious until she's ready—that she's the one for me.

I flash her a smile, waiting for her to say hello as well. But for the first time, she's not speaking. She's not even blinking. She's officially gawking.

At me.

Or more precisely, at my shirt.

I grab the palm tree–covered fabric. "It's new. It's what all the cool guys wear."

She purses her lips, nodding. But she still doesn't speak.

"That's what the lady at the shop said."

"What. Shop?" Each word comes out like she's biting them off a don't-laugh stick.

"Tren-day. You introduced me to the owner the other night."

She swallows and a laugh bursts through, then she slams her palm to her mouth.

I sigh. "Okay, so it's not a cool shirt."

She nods.

"Wait. It is or it isn't?"

She reaches forward, places a palm on my shoulder, and says, "Clothes are so dumb. Go naked."

That perks my interest. "Is that an option?"

She taps her chin, as if considering. "Maybe not while driving."

"So, maybe I shouldn't wear this?"

Finley reaches forward and plays with a button on the shirt. Just like that, my pulse spikes. "You know what? It's ironic. I like it."

"But I didn't intend for it to be ironic," I say.

She rubs her thumb over the button and raises her chin, meeting my eyes. My blood thunders, and what the hell am I going to do for the rest of the trip if I'm this affected by a single look from her? "What did you intend, Tom?"

For you to like it. For you to like me. For you to look at me like . . . Like you're looking at me.

I clear my throat. "I'm good with ironic. Let's go with the irony."

She squeezes my shoulder. "You know what? I'm going to get my Hawaiian shirt too. We can match. It'll be doubly ironic. Be right back." She spins around and races to her staircase.

"You have a Hawaiian shirt too?"

"It was for Halloween last year. My friend James and I dressed up."

"As tourists?" I call up to her.

She rounds the top step and snaps her gaze back to me. "No, I was Magnum P.I., and he was my red Ferrari."

I let that image soak in, sort of turned on, sort of not. "Don't wear the mustache, please."

She laughs as she heads out of sight. "I won't."

But you can ride me like a red Ferrari. Or vice versa. I'll play the beach-going detective, and you can be the car . . . and yeah, maybe I need another analogy.

A minute later, she bounces back downstairs, sporting a red Hawaiian shirt and the tiniest shorts I've ever seen.

"Nice duds," I rasp as I stare at her pelvis and then at her ass as she rounds the corner at the bottom of the staircase.

She glances at her own rear. "You like my short shorts?"

"Those are some hot pants."

"Let me get my suitcases," she says, heading toward what looks to be the kitchen.

"Suitcases? As in plural? Do you need help?"

"Nah. I've been pumping iron." She returns to the foyer wheeling two suitcases the size of steamer trunks. She could be traveling to Europe for the entire summer. "I'm ready now."

I blink, then point. *"Finley."*

"What? You said three days. That's less than a bag a day."

"How many outfit changes are there?"

"One every two-point-five hours. I thought you would appreciate the precision, being an engineer and all."

"I don't think there's room in my car."

"We could rent a U-Haul?" she offers, her voice rising in hope.

"Let me see if they'll fit in the back seat." I lift one of them. It's as light as a feather. I smirk. "You were testing me."

She wiggles her brow. "You passed. It was adorable that you truly thought I was bringing them, and that you wanted to make it work."

Okay, so I just won points I didn't know I was vying for. I can deal with that.

She grabs a lone green backpack from behind the door. "Want to see something super cool? Everything fits in here."

"You're the perfect woman."

"Why, thank you, Tom Bahama."

Rolling my eyes, I groan at the nickname. "And you're a button-pusher."

"And you love button pushing." She winks and ruffles my hair. "Also, your hair is fine."

"I deserved that, and I do love button pushing."

"I know," she says with a smile.

We leave, her prop suitcases staying behind in her front hallway, her light-as-air backpack on her shoulder, and the most fantastic shorts I've ever seen barely covering her ass. Yes, I'm going to have fun on this road trip.

"After you," I say, gesturing to the front steps.

I'm such a gentleman.

She walks down the stairs, and I fully enjoy the view as she heads to the car.

* * *

An hour later, she's nearly exhausted playing with all the bells and whistles on the dashboard.

"Enjoy it while you can. I'm going to swap this out for a rental."

"You are?"

"I figured having to charge it three or four times would be a pain, even though it fills up quickly. I made a reservation for a hybrid though."

She pats her chest. "My green heart is happy." Then she pushes a button that she hasn't fiddled with yet. It activates voice control for the entertainment input.

"Hello. What can I play for you?" the robotic voice inquires.

"Now what if that button had stopped the car?" I ask Finley.

"But it didn't stop the car."

"But what if it had?"

"Then the car would have stopped, but it didn't happen. Where is the button for snacks?"

"Did you say you wanted snack music?" the robotic voice of the car asks us.

"What is snack music?" Finley asks incredulously.

I hit the button to turn off the voice commands. "It's music you snack to."

"Oh, thanks. I couldn't figure that out."

"Fine. Do you want to hear the snack music?"

She shakes her head. "Nah, I'd rather have the snack rundown."

"You're hungry —" But I cut myself off from saying *already* since I'm pretty sure commenting on when a woman is hungry is akin to calling her hair *fine*. So I pivot. "You're hungry, and I'm at your service with roasted pumpkin seeds, seaweed strips, and tangerines."

She smacks my arm.

"Ouch. Also, why'd you do that?"

"Because that's the nicest thing anyone's ever said to me," she says, kicking off her flip-flops and tucking her feet under her as we head down 101 toward Marin County.

"That is the nicest thing?"

"Because it's all food I can eat. And it's all so healthy too. Or pseudo healthy. I like that."

The pride I feel is disproportionate to the achievement I just unlocked, but I don't care. I bask in the satisfaction of her being pleased with the food choices.

"So you picked out awesome snacks," she says, counting off on one finger as I head south on the slate-gray ribbon of highway. "You bought a new shirt, and you booked the hotel."

"You can just say it. I'm certifiably awesome." I flash her an over-the-top grin.

"You are absolutely awesome."

"Now, try not to get too excited, but what if I told you I made you a playlist of your favorite tunes?"

She laughs. "You did not."

"I did so."

As the road curves, she shoots me a quizzical look. "You don't even know what music I like. We've never even talked about music. Honestly, I don't even like 'Unzipped.'" She holds up her hands like she's apologizing. "Sorry, not sorry."

I laugh and decide to serve up some truth. "Confession—I was never crazy about it either."

"Really?"

"Really. It was never my thing."

"Did you pretend you were into it for her?"

I shrug. "Maybe. She liked it, so I did it for her."

"Like how she pretended she was into movie quotes for you?"

"Yeah, maybe."

"Do you know if she'll be there? I really hope this isn't all for nothing."

"I called the yoga studio and checked on her class schedule. The day we're in San Diego she should be teaching, so I have it all lined up. Told you I'm a good engineer."

She smiles briefly then stares out the window, her jaw ticking, and this is when I'd like to ask my brothers if I said the wrong thing again. But the wrong thing would be ignoring her reaction. "I'm not into her now," I add.

She snaps her gaze back to me. "That's kind of a one-eighty." But she doesn't sound combative—more like curious, and I can work with curious.

"Yeah, I can see that it would seem like a big shift."

She smiles. "Kind of, considering I found you on my lawn with a boom box, Lloyd Dobler."

And I'm fucking lucky that Cassie wasn't home, I want to say. The trouble is I can't quite say that to her yet. Finley's a little bit like a bunny cornered at the bottom of a yard. To reach her, I need to take small, quiet steps. I don't want to spook her. And even if I get close enough, eventually I have to let her come to me on her own.

But I can still be honest, and that's what I need to do—keep practicing change. "I was confused about some of my feelings," I say, doing my damnedest to just own it. "They were conflated with the past and mixed up with why I thought things ended with her. It wasn't till I understood the full scope of what happened that I was able to see that the feelings weren't real. They were tangled up with the last time I thought I really connected with someone."

She nods thoughtfully, like she's digesting this bit of intel. "Sometimes it's hard to sort through our own emotions. It's easier to see how others get all tripped up, but we can't always see it for ourselves till there's an 'aha' moment."

"Yes. Meeting you, talking to you, learning things with you. That was an aha moment."

She flashes me a sweet smile, and this conversation feels like a step in the right direction.

"And now . . . *poof*?" She mimes a magical explosion of abracadabra-ness. "Your feelings for her are 'now you see it, now you don't'?"

"Exactly. And I know it seems hard to believe that everything could shift —"

She laughs. "Just a teeny tiny bit, Lover Boy."

"But it's true. It's as true as . . ." I stop talking to search for the right words. "As true as how you feel about being the class clown, eating olives for every meal if you could, and how dates should end."

She laughs. "Fine, fine. You've made your case. I believe you. Tell me more about the playlist."

And we're done for now. Or at least she is.

Convincing her will take more than making my case once. I'll have to prove myself to her. Show her I know *her*. But that I can also listen to her by doing what she asks—talking about something else. "I'm going to play it for you. But tell me what type of music you like."

She looks at me, confused. "But you already made the playlist."

"Humor me."

She narrows her brow, then shrugs. "I don't listen to music that often. I feel sort of terrible saying that. Like it means I'm missing a basic part of being human."

"Why would you feel that way?"

"Because music is like sunshine. How do you dislike it? And it's not that I dislike music. It's that I love the sound of two other things more."

"What things?" I ask, eager to know more about her.

"Silence. I need silence when I write."

"Total silence?"

"For the most part. I don't know how people write with songs blasting in their ears. More power to them, but I need a blank slate aurally."

"And what's the other?"

"Talk. I like to listen to people talking more than I like listening to songs. Memoirs and old-time talk radio and plays and comedy albums and whatnot. What do you listen to? I bet you love rock and indie pop."

"I like music, but . . ." I feel a little like I have an ace up my sleeve. But now's not the time to show her my hand. "I like to listen to podcasts more."

"What kind?"

"I like to learn new things. I listened to one recently

on the science of food, and then another on the evolution of life. For instance, did you know sex was invented two billion years ago?"

"There was no nookie two-point-one billion years ago?"

"Sadly, no. Before then, new organisms could only come to be through random mutations. When reproductive sex was invented, that sped up evolution because two organisms could then exchange their DNA code."

She makes a sexy sigh and runs her hand down her bare thigh. "You make it all sound so sexy."

"Would it be sexier if I told you I also learned that organisms that like to get it on have more success with natural selection?"

She gives me a pouty, dirty look. "Oh yeah. Now that's getting risqué."

"What about if I said humans today like giving each other the DNA business?"

She murmurs. "Mmm. Give me your DNA, baby." She wriggles an eyebrow. "Sexy?"

She has no idea how much I want to give her the DNA. I mean, I don't want to mix chromosomes with her. Not now. But I do want to engage in the act of DNA trading though. Very much. "Genetic code is so hot," I say.

"Hey, now you're doing sex talk again."

"I never said sex talk was forbidden."

"Nor did I. I only said no sex talk on a first date."

That pings my radar even more. "Are we beyond the first date?" I ask, as cool and casual as I can manage.

"Tom, they're going to need a new word for whatever this thing is." She points from her to me. And that deflates me a little bit, but it also reminds me to keep trying with her. To try till we both know exactly what's happening between us.

"So, where is this mythical playlist? And since I told you I'm not a huge music fan, what on earth did you put on it?"

I hit a button on the screen, then issue a verbal command to the car. "Kitt, play Finley's playlist."

"You did not name your car Kitt."

I laugh. "I didn't. See, it's not even responding." I point to the dash. "Let me try again. Adler, play Finley's playlist."

Her mouth falls open in a no-you-didn't look.

"I needed a good name."

A cool, modulated voice answers. "Hello. I'll play Finley's playlist for you."

She clasps her hands to her chest. "You did all that for the sake of a joke? You're so cute."

I blow on my fingertips.

Finley stops talking when a voice fills the car.

It's Tina Fey.

"What is this?" Finley tilts her head, like she's the RCA dog, tuning in.

"I went on YouTube. Cut the audio from some clips for you. Made it into a comedy playlist." I sneak a glance at her, and the smile that's tugging at her lips grows even bigger, reaching all the way to her eyes, making them twinkle.

"I love this," she whispers, almost reverently.

As we drive across the Golden Gate Bridge, the Pacific spreading majestically to the right, the comedian chats about her affection for Larry Wilcox, followed by the voice of Amy Schumer riffing on how Rosario Dawson should have earned an Oscar for the movie *Zookeeper*.

We make a pit stop, dropping the car in the parking garage next to my townhome off Fillmore Street, then grabbing the rental I reserved.

Back on the road, the playlist goes to a Tiffany Hadish routine, then a bit from Ali Wong.

By the time we reach Santa Cruz, Finley is wiping tears of laughter from her face. When we park, she reaches across the car, grabs my cheeks, and kisses my . . . nose?

The tip of my nose.

I wasn't expecting a real kiss right now, but I wasn't expecting a nose smooch either.

The funniest thing is—I'll take it. I'll happily take it.

"That was the best playlist ever. Those are definitely all my favorite tunes," she says, and that's why I made it. For that look, right there, on her freckled face.

18

TOM

The white and red wooden tracks rise high above us, the crystal-blue sky and vast expanse of sandy beach forming the backdrop to the thrill ride.

Finley crosses her arms and stares at the big beast, talking to it. "All right, Giant Dipper. Impress me. Show me what Tom can do."

I laugh, shaking my head. "This one isn't mine. But it is seriously impressive. It was built in 1924, in forty-seven days, at a cost of fifty thousand dollars, and more than sixty million people have ridden it since then."

"You're showing me someone else's creation?" She arches a brow. "I want to see your handiwork."

"Tomorrow." I move closer, bumping my shoulder to hers and whispering, "But will it impress you if I say they added my safety feature to it a few years ago? It's part of the anti-rollback device."

Her eyes sparkle. "I have no idea what that is, but it sounds super-hot."

I tap my temple, glasses-free at the moment since I

can't wear them on rides. I switched to contacts when we arrived. "I have a million more little facts up here at your service. Let me know what you want to hear next."

As the line for the coaster snakes around a corner, she wiggles her fingertips, the sign for me to give her more info. "Give me some of those safety facts, Tom."

I serve up one of my favorite ones as we make our way through the queue. "Roller coasters may seem scary, but they aren't actually dangerous. There's *only* a one in twenty-four million chance of getting seriously injured on an amusement park ride, according to the National Safety Council. Which means," I say, raising my finger for dramatic effect, "you have a bigger chance of kicking the bucket by falling out of bed. There's a one in 423,548 chance of that happening, by the way."

She frowns. "Should I wear a helmet in bed?"

"Only if you're engaging in other dangerous bedroom activities," I tell her with a wink.

Soon, we reach the front of the ride, and we board the next car, the shoulder bars locking in place. I still get a thrill when I hear that noise. "I love that sound. It's the sound of knowing you're about to scream at the top of your lungs and enjoy it."

"You're such a geek."

"I am a geek."

The car pulls away from the platform, sliding into a tunnel, dropping and curving before it emerges and begins thrusting skyward, the clacking intensifying as we slowly climb the first hill. "That clicking noise when you go up the hill? It's an anti-rollback device," I say proudly.

"Oh," she says, her lips parting in a pretty *O*. "The thing you said you designed, right?"

"I didn't actually design the anti-rollback device—that's a standard safety feature. But I created an advanced component to the toothed metal ratchet that ensures the cars can't roll back if there's a power outage or a broken chain."

"I'm officially impressed."

"That sound is music to my ears. I think it's like how laughter is to you," I say as we near the top of the first hill.

"Like ride foreplay," she says with a wink as she grips the lock bar more tightly. "And you *can* feel the car rising higher."

"I take it that means you're having a good day at the park?"

We reach the top, and that second-long moment of suspension before gravity takes over, turning potential energy to kinetic energy and powering a fantastic fall.

"Yes!" she screams, and I hope it's a sign of how much she's enjoying this day as much as a response to the drop.

I shout too, and we fly, the car careening down the tracks, curving onto its side, and shooting us up, down, and around.

Finley never lets up. Her voice is an epic megaphone of exhilaration. It's the beautiful soundtrack to a ride well designed, the relentless pace of thrills—of chasing them, living them, making them.

She screams the whole time the wind whips by and the car speed-demons its way around half a mile of track, not letting up until it chugs slowly into the station, where it locks in place when it stops.

I rub my ear. "You're a screamer."

She wiggles her eyebrows and answers softly, "I am."

I freeze, staring at her for a few seconds. She's always been flirty, always skirted the naughtier sides of our conversations. I have too. But this feels different. Maybe because I want it to be. Or maybe because I know how her lips taste, and I'm determined to find out if the rest of her skin is as delicious.

Or more.

* * *

We tackle more of the park, visiting the arcade then playing laser tag and climbing the rock wall. After, we walk along the boardwalk as the sun makes its dip toward the horizon. "Thanks for inviting me," she says.

"Thanks for saying yes. I'm glad you did."

"You are?" she asks, her voice tentative, a touch nervous.

"Yeah. I'm really glad."

She studies me. "How do you see me?"

I furrow my brow. "What do you mean?"

"Are we friends?"

I scoff-laugh. "We better be."

She smiles. "Yeah, I think we are too." She stops walking, wraps her hands around the wooden railing of the boardwalk, and stares at the ocean. "I'm glad we're friends."

My chest warms—for maybe the first time on this trip, I feel certain that we're getting somewhere. Somewhere that's a step closer to where I want to be with her. "Life is pretty random, isn't it?"

"Are you going to regale me with more details about how horny organisms invented evolution?"

I shield my eyes, laughing. "Not at the moment. I was mostly thinking about how you happened to be in the window last week." *But it's more than random*, I think to myself. It feels like serendipity.

She nudges me. "And to think, you might have been road tripping with two burly bikers."

"Somehow I doubt they'd have taken me under their wing."

"Is that what I did?"

"Felt that way, for sure."

She juts up a shoulder and flashes a small smile. "Maybe for a few days. Truth be told, you're a pretty fast learner."

"I'm not sure about that, Finley." I sigh. "I feel like everything I thought I knew about women has been turned inside out and upside down."

"It's been unzipped," she says playfully.

I laugh. "Maybe it has. By the way, I'm glad I'm a fast learner. I'm glad you helped me. I was a stubborn bastard when I met you."

"News flash. You still are."

"But maybe not as much?" I ask hopefully.

"You're five percent less."

I pump a fist. "Progress."

She goes quiet for a few seconds, then turns to me, her brow pinched. "But have I changed?"

"Did you need to change?"

"Don't we all?"

"But what would you change?"

She parts her lips, takes a breath, but then shakes her head before she fixes on a witty grin. "Now's not the time to talk about the tires on my bike." She *tsks* me, and we both know she's not talking about her bike tires.

I don't know what she wants to change, or why she doesn't want to tell me. She turns to continue along the boardwalk, but I grab her arm, pulling her back, looking into her eyes. "What do you want to change?"

She swallows nervously. Shrugs. Looks down.

"Tell me. I'm a stubborn bastard ninety-five percent of the time. I'll be stubborn till you tell me."

She waits a beat, then lifts her chin. "I'd take more risks."

"What's the risk you want to take? You already ride all the rides, and you went skydiving, and you're taking a chance by writing this show. You're a risk-taker by nature."

She stares at me, and for a few seconds, it's as if her chatterbox mask slips away and sheer vulnerability replaces it. "Bungee jumping."

I furrow my brow. "That's the risk you want to take?"

She nods.

"Really?" I find it hard to believe this scares her. A woman who skydives is fearful of bungee jumping?

"Yes, but I'm afraid to go bungee jumping."

"Why?"

"It terrifies me," she says, deadly serious, but it almost seems like bungee jumping is a metaphor for something else. Only, I don't know what or how to figure it out.

I offer the one thing I have. "I'll go with you."

A faint smile spreads. "You will?" Her voice sounds breathy, but it's not the sexy, flirty kind. There's an undertone there, one I'm trying to understand.

"Yes. Say the word. Or words, really—*I dare you*. Three little magic words."

"Three little magic words," she repeats. Then she snaps out of it, announcing that she's hungry.

I point my thumb at the road. "There's an artichoke-themed diner a few miles away."

"Hello! Why didn't you mention that sooner?"

"I forgot," I say, laughing.

She presses her palms together like she's absolving me of a sin. "I forgive you for forgetting to mention the best thing ever. I'm going to have one of everything. Take me there now."

Since the diner seems to specialize in all things fried, Finley doesn't have one of everything. She does order roasted artichokes and an artichoke salad, while I take one for the team and order the artichoke fries along with a burger drenched in—you guessed it—artichokes. When the waitress leaves, I return to something Finley mentioned the other night.

"Remember when you said some dickhead broke up with you because you talked too much?"

"Why, thank you for reminding me of all my flaws," she says with a goofy grin.

"That's not why I brought it up. I mentioned it because I disagree."

"With why Jaxton Winkler ditched me?"

My nose crinkles. "That's a trying-too-hard name."

"He wore plaid pants and a bowler hat. He was a trying-too-hard-to-be-cool guy."

I pluck at my palm tree–covered duds. "Suddenly, this shirt looks pretty good." I wiggle a brow. "Anyway, I disagree because I don't think that's possible."

"To talk too much?"

I nod, folding and unfolding the napkin in front of me. "When I said earlier I've been holding on to this notion of the past? I don't know a thing about Cassie now, so I was basing my choices on all this old stuff. I haven't talked to her in years. How can you love someone you don't even talk to?"

She takes a drink of her water. "How can you even *like* someone if you don't talk?"

"You're preaching to the choir," I say confidently, feeling a new certainty about my decisions. With Finley, all we do is talk. All I've done the last several days is get to know her. And I don't want to stop. "I've been wanting to find someone I could truly talk to."

"I've never understood love at first sight. I think there's lust, but I think love comes from getting to know someone." Her eyes are wide as she stares at me. "Do you agree?"

"One hundred percent," I say, holding her gaze, wishing I could tell her I'm falling for her. But I'm not stupid. Move too fast and she'll say *see you later*. "What happened with your last boyfriend? You mentioned him the other night too."

She groans. "Is this the Finley inquisition?"

I smile. "Well, we both do like talking."

She narrows her eyes like she's pissed, but there's a

playfulness to her expression, then a darkness when she says, "He was in love with someone else."

That news hits me like a hammer. Does she think I'm cut from the same cloth, poised to hurt her? If she does, I don't know how I'll reassure her. I thought it would simply take time to prove myself, but now I don't know if I ever can, even though I know how I feel.

I focus on the other guy for now. "Did he cheat on you?" I clench my jaw.

"No. I don't think so. And I can't be mad at him for the reason it ended. He simply didn't love me the same way he loved her. I was the in-between girl. Trouble was, I wanted to be his everything girl."

A tornado of jealousy swirls in my gut, and I'm envious of that guy. Envious because she wanted so badly to be loved by him. By someone who didn't care about her heart the same way. But on the other hand, if he had cared about her, I wouldn't be road-tripping with her now, so I can't be too mad that he broke her heart.

Except I am, because I hate she was hurt. "Let me see if I have this straight. That ex was a dick for not seeing what was in front of him, and the other guy is a dick for saying you talk too much when, as I've mentioned, you talk the perfect amount. We talked most of the way down here when we weren't listening to your comedian playlist."

"Which, for the record, was an awesome way to road-trip."

"Will you write about the road trip in your show?" I ask after I take a bite.

"Eh, who knows." She pops an artichoke fry into her mouth. "Just kidding. Of course I will. The main characters actually left for a road trip at the end of the last episode."

That makes me ridiculously happy, that she already weaved this into her show. "Is that so?"

"Well, the hero invited his friend to go on one. She hasn't said yes yet."

I wiggle my eyebrows. "I bet I know her answer."

She kicks me playfully under the table. "Shh. Don't tell."

"It'll be our secret."

She takes another bite of her salad then sets down the fork. "I've been taking mental notes all day. And when I do sit down to write about it, I'll probably be required to use every road-trip trope known to writer-kind."

I arch a brow. "How so?"

"In every road trip movie or show, the following are inevitable," she says, then rattles off, faster and faster, "Forgotten Underwear, Car Breaks Down, Only One Room Left at the Hotel, accompanied by Only One Bed in the Room, followed by Inconvenient Knock on the Door That Prevents Kiss, then Wise Old Widower Remarks What a Good Couple They Make, then Hero Break-Dances, and then He Gets Tipsy and Falls Asleep Nude before They Can Have Sex, followed by Entire Sheet Wrapped around Body When He Gets Up. And of course, the pièce de résistance—the Epic Airport Chase Scene."

I stop with the burger midway to my mouth. "Sign me up. Well, except for the car breaking down and the tipsy part. I'd like to not fall asleep at the wrong moment."

"But you have to. It's the law of the tropes."

"Are we living in a TV show or a movie?"

She stage-whispers, "You never know. But those things happen in literally every road trip movie or episode."

"Will they happen in yours?"

"Should they?"

"What if I told you there was one room at the hotel?"

"I'd say you engineered it."

I sigh heavily. "I reserved two."

She snaps her fingers like she's disappointed.

I am too.

* * *

When we check in at Seascape Inn, I glance at Finley and mouth, *Waiting for the One Room trope*.

But the innkeeper, sporting a tweed vest and a matching hat I suspect is the height of hipster couture, hands us two keys. "One's by the pool. The other by the road," the innkeeper tells us. "Pool's the better view."

I hand her the key to that room, and she thanks me.

I walk her up the stairs, wishing that tropes were as common in real life as in the movies. Come to think of it, nothing that I thought would be like the movies has come true.

And that's both good and bad.

But mostly good, so I hope this un-movie-like moment will work out in an unexpectedly good way. I point to my room. "If you get hungry or bored, come see me."

She mimes typing. "Time to make the donuts. Thanks for a fun day."

I shoo her away. "Go. Write. You can't lollygag with me any longer."

"Hey, did you ever think that lollygag sounds like something that happens with a blow job that takes too long?"

"That's not a thing."

"A blow job that takes too long?"

I shake my head vehemently. "That's never happened and it will never happen." I snap my fingers. "Wait, wait. You said something about being bad at blow jobs."

She groans in obvious frustration. "Thank you for reminding me of my shortcomings."

"Hey! No one ever said you were short with coming."

She rolls her eyes. "We are not discussing blow jobs right now."

"But eventually?"

"Good night, Tom." She heads into her room, and the door closes with a dull thud.

That sound is the end of my night, and I have only two more to win her heart.

Inside my room, I take a shower and power through some work. When I check the clock and see it's ten thirty, I pick up my phone to text her to see if she's gone to bed.

But as I tap out her name, there's a knock on my door.

19

FINLEY

This tune is driving me insane. Every song is driving me crazy. Most of all, the guy playing them is making me lose my mind—this shirtless, long-haired, ankle rope bracelet–wearing surfer dude strumming tunes on the loudest guitar in the universe.

Outside my window.

The window is shut, but I can still hear the instrument crying through the glass as he sings and plucks by the pool, and it's enough for me to WANT TO DIE.

I drag a hand down my face. "Ugh."

I turn to the window again, yank it open, and fix on my best oh-so-kind face. "Hi there! Any chance you could play a little quieter?"

But he doesn't even look up.

I shake my fist at him, pivot, and march dramatically to the hotel phone. I call the front desk, and Hipster Hat Dude gives me a sympathetic, "I know, I hear ya, I get it. As a harmonica player myself, I try not to music pollute."

"Thank you," I say. "So you can handle this aural assault?"

"Well, it is a free country," he points out.

"So you can't help?"

"I'll see what I can do. I appreciate you letting me know."

Only mildly relieved, I hang up and return to my laptop and do my best to put blinders on my ears, so I can focus on the scene in front of me. Since I worked all day yesterday, I'm more than halfway through episode three, and I've managed to write another scene tonight. The homestretch for this episode is in view. Inspiration and I are tight these days.

But this pivotal scene between the hero and heroine, where they're talking *about* other things without saying what they really mean, is bedeviling me.

I'm close. So close. What if the hero says—

A harmonica reverberates in the air, breaking my concentration. I snap my gaze to the window then stomp over, peering through the glass.

"Are you kidding me?" I mutter.

Tweed Hat Guy is outside now, one booted foot parked on a lawn chair, playing his harmonica, jamming with Surfer Guitar Dude. This is why he appreciated the tip—so he could play, front desk duties be damned.

I become the demon baby in *Incredibles 2*. I'm fuming, filled with smoke and fire and rampant irritation. I seethe, clomping my way to the bathroom to lock myself in there and write in the freaking tub, when I realize something.

It's both a face-palm and a glorious chorus of angels.

Tom's room.

It's on the other side of the hotel.

I stuff my laptop into its case, grip it tight in my arms, and march to his room, banging hard on the door. When he answers, a slow smile spreads across his face, an easy grin that makes my heart kick.

That grin, those teeth, his lips.

His hair.

His eyes.

I smile too. "Hi."

I nearly stumble when I hear the timbre of my own voice. I sound like a girl greeting a guy she likes. But I also sound like someone else.

I sound like Tom did this morning when he picked me up. He "hi'd" me the same way. The start-of-a-date hi. An I-like-you-so-much hi.

I blink in surprise then double surprise when he says it again.

"Hi."

My heart flutters. My skin tingles.

I'm supposed to be angry. I'm supposed to be completely annoyed and frustrated over harmonicas and twangy guitars. But I'm neither of those anymore.

I'm happy. I'm flirty.

"Fancy meeting you here," I say.

His eyes sparkle. "I assume all my prayers that you'd wind up hungry or bored have been answered?"

I'm not the only flirty one. He's doing it right back to me. With me.

My mind slingshots to the first night at Red, White, and Rosé. I joked that Tom was easy to say in bed.

Maybe you could show me what that sounds like, he'd said.

Have we been flirting from the start?

What if it's true what he said in the car today, that all along his affection for Cassie was misplaced? That it was rose-colored glasses tinting the view? That he hasn't felt anything for her in ages, and it took a light-bulb moment to see that clearly?

In this moment, I believe him. Because he looks at me the way I imagined he looked at Cassie.

But then I think of Anthony and his parting words. His I'm-just-not-that-into-you-since-I'm-totally-into-someone-else words. Even if Tom looks at me like I'm the one he wants right now, that doesn't mean he feels for me the way he once did for Cassie. I'm not that girl to him. I'm the replacement, and I don't intend to play that part with him.

Keep it light. Keep it breezy. Focus on friendship.

"There's a new trope I encountered tonight."

He arches a brow. "Do tell."

"It's the Horrifically Loud Guitar and Harmonica Duo Playing by the Pool trope."

"Which obviously leads to Only One room Left at the Hotel." He opens the door wide, gesturing for me to come in. "There's also Only One Bed in the Room."

As I wander in, my eyes drift to the king-size bed. "It's so blissfully quiet. Can I write here for a bit?"

"Be my guest. I'm just going to get tipsy and wrap a sheet around my waist."

I swat him, because I still like flirting with him, even though I won't let it go anywhere. I can manage this flirtation and keep him at arm's length. Just like I can safely get out of bed without a helmet.

I write for an hour, maybe more. I'm dead-focused the entire time, and when I tear my gaze away from the screen at last, Tom's lounging in the hotel chair, reading.

"You're the perfect writing companion. You're like a church mouse."

"You did say you liked quiet," he says, setting down his e-reader, rising, and walking over to the bed. He sits on the end of it. "How's it going?" He tips his forehead to the laptop.

"I'm almost done with another episode," I say, a huge smile spreading across my face.

"Can I hear some of it?"

I flinch, surprised by his request. "You want to read it?" I ask, as if he suggested we speak in Arabic tonight.

"No. I want *you* to read it to me. Read me a scene."

"Like a bedtime story?"

"Well, hopefully it won't put me to sleep."

He scoots up on the bed, parking himself next to me, and my body goes up in flames. I rein in a shudder and hold back a sigh. But even as I feign stoicism, it's as if I'm wearing a bright, flashing sign broadcasting my heart. *I like you. I want you.*

I should move away from him, but I don't want to move at all. I want him to come closer. I clear my parched throat and do my best to concentrate on the words on the screen, but they hardly seem legible.

It's more than *like* that I feel for him.

It's so much more.

"Want me to read Lane in this scene?" he asks gently.

I only nod, because forming words that aren't *I'm falling for you* is too hard.

"Question. Why are you bringing two umbrellas?"

he asks, and he sounds so eerily like my hero that it takes me a few seconds before I can *see* the words on the screen. The damn words I wrote.

"It might rain," I say as Amanda, and I'm grateful I have a script, that I don't have to improvise my way through a conversation right now on his bed. I pat his arm since that's what Amanda would do, and since I like touching him as her. I like touching him as me too. His arm is strong and toned, and the second I make contact, I picture those arms wrapped around me, spreading me open, pinning me down. Heat shoots across my skin, fiery and bright. I force myself to focus on the screen. "You can use one of mine if it rains," I say, reading the next line.

"I'm not going to use an umbrella," Tom says.

The next few lines swirl in front of my eyes. I don't need to read this to know what's coming next. Words we've said. Words I say to him all the time. He already knows he's my inspiration, but will he know he's becoming more?

My heart rises into my throat.

"You're such a guy," I say as Amanda, fighting to stay light, breezy. I desperately want to stay in character.

"News flash. I am a guy," he says, just like Lane, just like Tom.

Slowly, Tom turns his gaze to me. He taps the screen. "You've said that to me before. *You're such a guy.*"

His brown eyes linger on mine like he's found some hidden meaning in them. "You've said that back to me. *I am a guy,*" I say, too breathy for my own good.

But I don't know how to speak like me anymore. I

don't know if I'm the character or the creator or the woman who's been swept away by what she's living.

My heart thunders a demanding rhythm that he has to notice, has to hear.

"What's next? What will you write next?" he asks, since that's the last thing on the page.

The room is so quiet, I can hear the fabric of his shorts rustle against the comforter. I swallow, trying to find words as he slides closer. But it's not words I need. It's guts. The ones to match my emotions. The man told me less than three days ago he wasn't into the woman I've been helping him win back, and now all I want is to grab his face and yank him against me.

I should run.

I've been there, done that, have the scars to prove it. I've been this girl before, the one cast aside. The second choice.

I don't want to be that girl with Tom.

But I also don't want to spend another second with this knot twisting in my gut. The pain of not telling him what comes next is clawing away at me.

I don't want to run from him.

"The network wants," I say, my voice bare, "a fake kiss."

"Fake? Like ours the other night?"

The tingles are everywhere, slip-sliding all over my body. "Yes."

"The network wanted that?"

"I mentioned it to Bruce, and he jumped all over it. I need to write it next."

"But will it be a fake kiss or a real kiss?"

I lick my lips. "He wants it fake. Like they don't

know they're kissing for real yet. Do you know what I mean?"

"I do." He takes the laptop from me, gestures that he wants to close it, and I give him my permission. He flips the lid and moves it down the bed. "Was our kiss fake or real?" he asks, and his voice is so raw. He's as desperate to know as I am.

But I'm still afraid, still so scared. "How did it feel to you?"

His lips quirk. "I want your answer." Closer. He moves closer.

I take a breath and find my courage. It's somewhere near my heart, and my heart wants what it wants. It wants him. I raise my chin. "It felt exactly like how this feels now. *Real.*"

He lifts his hand and brushes strands of hair from my cheek. My eyes float closed for a few seconds, then I open them. He's staring at me, heat in his eyes, desire blazing like flames.

He spreads his fingers through my hair. "Is the way I'm touching you fake or real?"

"Real."

He lets go of me and takes off his glasses, twisting to set them on the nightstand. It's such an honest move. Such a vulnerable one. It tells me he wants to kiss. He turns back.

"Do you want to kiss for real?"

I look into his eyes, and I see him so clearly. This flawed, beautiful, stubborn, ridiculous, funny, smart man.

Who wants to kiss me.

"So much."

20

TOM

"Ask me the question," I say.

The air between us is charged. Crackling. The room is stone-quiet, but the silence blankets us and beats louder than music or song. It's the sound of desire.

"Ask you what?"

"How much I want to kiss you."

She trembles. "How much do you want to kiss me?"

I end all this talking, all this wonderful, incredible talking that only makes me want to kiss more. I end it with my lips. There is nothing fake in this kiss. Nothing inauthentic in the way my lips slide across hers, how I nip on the corner of her mouth.

Everything is true as she loops her hands around my neck.

This kiss is long overdue.

We may have kissed already, but this is our first kiss too. The first between just the two of us, no audience, no objective. It's not a rehearsal or a practice round. It's full of possibilities, but now they're only for us.

I want all the possibilities with her. I want more than kissing. My hand finds its way into her hair, and she sighs against my lips, angling her body toward mine like she's saying *keep going, give me more, give me so much more.* The closer I get to her, the closer I want to be. I want to kiss her so hard that it erases any doubt she felt moments ago. That it blots out any worry that this kiss could have been anything but true.

She returns the kiss. Fiercely, and with the same kind of passion I've seen her pour into her show. Right now, I'm the lucky bastard who gets to receive that passion.

And she gives so damn good.

She gives right back to me, urgency in her touch, like we're running out of time. She tastes hungry and needy. Her hands clasp my face then thread through my hair, and soon the kiss becomes a blur of heat and need and hands and lips and clothes.

She's under me.

Wrapping her legs around my hips. We're no longer sitting up in bed kissing. We're lying down, and everything is hot and heavy.

This is what I've been chasing for years. This desperate connection between body and mind.

I break the kiss, breathe her name.

Her eyes flutter open. They're hazy and wild.

"You're so pretty," I tell her. Because she is, because I should have said it sooner, but mostly because I can say it now.

"So are you," she says on a panting breath, then rolls her eyes. "I mean . . . you're handsome. You're hot.

You're cute. You're so fucking good-looking I don't even know what to do with myself."

Pride suffuses me, filling my whole body. Not because she thinks I'm handsome, but because of one word. "That's the first time I've heard you swear."

She laughs, miming throwing up words. "Everything just sort of spilled out."

"You can compliment me anytime," I say, then lower my hips against her, letting her feel the outline of my erection.

She throws her head back and moans. "Ahhh."

"*Finley*." I don't know if it's a question or a command or simply the sheer relief of *finally* saying her name like this.

"Kyler," she says low, under her breath.

I grab her chin. "Why are you calling me that now?"

"Just seeing if I like it."

"Do you?"

She shakes her head. "I like Tom."

My heart pounds as I brace myself on my hands and bring my lips to hers once more, pressing another kiss to her soft, sweet mouth. This feels like a new beginning, like we could be an *us*. But I also know the possibilities are tender and new, and I don't want to crush them.

"I like the way you say it," I tell her. I run my finger across her lip. She nips on the pad. "I like how it sounds on your lips."

She demonstrates again for me. "*Tom*."

I groan, pressing against her. "Say it again."

She moans my name and draws my finger between her lips then stops. Tenses.

"What's wrong?"

"To answer your question from before—I'm terrible at blow jobs. I can't even simulate one."

I laugh.

"Don't laugh at me."

"I'm not laughing at you. I'm laughing because I love that you just blurted that out, and I've been dying to discuss blow jobs with you."

"Wait. Let me guess. You're obsessed with them."

I wiggle my eyebrows. "I am a guy, after all." I move off her, lying next to her, running my finger down her side. "So what's the story?"

She sighs. "Are we doing this?"

"The blow job story?"

"Yes."

"Well, you were privy to one of my most embarrassing moments. In fact, you kind of know most of them."

She sinks her head against the pillow, dragging a hand through her hair. "This guy I went out with, maybe four years ago, told me to stop in the middle of one. He said it felt like my mouth was a wet napkin on his dick. I kind of stopped giving them for the most part."

My eyebrows rise. "Entirely?'

She swats my shoulder. "It's not like I had a blow job stand that I had to take down."

I laugh. "Glad to hear that."

"Why are you asking? Are you angling for me to lollygag? And also, why would you want a bad blow job?"

I lean over and kiss her. "I know it wouldn't be bad."

"How do you know?"

"Because your lips are spectacular, because I like you, because my dick would be very happy. But look, I'm not angling for one." I let my voice trail off then toss out a very appealing option. "Unless you want to practice."

She laughs, arching a brow. "So you are angling for one?"

"I'm open to teaching the fine art of blow jobs."

"Are you now?" Her eyes are intense, like she's seriously considering my offer.

"Completely." The prospect of being her test case for how to give a blow job is intensely alluring. "Let me be your dummy. For the sake of education."

She rolls her eyes. A dart of worry hits me. "Did I say the wrong thing again? Tell me. Tell me if I did." I finally have her where I want her. *Happy.* I can't fuck it up. "Did I say something wrong by saying I'd like to teach you how to give a blow job?"

"No." She slides her hand down my chest. A shudder wracks my body. "That feels good," I murmur.

She travels lower, to my shorts, and I thrust against her, asking silently for her touch. She covers my hard-on with her palm. "That feels incredible," I say.

"Yeah?"

"So good," I rasp out. "And it'd be so much better if it were your mouth."

"Do you mean that?"

"You have no idea how much."

"Tom?"

"Yes?"

Her eyes are wide, etched with nerves, but guts too. "Will you please teach me?"

No one has ever said anything sexier in my life.

No combination of words has ever been more arousing.

I say the only thing I can. "Yes. Now. Please." I practically rip off my shirt as she crawls over me, unzipping my shorts and tugging on my boxers till my cock greets her with a spirited salute.

She whistles her appreciation then bounces lightly on my thighs. "Now what? How do you like it? I want to learn how to do this." She rubs her hands together, an eager student.

I'm naked and she's dressed, ready to learn. But I think this power play is important to her. And I want this to be good for her. This is a gift to be able to teach a woman—not just any woman, but *the* woman I want—how I like it.

"I'm going to tell you a secret. There's no art to a blow job. There's one thing that makes it good. Want to know?"

"I do."

I reach for her hair, bringing her face closer to mine. "When the woman is into it."

A sexy little sigh seems to fall from her lips. "That's it?"

I lift an eyebrow. "That's all. So . . . do you want to suck my dick?"

She drops her forehead to mine and breathes out a shuddery *yes*.

My cock throbs its satisfaction with her answer.

"Then trust that it'll be good for me." I bring her mouth to my lips first and whisper, "Kiss the tip."

She moves down my body, smiling shyly, stopping right where I want her. When she wraps her fist around my shaft, pleasure shoots through my veins like wildfire. She grips harder, strokes once, twice, then lowers her lips, planting a too-soft kiss.

It's good, but I want more. "More," I tell her. "More lips. *Use* them."

She opens her mouth and licks the head, and my hips jerk up. Her lips curve into a smile, and I tell her to lick and suck on the crown. "Treat me like I'm candy."

She does as instructed, licking lines that start to drive me wild with pleasure. I moan and close my eyes for a few seconds, savoring the teasing taste of her lips.

But it's not enough. I'm dying for her warm mouth. "Finley, I'm going to tell you what else I like."

"Please do," she says desperately. "I feel like I'm flailing."

"Play with my balls."

Her eyes light up and she dips her hand lower, cupping them. "How?" she whispers.

"Gentle, but not too gentle."

She rolls them lightly in her palm. "Like this?"

A wild thrill rips through me, and I pant out a *yes*.

"And do you want me to suck your dick at the same time?"

I love how she's breaking this down to a step-by-step diagram. "God, yes."

"But what do I do when your dick is in my mouth?" Her voice rises. "So it doesn't feel like a wet napkin to you."

"*Suck.* Just like a lollipop and you're dying to get to the candy center. Only don't bite."

"Don't bite," she repeats with a dutiful nod then quirks up her lips. "How do I make sure I don't bite?"

"Wrap your lips around me and kind of cover your teeth with them." I demonstrate, and she imitates me. "While playing with my balls," I add with a wink.

She kisses the tip again, and wild pleasure sparks down my thighs.

"Yes, like that," I groan. "Fuck. Yes."

"Wait. Was that a good *fuck*?"

"Yes. That was a very good *fuck*."

She kisses my dick again then draws me in farther, past the head, down the shaft.

My thighs shake as I watch every move. It's like every single inch is a learning experience. I'm halfway to filling her mouth, and she's awkward and curious and the sexiest woman I've ever seen because she's using my dick as a test case.

She's trying to learn pleasure from my cock, but I'm truly the lucky one. In this moment, I decide I can't lose her. Not because she has me by the teeth. But because she trusted me enough to let me show her.

She stripped bare for me. Opened up. Asked for help.

This is the woman I want.

Her.

And that thought turns me on so damn much. I thrust up into her mouth, reveling in the feel of her.

But I push too hard, and she coughs. I jerk back, pulling out. "Are you okay?"

"It just surprised me. Did I do something wrong?"

"No, I was getting into it. I was enjoying it."

A smile tips the corners of her lips. "You were?"

I grin wickedly. "I was thinking about how much I want to fuck your mouth."

"You do?"

"I do."

"I'm nervous I won't be any good," she says softly.

"I'm not worried about that in the least."

She laughs.

"And if you're worried, we can do it a few times. To be sure."

That earns another laugh, then I thread my hand through her hair again and gently, but firmly, tug her back toward me. "I need you to do something right now."

"Tell me."

Her eyes lock with mine, and I hold her gaze, running my thumb over her mouth. "Suck my dick, please. Suck my dick till I come in your mouth."

Her eyes are wild, fierce, and she's the best student ever as she lowers her mouth to me.

I'm not all the way in. Not even close, but I don't care. It feels extraordinary, the way she holds the base with her hand, how she moves her fist. There's no finesse. It's not an artful blow job. It's not a show-off suck. It doesn't need to be. She breathes hard as she takes me deeper. She keeps it simple, up and down but the pleasure builds in me. It coils in my belly, tightens under my skin, and turns electric. I want to close my eyes and let go, but I want to watch her more. I push up on the pillow, push her hair from her cheek. "I fucking love watching you do this," I tell her, since I think she needs praise.

I see her smile with my dick in her mouth, and if I were the dick pic–taking kind, I would want this shot. "My dick has never looked so good."

Her eyes close for a second, like the pleasure is too much. It is too much. It's far too much for me. It grabs hold of my senses, knocks out wires, trips fuses.

"Don't stop," I command, or maybe I beg. "Don't fucking stop. Don't you dare fucking stop."

And she doesn't. Her noises are messier, her breath is harder, and the storm brewing inside me bursts in one fierce explosion of ecstasy. It spirals through me as I come in her mouth.

When I open my eyes, she lets me fall from her lips, raises her face, and thrusts her arms high in the air.

"Oh yeah!" she shouts.

I have no choice but to crack up. "You can do a victory dance too, if you want."

She shakes her hips on me. "And that's how you lollygag!"

"If that's lollygagging, you can do it to me every day."

She bends closer, her voice going more intimate. "Thank you for teaching me."

I shake my head. "No. *Thank you* for being such a willing student. I assure you, the pleasure was all mine."

"Actually," she says, her tone flirty, inviting, as she wriggles against me, "the pleasure was also mine."

That's an open invitation if I ever heard one. I slide my hand between her legs, cupping her through her shorts to find she's soaked.

I groan with desire. "Finley, I don't know how to go down on a woman. Would you teach me?"

She swats me. "You lie."

I hold up a hand like I'm taking an oath. "I swear."

"I don't believe you. But I have to go. I have to write more, and I remain ever hopeful that the harmonica guitar session is over."

"You're only using me for blow-job lessons."

"Yes, that's it."

I tug her closer, stroking her between her legs even through her clothes. "I want to taste you, and I'm not above begging, pleading, cajoling, or paying those guys to keep playing harmonica and acoustic guitar."

"I want that. Well, not the hipster-surfer duo's music. But if I don't write more, I won't hit Bruce's crazy deadlines."

"Can we practice again tomorrow, then?"

She smiles. "Let me see if I can fit you in."

When she leaves, I wonder if our lesson will make its way into her show. Somehow, I doubt it. Her show's not that racy. But I hope that it inspired her to at least want to keep me around. Only, I'm not entirely sure how to get there with her. In the past, I'd have winged it, turned to the movies, or charged forward, sledge-hammer-style, like the blunt instrument I often am. But this is the present, and I need to approach this differently. So I call in the reinforcements, starting with Nash.

Tom: I want to do something nice for Finley.

Nash: Remember that time I taught you how to French braid hair? Do that.

Tom: You never taught me to French braid hair, and may you never.

Nash: Hair-braiding is a skill you should have. Women love that. But that isn't something I can tutor you on via text. Talk to me. How can I help?

Tom: You know how some women like flowers and some like cake? Well, she likes jokes. I want to do something that will make her laugh.

Nash: I'm trying really hard to resist making a joke about showing her your dick.

As for me, I resist tossing out a zinger about how I already did, then came, saw, and conquered.

Tom: Anyway . . .

Nash: Cut me some slack. I can't change overnight. But I'll roll up my sleeves and work on this. What's funny to her? Can you tell her an inside joke or something?

Tom: Yes! That's it.

Nash: Um, how is that it?

Tom: It is, and you're a steely-eyed missile man and so am I. See ya, man.

Nash: I have no idea how I helped, but may the Force be with you.

I wake up early the next morning and get to work.

21

FINLEY

It's seven forty-five on a Wednesday, I've had four hours of sleep, and I'm giddy.

Just look at me. This never happens. I'm having a fantastic hair day. The shampoo gods are smiling on me, and they blessed me with curls that are springy and cute.

A day like this, you can do no wrong. Also, there's one other reason to celebrate.

Fine, two.

First, Bruce emails me. *"Things are looking good, Peaches. Since you're on your road trip, any chance you can stop by the network tomorrow? Some face time with the brass would be good."*

I squeal as I reread the note. Now, I suck *good*.

As I consider my reflection, I wonder if everyone will be able to tell I've acquired a brand-new skill. I raise an eyebrow, studying my face. Do I look like a woman who learned to play the skin flute last night?

"Yes, you do. You look like a virtuoso," I tell my

reflection, then I close my eyes and replay last night. His reactions, my responses. But also something else. How I felt inside when I did that to him.

I felt . . . *right*.

I felt like he's the one I want to do all those things with, the one I want to experience new tricks with, new ways of coming together.

I'm not innocent, not in the least.

But at the same time, there's so much to explore, in bed and out.

Tom feels like the Lewis to my Clark.

He's my co-explorer.

He's also the man I want to kiss over and over. I run my fingers over my lips like I can reactivate the kiss that shook my entire body. A kiss I felt from top to bottom, from sea to shining sea, from the ends of my hair to my toenails.

Yes, a spectacular kiss can evidently resonate in the toenails. How else would toes curl?

But I'm not only giddy. I'm nervous as hell too. What comes next? Do we kiss more today? Do we go out? Are we a thing?

I have no clue, so I tug on shorts and a black scoop-neck top with tiny white polka dots, hoping for clarity this morning.

I find Tom easily in the dining room downstairs. The second I make eye contact, the butterflies launch a full-scale sweep. Warmth spreads over my shoulders and down my arms, making goose bumps rise across my flesh.

Tom smiles at me, slow and easy. I walk over to him at the table, and he rises, pulling out a chair for me. I sit, unsure what to say. There's something so awkward about the morning after a night like that. You both know each other better, and know each other less. Because you don't entirely know if it was sex, or sex and the start of something more.

"How was your night?" My voice is jittery, like a cup of strong coffee.

"It was . . . illuminating."

"How so?"

"I learned that Crash Davis was right."

"About the designated hitter or soft-core porn?"

He nods his head approvingly. "Dirty girl."

"Dirty guy," I counter.

"He was right about kissing."

Sparks race down my chest, and I know where we're going. His gaze holds mine tight and we speak in unison, reciting one of the sexiest lines from *Bull Durham*, from any movie. "I believe in long, slow, deep, soft, wet kisses that last three days."

I am a puddle.

I've melted onto the floor, and all that remains is my great hair and my squishy heart.

He slides a menu to me. "Want breakfast?"

No, I want to jump across the table, clasp your face in my hands, and smother you in kisses that last three days.

So I decide to tell him. Maybe that lesson last night unlocked something else in me. Maybe it unlocked a little more courage to speak my mind and take a chance. It's not the riskiest of moves, but even so, it's risky for me. "Yes, and then I want to kiss you for three days."

He groans, drags a hand down his face, and makes a show of spreading a napkin carefully across his lap.

"And you will never hear me telling you to snap out of that."

We pat ourselves on the back for our movie-quote skills, and I don't care that he used to do this with Cassie. From what he's told me, she didn't like them as much as he does. Or as much as I do. And I *like* movie quotes. I like that he does them with me, that we do them together.

We order, and we talk about the park we're going to visit that day, then about Bruce's latest email.

"We should stop in Los Angeles, then," he says.

"Will that interfere with your plans to see Cassie?" I ask, and I want to vomit. Saying her name again twists my stomach. Movie quotes or not, I'm wickedly jealous of her, even though he says he's not into her. But the fact that she's his final destination weighs on me. It's the reminder that he has unfinished business with his ex.

He shakes his head quickly. "No. This meeting is important. We'll make it happen."

"Also, how are we getting home once you're done in San Diego?" I ask, biting off more of this bitter pill.

"Drive or fly?"

I shrug. "Why don't we do it the Indiana Jones way?"

He lets out a sexy sigh. "I'm just making this up as I go along," he says, quoting from *Raiders of the Lost Ark*.

After the waitress brings us my oatmeal with blueberries and his scrambled eggs, an older couple strolls by. She wears a red polo and he sports a blue one. They're holding hands, and she motions for him to check out our plates.

"Don't those blueberries look heavenly, Harry?"

He smiles at her. "They sure do, Mary."

Harry and Mary. Too cute.

"Are they as good as they look?" she asks me.

"They're the stuff oatmeal dreams are made of."

She laughs. "And how are your eggs, young man?"

"The chickens were happy, and they'd be very proud, I suspect."

She presses her hand to her chest. "You two are such a cute couple."

They shuffle away, and I raise my eyebrows at Tom, pointing silently at them. "It happened. A kind old couple said we look cute."

"And you said tropes don't come true."

I hold up my hands, surrendering. "I stand corrected."

A little later, while we're loading our bags into Tom's car, the notes of something that sounds like LL Cool J land on my ears.

I spin around, looking for the source. On the stone path cutting across the hotel grounds is the man in the blue polo shirt.

Break-dancing.

Harry is freaking break-dancing, holding his iPhone, blasting LL Cool J.

He tips his imaginary hat to us and moonwalks away.

Under the morning sun, I raise my pink shades and regard the man in front of me holding open the trunk of the car.

"Next thing I know, there will be an airport chase scene," I say, a little amazed.

"Wouldn't that be something?" he asks, like a man who has all the tricks up his sleeve.

"Did you plan that?" I ask, though I'm pretty sure I know the answer.

"If I said it was random, would you believe me?"

I shake my head, my smile taking over all the real estate on my face. "You did plan that."

He wiggles his eyebrows, ridiculously pleased. "I thought you would get a kick out of the Kind Old Couple Remarks What a Cute Couple They Make, followed by Kind Old Guy Break-Dances."

"How? How did you do that?" I ask, amazed that he pulled this off for me.

"I wandered around the hotel, found this couple, told them there was a girl I was trying to impress . . . and there you go."

I throw my arms around him, and give him a long, slow, wet, deep kiss that Crash Davis would approve of.

That's the moment when I fall completely in love with Tom.

Hopelessly. Helplessly. In a way that makes me feel both sick to my stomach and on top of the world.

As we slide into the rental, and the final destination on his GPS blinks *San Diego*, I'm reminded that a few days ago, Tom was planning on seeing Cassie to declare his love for her, rather than to apologize for hurting her.

Heck, a week ago he was singing to her outside my window.

Can the heart truly do a 180-degree turn in a week? Can he possibly feel for me the way I feel for him? What if his feelings for me are misplaced? What if they're conflated with this newfound freedom from being on the road? We could simply be on a honeymoon. A wonderful, delicious, rebound honeymoon for him, and then the bubble will burst when real life sets back in.

When we're living our regular lives, him in San Francisco, me more than an hour away up the coast.

This bubble of time with him feels so real and so unreal at the same damn time.

So much of my life is up in the air—my show, this man—I don't know what's solid and what's lasting.

I think about Christine's parting words. *Be careful.*

I try valiantly to do that by focusing on enjoying today for what it is—a *day*.

As we wind down the coast, the ocean waves framing us on the right, showing off their vastness, I try to shove all the questions from my mind. We stop at a roadside fruit stand and buy blueberries, eating them as we drive on, listening to '80s tunes, then turning off the music to talk about why some big gestures in movies were overrated.

"The thing about the boom box is this," I say, popping a blueberry into my mouth. "She never even came to the window."

He nods thoughtfully. "True."

"But I think we all forget that part. Lloyd Dobler just stood there in her driveway, lifting it higher and higher and playing the song, and Diane didn't even get out of bed."

"So it was the wrong big gesture?"

I shake my head, reaching for my iced tea and uncapping it to take a swig. "In the end, she was the one who had to go to him, remember?"

His brow pinches, and he must be thinking of the movie. "At his kickboxing studio?"

I offer him the bottle, and he takes a gulp then hands it back to me. "Yes, exactly. She had to win him back because she'd already broken his heart."

"Maybe that's why it didn't work for me. It wasn't supposed to work."

I nod. "Maybe."

"Or maybe it was the wrong girl," he says, offering a hopeful smile before he returns his gaze to the road.

My stomach squeezes again. "But what if she was there?"

He shrugs. "I don't know, Finley. That's not what happened."

"I know," I whisper, and what happened is so much better, but also so much more terrifying.

We reach the amusement park that's an hour outside Los Angeles.

"This one has the Spinning Devil," he says. "And it's one hundred percent mine."

I smile. "I can't wait to ride your ride."

He enters the park like a civilian, and I tease him. He waits in line like an everyman too, even though I keep telling him that all he has to do is swagger his way to the front and break out the "hey man, that's my ride."

He won't.

Instead, when we're in line, he tugs me close, slides a hand through my hair, and kisses me.

It blots out my fears. It erases my worries, and it takes my breath away.

When we make it onto the Spinning Devil, his work takes my breath away.

And taxes my lungs.

Because holy speed.

This ride is a whirling dervish, zipping and careening and flipping us upside down again and again.

By the time it ends, two and a half minutes later, my hair is a wild mess, my heart is beating outside my chest, and I'm in awe of this man.

Once we're off the ride, I grab his face and kiss him hard. A little dirty, a lot sexy. Because I'm turned on by what we did. By his mind and his talents and his abilities.

And it's killing me that I fell for him at the wrong time.

In comedy, timing isn't just everything.

It's the *only* thing.

It's the same in love. You need the right person, true. But you also need the right person at the right time for it to work. He might feel like the right person, but he seems to have arrived at the wrong time in his romantic life.

When I let go, he tugs me right back to him. "Would you like to ride another ride?"

"I would," I say, excited, as I scan the park. "Which one?"

"That's not what I mean, Finley."

I feel the press of his erection, and my thoughts go hazy and straight to the bedroom. "Oh."

* * *

"One room or two?"

Inside the motel lobby, I wait for him to answer the question from the clerk, even though I know his answer. I know he wants me tonight. I want him too.

"One."

* * *

We stumble into the room, dropping our bags in a flurry, grabbing at each other like we haven't seen each other in days. *Years.* It's only been minutes since we had our hands on each other, but this is the way of new lovers. We scramble and scurry and we *need*.

My pulse rockets to the moon as he ropes his hands through my hair and pulls my head back, kissing my lips, my jaw, then my neck.

Dear God, my neck is on fire. He travels down the column of my throat, mapping me with kisses.

Then he guides my head back up and stares at me. "The best thing that's ever happened to me was you being at that window."

My heart tries to leap into his arms. I want to blurt out my truth too—that I'm in love with him. But that fear is still lodged in my chest, so rather than say the L-word, I echo him, and it's completely true. "Same here."

He kisses my neck, then grabs my face like he has to make sure I see him. But I do. I do see him.

"This is crazy and so out of the blue," he says, and my doubts start to crumble. But I'd be a fool to sweep them away completely. I'm not ready to play that part yet. I need him to lead.

So I agree, because I do. "I know."

"I didn't think this would happen," he murmurs, and nips on my ear, and I want to float away to the stars because that's where he takes me. "I didn't know you a week ago. And now I'm crazy for you. It almost doesn't feel real."

"Is it real?" My pitch rises.

"Yes."

"It's so real for me."

Then words scatter to dust as we claw feverishly at clothes, stripping off shorts and shirts, and soon, he has me down to my bra and panties.

I stop, needing a second to catch my breath.

"Are you okay?" he asks.

"I've seen you naked, but you haven't seen me."

He smiles. "You do know that can be remedied in seconds, right?"

I love his sense of humor. I love how he disarms my fears. "Can you please remedy that, then?"

"Consider it done." He loops his hands behind my back and unhooks my bra, then whistles in appreciation, his hands darting out to cup my breasts. I'm not a busty woman. I'm average, a standard B, but he doesn't seem to care that I'm not posing for Cleavage "R" Us ads.

He fondles me like it's all he wants to do, before sliding one hand between my legs.

He groans. "You're not stopping me from going down on you tonight, are you?"

His fingers are sliding across the wet panel of my panties, sending me into a frenzy, so I doubt I'm capable of making him stop.

"Don't stop."

We make it to the bed, and he tugs down my panties, then kisses the inside of my thighs, and my vulnerability shoots up ten thousand times. I haven't been touched like this, in a way that makes me feel cherished, in ages. He kisses me that way, with affection and adoration, and it's such an elixir to the heart.

He touches me like I'm not second best.

He kisses me like I'm not a rebound girl. As he spreads me apart and curls his arms around my hips and brings me to his mouth, I don't feel like I could be anything less than first.

For now, I let that sensation wash over me as he

drenches me in wild, hot kisses, as his tongue strokes me and his lips devour me.

Soon, I'm moaning and panting and letting go, grabbing his hair, sliding my fingers through it, and he's not just licking me—I'm fucking his mouth.

He moans and sighs and urges me on, and it's hardly necessary because I'm there. I'm already there with him, as I reach the edge and fall over.

It's more exhilarating than skydiving.

When I come down from the intensity, I think I might be glowing. "You were right," I say, my breath still coming fast and hard. "You really do need a lesson in that."

He grins and plants a kiss on my belly. Then higher. Moving up to my breasts. "Yes, I was thinking I should spend a lot of time down there, eating you."

I laugh. "You need *so* much practice."

"God, I really do. I'm so bad at it. Teach me, please," he says when he reaches my face.

I stop laughing when I meet his eyes. They're so earnest and so entertained, and I want to ask how I got so lucky. But I know the answer. The answer's in San Diego.

And I'm so tired of thinking of her.

So tired of thinking of anyone but us.

I vow to believe in us for the rest of the night. "What comes next?" I ask.

"You're the writer. You tell me."

I pull him close and whisper in his ear.

23

TOM

Few words are better than *I'm on the pill*.

There are probably only two that can best that.

After she tells me we can go bare, she nips on my ear and murmurs, "Fuck me."

That's all I need to hear.

She scoots up higher on the bed, her hair falling across the pillows, and I position myself between her legs, notching my cock against her wetness.

"How do you like it? Hard, deep, slow?"

She nibbles on the corner of her lips. "I'm open to all of the above."

"Let's start with deep." I sink inside her, and my head falls back as I savor the intensity of that first moment when she clenches around me. When her heat hugs my dick. When she releases a shuddery moan of pleasure.

This woman has thrown my world upside down. She's sent me into a beautiful kind of chaos, a whole new starting over.

And I couldn't be happier, or luckier.

Or honestly more turned on right now.

I shove off those other thoughts as my breath comes faster and desire blares through me.

Admittedly, I've thought about fucking Finley since the night I met her. At first, it was an offhand thought, then it became more persistent.

But I didn't know what she'd be like. If she'd give in to the pleasure, if she'd let go to the sensations. She's in her head so much of the time, but right now I'm seeing she has no problem letting her body lead. The sounds she makes—moans of pleasure, sighs of desire—are like a wild drug, and that drug has quite an effect on both of us.

I'm in another world of erotic bliss as she parts her legs wider, digs her nails into my back, and moves her hips at a frenzied pace. I match her, fucking her deeper, harder, my hand anchored at her waist, the other one hiking up her leg, opening her farther.

She lets her head fall, exposing her neck, and I kiss her roughly, nipping at the flesh.

"Oh God, that feels so good," she moans.

Naturally, I do it again. Heat blasts through me in waves as we chase pleasure. The sounds I make are hoarse, animalistic, as white-hot lust runs roughshod in my body, over my skin, and through my mind.

It's never been like this.

I brace myself on my hands, swiveling my hips as I watch her face. Her expression twists with exquisite torture.

"God, you're so fucking pretty like this. You're so fucking pretty when you're about to come."

She trembles, and her lips part, and she grabs my shoulders, jerking me close. "I'm coming," she whispers, husky and sexy and so full of abandon.

Then she screams.

Holy fuck, does she ever scream, just like she said she would.

Louder than on the roller coaster, like she's soaring higher, flying farther, speeding into blissful oblivion.

"So good, so good, so good," she chants, and it doesn't stop. She keeps going, and it sends fiery sparks down my spine as my own climax barrels through me, and I chase her over the hill, around the tracks, and into a wild high that only this kind of sex can bring.

Sex with love.

I fucking love this woman, and now I need to convince her, beyond a shadow of a doubt, that it's the real thing.

* * *

But I don't have to yet, since Finley has a bigger appetite than I expected, and sex is keeping us both busy. My brain and my body are completely occupied with her pleasure.

She's ready to go again a little later, and since I'm a generous guy, I let her ride me. I know, it's totally altruistic, and not at all because I can get my hands on her tits, her ass, her belly, her crazy hair. It's not at all because she looks spectacular riding me like a bucking bronco.

She comes hard and, somehow, even more loudly.

Which triggers a primal urge in me to flip her to her hands and knees and take her that way.

After, we're lying in bed, and I run a hand down her side, figuring maybe now is a good time to talk. I decide to ease her in, asking if she's going to be writing tonight or early in the morning. Maybe that'll lead us to where she's at in her storyline. If she lets on, I can figure out where *we* might be, and what to do next.

Art imitated life, but now life may be imitating art too. In it, I could find the clues I need about her state of mind and heart.

"Do you need to write again tonight?"

She yanks a pillow over her head, groaning. "Don't remind me."

"Does that mean you're done for now?"

She mumbles from under the pillow. "I sent them three scripts in about a week. I'm dead from writing. I usually work with other writers on the show, but since this was on spec, it was all me, so I'm extra dead."

I hum. "Hate to break it to you, but you were pretty alive when I fucked you."

She flips over and tosses the pillow at me, then unleashes a magnificent yawn. "And if you do it to me one more time, I will be literally dead. Do you want that on your conscience?'"

I shudder, aghast. "God, no." I take a beat. "Is there anything I can do to help? Read another scene? Bounce ideas off you? Practice fake kisses, real kisses, or any combination thereof?"

She grabs my cheeks and kisses me hard, our tongues skating together. Her fingers twist in my hair, and my dick springs to life again. Holy fuck, is she ready for another round? I believe I am.

But when she yawns in the middle of a kiss, I have my answer. "Go to sleep, Finley."

She smiles at me, her eyes fluttering closed as she snuggles into the pillow. "If anyone calls with free candy or money, take a message for me."

In record time, her breathing is even and steady.

I stay next to her, wide awake, my hands parked behind my head. I need to do things differently this time around. I need to say the right things at the right time.

And do the right things.

Finley said big gestures don't work like the movies make us believe.

Finley also loved the staged tropes earlier today.

Somehow, I need to combine these two ideas.

Before I can figure out how to make two plus two equal four, her phone rings.

I glance at her, but she's sound asleep, conked out on her belly, her hair falling across her face. Peering at the screen on the nightstand, I see "Spam Likely" is calling her, so I hit ignore, as she would do herself.

A little later, I slide into slumber, and I don't rise till the sun is up on Thursday morning.

I rub my eyes, grab my glasses, and sit up in bed. The patter of the shower fills the room. For a brief moment, I consider joining her.

But I don't know if she'd want that. Maybe she's in Business Finley mode. When she's done, I toss off the covers, mumble a *good morning* when she exits, and head under the stream of hot water.

By the time I'm out, Finley is pacing, her hair yanked

back in a tight bun. She wears a pair of slacks and a silky tank top.

"Traffic is brutal. We should go," she says, tapping her foot as she fidgets with the strap of her backpack. "Do you mind if we just grab a bar or a piece of fruit?"

"Breakfast of champions," I say, then dress quickly and get the hell out of there.

* * *

She taps her knee constantly on the ride down.

Even if I'm oblivious to some clues from women, that's one I can read without my 20-400 prescription. "It's going to be great. They love the episodes so far."

"Yeah," she says, absently picking at her cuticles as she stares out the window. "I haven't been to the network offices in a year. Not since they picked up the show." She turns to look at me. "I feel like I'm walking into a shark tank."

I give her a sympathetic smile. "Then you're going to need a bigger boat," I say as I exit the highway, and she chuckles lightly.

That's all I can do for her now as we head toward the network's offices, battling stop-and-go traffic in Burbank the whole way. I drop her off, wish her luck, and duck into a coffee shop across the street, where I touch base with my client in Singapore via email while I drain half a cup of coffee. Before I can finish the drink, she texts me.

Finley: Done early.

I leave the rest of the coffee and dart across the street, figuring since she's probably in a good mood, now might be the right time to tell her how I feel. As I wait outside the revolving glass door, my brother Nash texts me about a celebrity who showed up at his restaurant, and I respond to him quickly, then glance up and see her.

She looks shell-shocked, and that must mean they shocked and awed her with a terrific offer.

I give her my best smile and dive right into the deep end. *"'All my life, I've been waiting for someone. And when I find her, she's . . . she's a fish.'"*

She stares at me like I'm a merman.

So, yeah, maybe the old toolbox was the wrong one to use.

24

FINLEY

LGO doesn't skimp on air conditioning.

The white offices are chilled to a crisp. A squirrel-like intern with a Bluetooth riding sidesaddle on his ear escorts me to the second floor toward Tad Hansen's office.

"Tad and Chad will be with you shortly," he says, in the kind of deep baritone that tells me he wanted to be an actor, too, and is cursed with having a good voice, a good face, a good body, but nothing great.

"Do you need anything? Water? Vitamin water? Nutrient water? Sparkling water?"

I didn't know there were so many varieties of water. I shake my head, say "no, thank you," and sit on the leather couch in the reception area outside of Tad's office.

"Is Bruce here yet?" I ask, my voice stretched thin with worry.

The intern smiles robotically. "I'm sure he's on his way."

"Okay." But I'm not sure Bruce's absence is okay. The man is punctual, even in the land of everyone's-late-because-of-traffic.

The squirrel-man-boy spins on his wingtips and heads in the other direction. I smooth my hand down my slacks and turn my phone to Do Not Disturb. I don't want to be distracted, and I don't want Tad and Chad to see me fiddling on the screen.

I wait.

I wait a little longer.

I check the time.

My stomach rides a dozen roller coasters while I wait for them. Finally, twenty-five minutes later, a plastic blonde Barbie emerges from somewhere, nods at me, and says, "Tad will see you now."

She escorts me into a corner office with a view of the hills, thick with smog.

Dark-haired Tad stares out the window, chatting on the phone, the sleeves of his crisp green-and-white checked shirt rolled up. "Definitely. We love it. It needs a little minor tweaking."

He pauses, still gazing out the window.

"I'm spitballing here, but think about this. How about a new love interest, for instance?"

He pauses.

"That. Yes, do that. Or you could give the lead a new career."

He turns around and waves at me, flashing the biggest grin I've ever seen, then gives me the sign that he'll be ready in a minute. His eagerness settles my nerves somewhat.

"Or what you could do is maybe move the setting

from New York to Los Angeles. Think about that. Does it have to be a cramped-in-the-city show? It could be a stuck-in-traffic show."

He takes a beat.

"It's not that big a deal. It's the same but a little different."

Another pause.

"Right. Yes. You got it. Do a little bit of that, but not exactly. But then, do *that*."

Whoever he's talking to must be experiencing whiplash with his vague directions. But that's how it goes in Hollywood when executives direct writers.

The second he hangs up, the blond Chad strides in, as if the two of them can send each other telepathic messages, like *Time to start the meeting now*. Chad wears a shirt that likely costs more than all of my belongings. He extends a hand and shakes confidently. "So good to see you, Finley."

"It's good to see you too."

Chad flashes me a gleaming grin that matches Tad's. Perhaps they had teeth whitening at the same spa.

Tad gestures to a chair. "Sit, sit."

I take a seat and the Almost Twins sit too, each parking an ankle on a knee, like synchronized executives. "What brings you to L.A.?" Chad asks.

Okay, so now were doing the personal chitchat portion of the meeting. "Road trip," I say, keeping it light. "I road-tripped down here with a friend."

Tad laughs. "Road trips. We love road trips. We love, love, love road trips."

Chad points at me, then turns to Tad. "She should do a road trip show. Right?"

Tad thrust his arms in the air. "Brilliant!"

I want to remind them that I do have an episode on a road trip. But that must be why road trips are on their minds. Or *mind*, singular. Maybe they share one. I glance at the door wondering when Bruce is going to show up. Is that why they're making small talk? Are they killing time till Bruce arrives?

"What else did you do on the road trip?" Chad inquires.

"We visited some amusement parks and rode some roller coasters."

Chad cracks up. "Roller coasters! You need to include a lot of roller coasters in your road trip show."

They seem excited, so I take that as a good sign.

Chad clears his throat and rubs his hands together. "We are so glad you're here. So, so glad. We pride ourselves on all of our 'human' skills here at LGO," he says, stopping to draw air quotes. "We love the personal touch of being able to do these types of meetings in person."

Tad chimes in since they're tag-team executives. "It's like FaceTime. But the real face time."

They smack palms as they laugh at their own cleverness.

Tad turns back to me. "And we especially like this kind of repartee when we have news to share."

My chest plummets, and I grimace. They didn't say *good news*. They only said "news."

Chad scratches his jaw. "You see, we admire you so much and we love you so much and we have been so thrilled to work with you, and that's why we wanted you to know in person . . . that we're canceling the show." He shoots me the biggest smile of the day.

"What?" I ask in a tiny voice because his tone and his expression don't match the words. His face says happy and his mouth says, *We are screwing you over with a power drill up the wazoo.*

"We love it and we love you. But we have to cancel *Mars and Venus*."

The floor buckles beneath me.

Tad brings both hands to his chest like he's speaking from his heart. "Please know it has nothing to do with you and it's all about us."

Did he really use the "It's not you, it's me" line?

"You don't like the new direction?" I ask, confused and trying desperately to understand.

Tad chimes in. "We love it. We love it so much. But we still have to cancel it. At the end of the day, it just doesn't fit in the lineup anymore."

"But I thought you were waiting for six episodes?"

It's Chad's turn. "We were, and we just love it so much. But you know how it goes. The show is all that," he says, snapping his fingers, "but we need a little more of *this*."

"Can I get you more of *this*?" I ask, and I hate the way my voice borders on begging. But I would do anything to save this show and to save myself.

"Interesting idea. More of *this*," Tad says, nodding, like he's considering it. But then he shakes his head. "Let's think about *that*."

"That?" I ask, wondering what the hell we're talking about now.

"We love you, and we want to work with you. We want the first look at your new road trip show. Write *that* and give us some of *that*. That would be so, so, so fantastic."

My entire body runs cold like they've thrust me into a freezer.

I blink and fight back tears, remembering *A League of Their Own*. There's no crying in baseball.

"Where's Bruce?" I ask, gingerly, so I don't spill tears as I speak.

Tad laughs.

Chad chortles. "We love Bruce. So much. But we did have to let him go yesterday."

Tad rises and extends a hand. "So glad we could do this in person. Do you want a vitamin water on your way out?"

I shake my head. I've been whiplashed into cancellation. I have to get as far away from this place as possible. I text Tom and hustle my way out of the spaceship, holding in all the waterworks till the revolving door kicks me out into the hazy sunshine of the Los Angeles street.

Tom is speaking in tongues.

Or maybe it's movie quotes. It sounds vaguely like *Splash*, but it feels like Russian, and I can barely comprehend a word.

All I can hear is the echo of that conversation with the Twins. All I can feel is the hollow space in my chest, like someone has excavated my hopes and dreams with a bulldozer.

It's over.

My show is over.

My baby, my dream, my passion.

My *job*.

I've been chopped off at the knees, and I have no clue how this happened or why they led me on like this.

"Are you okay?"

I swallow, but I can't get words past the river rapids in my throat. I've cried countless times, but the tears welling inside me are geyser-strength. Part of me wants to let them rain down and cry all over Tom, but another part says no effing way.

And I don't know why.

I don't understand why I can't let go in front of him. We can drive and laugh and screw and kiss and talk and dare and dream.

But I can't, or I won't, cry in front of him.

These almost-tears are a hard knot in my throat that wants to untangle.

"Finley, talk to me. What happened?"

"They canceled my show," I blurt out, and he wraps his arms around me and pulls me in for a hug. As he holds me, says things to try to soothe me, I realize why I'm strangling back tears.

I don't know *what* we are.

Yes, he's a friend.

Yes, I've been his bedmate.

But am I his girlfriend or his rebound or his one-week lover?

I don't know who we are or what we're doing or where we're going. I desperately want him to love me the way I love him, but he hasn't said it and I haven't said it, and I can't take another pummeling right now.

I want him to be my rock, but I don't know if we are each other's rock. I want to blurt out, "Hold me and tell me it'll be okay because we have each other," but we aren't there yet. He's still on the road to amend his past, and I've been kicked back to the starting line.

"Why would they cancel it?" he asks quietly.

"I don't know. Bruce wasn't even there. I have to call him and see what's going on. They said he doesn't work there anymore."

He sighs sadly, running his hands down my back. "I'm sorry, Finley. I don't even know what to say."

"Me either," I whisper, my voice cracking.

"I feel responsible too. Since I was trying to help you."

I shake my head, giving him a sharp stare. "No. Don't you do that. Don't you dare think that. It wasn't your fault."

"We were on such a roll, it seemed."

"You were amazing. You were incredible. You were inspiring. It's not your fault they have the emotional intelligence of a gnat. Yes, one gnat between them."

He smiles faintly.

I swallow harshly, wiping a hand across my face. I take a deep breath and try to collect myself. "Did you say something about a fish a few minutes ago?"

He waves a hand. "It was nothing."

I blink. "Nothing? I thought it was *Splash*," I say, and I try to remember a line about fish, but honestly, there were probably a lot of lines about fish in a mermaid movie, so . . .

I meet his eyes, searching for something.

Anything.

But I feel nothing except misery, so it's hard for me to see beyond the blur of self-loathing. I want to fall into his arms. I want to tell him I'm crazy about him, but more than that, I want to curl up into a ball.

I need a rock.

I need a 100 percent certified, no-questions-asked rock.

Briefly, I think of Christine, and I know she'd be there for me. But there's someone else I need right now.

Someone I haven't been honest with about my career. Someone I should be starkly truthful with.

My father.

The instant I think of him, the tears start to fall. I swipe at my cheeks, futilely trying to wipe the evidence away. "I think I need to go. See my dad. Be alone. Wallow in Chunky Monkey."

Tom is quiet at first, like he's digesting this news. "Sure. Right. Of course."

I glance around, like I can find a porthole and teleport back to Hope Falls.

Then I see it. A sign at the end of the street. A green street sign indicating we aren't far from the Burbank airport.

"You need to go see Cassie. Doesn't she have a yoga class this afternoon?" I ask since we called the studio earlier in the week to check her teaching schedule. "I know I said I would help you, but I don't think I can handle it right now. Is that okay?" I ask, seeking absolution.

"Of course," he says, waving a hand like it's no big deal. "Honestly, I should do it on my own."

A slight twinge of jealousy pinches my chest since he'll be alone with her in a few hours. But I do my best to sidestep the envy, since I need to go. "Good. Yeah. You've totally got it under control," I say, punching his arm, like he's an old buddy, old pal.

He pretends to wince, rubbing the spot where I hit him. "It's under control."

"I'm going to see if I can get on a Southwest flight. They're practically like buses back to San Francisco."

He points a finger at me, like he's approving my

plan. "Great idea. I should try to catch a flight back from San Diego tonight. I can drop the rental at that airport."

"That's a great idea too," I say, and I can't even deal with how much I hate the way I'm acting like this is all such a fantastic plan.

As he drives me to the airport a mile away, I call Bruce's number. But it goes to voicemail. He must be so embarrassed by me. I bet the failure of my show played a part in him losing his job. I hang up without leaving a message.

"I'm sorry the trip ended early."

He shakes his head. "It had to end eventually."

He's talking about the road trip, but he might as well be talking about us. We aren't slated to be a long-term thing. We were always a road trip affair. I inhale sharply, fighting off a new round of waterworks.

When we reach the airport, he pulls up to the DEPARTURES sign, the engine idling. For a fleeting moment, I consider blurting out the truth of my heart. *I love you, this hurts so much, come see me tonight and make it better.*

But I can't bear any other answer but yes, so I don't take the risk of a no.

"So I'll see you in San Francisco some time?" I ask.

He holds my gaze for a beat, like he's studying me. "Yeah, sure. Sounds fun."

Sounds fun?

That's all I get? *Sounds fun?*

The security guy on the sidewalk brings a megaphone to his mouth and shouts at us, "Move along!"

I reach for him, dot a kiss on his cheek, and leave. I

trudge inside, defeated, and buy a ticket for the next flight home.

After I go through security, I call my dad.

"When do you leave for your trip?" I choke out.

"Later tonight."

"I'm sad. I need to see you."

"Of course, sweet pea. I'm driving toward San Francisco now. I was going to run a few errands in the city before my flight tonight. Meet me for a bite to eat?"

We make plans, and I turn off my phone and board my plane, wishing I knew where I was heading.

26

TOM

The traffic gods shine on me.

That's about the only good thing I can say for the next few hours as I head south to my final stop.

Mostly the drive sucks, since I messed up.

I said the wrong thing. Or I didn't say the right thing. Or maybe I didn't say enough.

I have seriously failed at romance once again.

I replay the revolving door bit when Finley left the network and I somehow thought that was the perfect moment to line-drop *Splash* on her. What the hell was I thinking? Honestly, it's not even a romantic quote unless you know the film cold. It's like I reverted to another version of me, the one who says her hair is fine, who tells her he doesn't want to sleep with her, who croons to the wrong woman.

The guy who says the wrong thing at the wrong time.

Because I'm pretty sure you don't say "I love you like you're a fish" when she just learns she HAS NO JOB.

But I know this—I can ask for help. As I cruise along the highway, I call Ransom and give him a basic overview. "I feel like I messed up because I was trying to help her with her show, and then, in the end, it all went belly up."

He sighs sympathetically. "Man, it sucks when your woman gets bad news and you don't know what to do to help her."

I flinch. My woman? "She's not my woman. Not yet, at least."

"What? You said you were into her."

"Yeah. Just a little bit."

"What's the problem, then? Why isn't she yours? Did she turn you down?"

I wince, and this is the real eff-up. I didn't tell her how I feel. "Um . . . she doesn't know?"

Ransom is quiet for a moment. But soon, he hoots. He hollers, and he laughs. "Hold on. Be right back."

A few seconds later, he clicks back, and he's patched in the peanut gallery.

"You asked us to help you," Nash sing-songs.

"And we're helping you," Gannon chimes in.

"This is brotherly love and wisdom all at once," Ransom adds.

Then together, as if they'd practiced it, they shout: "You're a dipshit!"

I roll my eyes. "Thanks, dickheads. Can you see me flipping you the bird as I drive?"

"Nope. Can't make it out, since you're in the doghouse for having no balls," Nash says.

"Do you need help finding them, so you can tell her you love her?" Gannon offers, in a mock-serious tone.

"All right, fine. I get it. But it's not that easy."

Ransom cuts in. "It absolutely is."

As I hit the blinker for Cassie's exit, I privately disagree. It's not easy at all because I'm not done. I need to finish my shit before I can move forward. I need to close the door on the past before I can reach for the future.

"I need to go," I say to the dickheads I love, since the GPS lady is telling me how to find Cassie.

"Tell her about it," Gannon croons, channeling Billy Joel.

"Are you singing to me now?"

"Sometimes it's not the movies you need," Nash says, and he's right.

But at this moment, I need to do something without a script and without lyrics. I pull onto the stretch of block that houses Cassie's studio, park, cut the engine, and end the call.

I head inside and ask the blonde pixie at the counter when Cassie's done with class. She's not the one who answers me.

"I'm all done. How can I help?"

I turn and set my eyes on the woman I thought I loved.

27

FINLEY

I'm twenty-nine years old, I don't have a job, I don't have a man, and I'm crying on my father's shoulder in a taco shop in the Mission District. The salsa here is so good it can induce tears of joy, but that's not why I'm bawling.

"What's wrong, sweet pea?"

"I'm a big, fat, stinking, stupid liar," I say as Dad wraps his strong arms around me, petting my hair.

"What do you mean? This isn't the best taco shop in the city?"

That's where I told him to meet me for a late lunch, which has turned into an early dinner because my plane was three hours delayed. When I sank onto the seat across from him, an iced tea waiting and peppy Latin music playing, I let the tears fall. He'd wordlessly moved to my side and patiently waited for the worst to pass.

When I'm done, I wipe my cheeks. "My show was cancelled."

He looks crestfallen. "Oh no, I'm so sorry."

I shake my head and take a deep, fortifying breath. I need to put on my big girl pants. "But that's not the big issue."

"It's not?"

I brace myself for something I thought would be hard, but at the moment of truth, the words come remarkably easily. Because my dad doesn't judge, and he's never put me down. He doesn't treat me like I'm second or third best. I can tell him, and he won't be disappointed in me. He'll be disappointed *with* me.

"It's been hanging on by a thread for weeks, Dad."

He shoots me a confused look. "It has? I thought they loved it."

"The ratings suck, it's been on the fence, and I didn't want to tell you how close it was to being canceled."

"Why not?" he asks so gently, so sweetly, that I know I should have told him sooner.

"Because you were finally happy. Or at least you weren't sad," I say, sniffling.

He hands me a tissue, and I realize he has a packet in his messenger bag for his trip. "Do you have allergies?"

"No, I have a daughter who's sad, so I stocked up."

I smile at that, at how well he knows me, at how good he is at being my dad. "I've been a bad daughter."

He scoffs. "Never. You've never been a bad kid." He tucks a finger under my chin. "And I want you to know you can tell me when things aren't perfect. You can lean on me when you're feeling down or when you need anything at all. I'm so lucky you've helped me through a tough time. I don't know what I'd have done without you, but it's not your job to worry about me." He taps his chest. "It's mine to worry about you."

"But I do worry about you. You miss her so much," I say, my voice breaking for him, for his still-broken heart.

"I do, but I'm going to be fine. I have Mister Dog, and my kids and my friends and all the ballparks." He offers a sympathetic smile. "And I know you weren't that close with your mom. I know you had a complicated relationship with her. But she was hard on you because she was worried life would be too tough if you chose a creative career."

I scoff. "It hasn't been easy."

"Maybe she didn't always show it in the best of ways, or at all. But I feel certain she'd be proud of you. As proud as I am."

My throat hitches. I love him. I love my dad so much, and with his words, he makes it easier for me to let go of some of the lingering hurt over my mom. "Thank you."

"Now tell me about the show and what happened."

I take a deep breath. This is going to require food fortification. Good thing this really is the best taco shop in the city.

Over nachos and salsa and iced tea, I tell him how my show unraveled. I tell him everything I didn't say before. He pats my hand, listens, and offers a sympathetic ear. He does what he has always done. He supports me.

"I should have told you sooner."

"Yes, you should have. But I'm glad you're telling me now."

"Me too." I take a drink of the iced tea. "What do I do now?"

"You cry if you want. You talk to me or to Christine. And you go back to the drawing board. You've tucked some money away, you're not going to starve, and you're a damn good comedy writer. You'll write another show for another network. I don't doubt it."

He's always believed in me, and it's the most wonderful feeling in the world. The only feeling better than this is . . .

I dismiss the thought.

But I can't, because my father poses another question. "Now, what does your *friend* think?"

I furrow my brow. "Christine?"

He shakes his head. "The guy you're in love with."

My jaw comes unhinged and lands on the tile floor of the taco shop. I pick it up and ask, "How do you know that?"

"It was kind of obvious when you left on a road trip with him," he says, giving me an I-know-these-things smile.

"Was it?"

"Completely."

I sigh heavily. "He was supportive. He encouraged me. He offered to help."

"Sounds like he's in love with you too."

I sit bolt upright. Is he? Does Tom feel the same?

I cycle back, replaying the last few days, starting with the way he invited me on the road trip, how hard he tried to ask in just the right way. I flash back to the morning he picked me up wearing a new shirt he thought was cool. A shirt he probably wanted me to like.

I flip ahead to the drive, to the snacks he picked and the playlist he made. The *gift* he made that was utterly perfect.

He listened to me. He learned all the things I liked.

He didn't sledgehammer his way through anything. He paid attention to everything.

In Santa Cruz on the boardwalk, we walked and talked. At the artichoke diner, he asked about my exes. He told me the guy who said I chatted too much was wrong. Tom likes talking with me, and we talk about every single thing.

That's how we've come to know each other. How he knew exactly what to do to impress me—finding the couple to play along with the Spot-the-Tropes game.

My heart jitterbugs around in my chest as I recall each thing with crystal clarity—moments that led to the way I feel now, to how we touch, to the words he said the last night in the hotel room.

The best thing that's ever happened to me was you being at that window.

My whole body warms at the memory of those words, and I'm floating.

Because it's the same for me.

The best thing that's ever happened to me was him being at the window, singing badly on my front lawn. It's the best thing because I fell in love with someone who loves me for me.

It doesn't matter that I'm twenty-nine and unemployed. It doesn't matter that he hasn't said he loves me yet. None of that matters. I love that man, even if a week ago he thought he wanted someone else.

I'm pretty sure he wants me now.

But I'm 100 percent positive I want him, and that's why I need to fight like hell to win him.

God, I love the power of nachos, a good cry, and a great father to lean on. Now all I need to do is figure out how to make Tom mine.

28

TOM

Her ponytail still bounces. Her nose is still tiny. Her eyes are still green.

She's still the kind, thoughtful girl, and I know that too, because she smiles at me then holds her arms out wide. "Kyler Sutcliffe, what on earth are you doing here? It's so great to see you."

She strides over to me on bare feet and pulls me in for an embrace in the center of her studio lobby, surrounded by candles and meditation books.

"Good to see you too," I say, relieved that she's not tossing incense or yoga bricks in my direction.

She hugs hard and purposefully, and I feel nothing romantic, nothing physical.

It's merely a hug from an old friend. It's not a contact high from an old lover, and I honestly didn't think it would be. But I like the confirmation that there's nothing here. How could there be when my heart belongs to someone else?

When we separate, Cassie smiles and waits.

The greeting is over, and it's my turn to take care of business.

I'm nervous, but not. I'm excited, but not. Mostly, I'm determined to fix a mistake and move on.

I square my shoulders. "Any chance we could speak privately someplace?"

"Sure, I have a minute between classes." She guides me to one of her studios and spreads out a mat on the floor for me. I sit cross-legged on it. She pretzels herself into a bendy position. "So . . . I can only assume you're here since the Honey Sticks got back together."

I laugh, glad the tension is eased. "But of course." I clear my throat. "So, listen. I've been taking stock of some things lately and assessing my life," I say, then I hear how it comes out, and I sound like a douche. If I were listening to me, I'd tell myself to be straightforward. "Let me start over. I was a dick when we broke up. I was a dick after we slept together. I was a stupid twenty-year-old, and I didn't have a clue, so I sent that dumb text and you were right to dump me and I didn't realize it till a few days ago, so I came to say I'm sorry."

Her face is impassive at first, her eyes narrowed, but the wheels are turning. Then she laughs lightly. "That's what you wanted to say? You're sorry?"

"Yes, I was an ass, and I deserved to be dumped."

She laughs, patting my knee. "You were an ass, but I forgave you long ago, and I swear I'm all good now."

"But you said that thing on a blog about a bad relationship?"

"My blog? I wrote that years ago. I was sad and frustrated, and I didn't like how it ended. But I moved on. I'm so happy now, and I feel good about myself. I love my life and my practice and my friendships. I also think it's amazing you came to say what you said to me. It's rare. So few people do, and I appreciate it. But you don't have to worry. Now, tell me, what are you up to?"

And that's it. That's all. It's easy.

I've said my piece, and the burden's been lifted.

I don't need to hold on to it anymore, but I'm so glad I made my way down here. It was the right thing to do. Cassie's not holding a grudge, and I learned a valuable lesson. Don't retreat. Speak your mind with kindness and grace.

Be a man.

And that's exactly what I should do with Finley.

Answering Cassie's question, I tell her what I've been up to, including Finley and including the fateful night with the boom box outside Cassie's Airbnb property.

She laughs and smiles and whistles, and then she shakes her head. "She sounds fantastic."

"She is. She's incredible. It's crazy and random, but it's perfect in its own way too."

"You need to do whatever it takes to keep her, Kyler," she says, her tone serious.

"I do."

"She's a winner. A woman who'd do that for you? Who'd help you win someone else? She's the real deal."

"She definitely is."

She tilts her head to the side as if considering. "If you really want to move on, you ought to do things differently starting now. Tell her you love her before it's too late. Don't let her slip away."

I jump up. "Shit, you're right. You're absolutely right."

It's *When Harry Met Sally*. When you realize you want to spend the rest of your life with someone, you want the rest of your life to start right now.

And I know how to do it. It's not rocket science. It's not a script. It's listening. Finley told me how to do it herself the first night we went to dinner.

Keep it simple. Knock on her door. Send her a note. Heck, send her flowers and ask her if she'd like to go out . . . Speak from the heart, not a script.

Now all I need is to get out of town.

29

FINLEY

If this were a movie, I'd gather the troops, scurry across San Francisco in a tiny car, shout "go, go, go" at the traffic lights, and race breathlessly to the finish line, praying the clock hadn't run out.

But this is real life. My needs are simple. Office supplies and information. Office supplies are easy. Information is hard. Searching on my phone, I scan my options, frustration digging in at the endless list of possibilities.

I might as well throw a dart to pin the tail on the donkey.

"You could just ask," my dad suggests as we turn into the parking lot near the airport.

I scoff at him, rolling my eyes dramatically. "What's the fun in that?"

"Getting an answer and doing this properly," he suggests, deadpan.

"Fine," I grumble.

He is right, so I text Tom and ask what time he

expects to arrive. But he doesn't reply. Is he in the air already? Is he ignoring me? Is he with Cassie?

My dad leaves his car in off-site parking so he can pick it up in a week when he returns, and we grab a shuttle bus to the terminal. I give him a hug at security and wave as he weaves through the checkpoint.

Then I turn on my heel and get to work on the next thing I need to do.

I'm jobless, but I'm no longer hopeless.

30

TOM

As I board the plane in San Diego, I calculate the time it'll take me to drive to Hope Falls. My car is at my house in the city. I can Uber over to Fillmore Street and then cruise along the highway heading north into wine country. It's 5:05 now. I land at 7:15. I'll be in my car by 7:50, and I could be at her house by about 9:20.

I do need to pick up flowers, but I reason I can grab some at the airport, and I don't think Finley will mind if I bring her airport flowers. She doesn't want a big production anyway. I know what she wants. She wants my heart, and she has it, absolutely. All I have to do is tell her.

But I figure I should probably start by letting her know I'm on my way. She'll appreciate the heads-up, and I don't want to leave anything to chance.

I find my seat in the eighth row, stuff my bag in the overhead bin, and open my text messages to start one to her.

A burst of excitement shoots off in my chest when I

find a note from her. It's the simplest question, but hope rises in me that maybe we're on the same page.

Finley: When do you arrive?

I write back instantly, but she doesn't reply—not for the next twenty minutes as the rest of the passengers board, not as we taxi, and not as we finally start to take off. At last, I turn my phone to airplane mode and hope I see her on the other side of the flight.

31

FINLEY

Why didn't he write back? Did he fall back in love with Cassie?

I cringe at that thought and howl at the moon.

But in my heart of hearts, I know he didn't fall in love with Cassie. He didn't go to San Diego to reconnect with her. He went there to earn a clean slate. I hope he has it. But I hope he sees my message too.

I pace through the terminal, and my mind whirs. Maybe I'll write about something like this for a new series. Maybe I'll do it for the Web. I'll get in touch with everyone I've worked with in the past. I'll reconnect with *Kiss and Tell*. I'll reach out to the late-night shows I've worked on. I'll cast a wide net. Bruce wasn't my only contact, and LGO isn't the only network familiar with my work.

I'm a writer. I write. I create. I have ideas. I observe life, and I spin my observations into humor. I will keep going even when I'm set back.

But the bigger, immediate setback is there are ten flights from San Diego arriving in the next three hours.

Then it hits me. What if he doesn't fly into San Francisco International? What if he flies into Oakland? I groan. I'm so screwed if that happens. There is no way I can hurry to the Oakland airport in time.

Grabbing my phone from my pocket, I stare at the empty screen once more. Why aren't there any messages from him?

I'm going to have to play *eeny, meeny, miny, moe* with these flights.

I find the flight board listing the incoming planes.

Shoot. There's one from San Diego that lands in ten minutes. Is that his flight?

Why won't he tell me?

Come to think of it, why won't anyone tell me anything? No one has written to me all day. I know I'm not the most popular person in the world right now, and I wasn't expecting to be besieged with messages or job offers, but I thought at the very least Old Navy would inform me about a discount paisley sweater set, and that hasn't even happened.

Then, a billboard flashing the word *dumbass* mocks me.

I turned on the Do Not Disturb function on my phone because I couldn't deal. I never turned it off. The only person I've seen today was my dad, and I called him.

I toggle the Do Not Disturb button to the right and wait.

In fifteen seconds, my phone is a slot machine, and I've

made it rain. The emails are cha-chinging, and so are the voicemails, but I don't care about either. Besides, the voicemails are probably from the dentist, reminding me that I have an appointment. I believe in staying on top of plaque.

But that's not the point. The point is—did anyone text me? And the answer is . . . yes. I jump. I squeal. I point at the screen.

Tom: Hey! I land at 7:15. Are you home tonight? I'd like to stop by.

I dance. I jig. I might even sashay. I want to shout to the sky, but then security would probably lock me up or toss me out, and that would ruin my entire plan.

I check the time.

It's 7:10. My pulse spikes. He'll be here in five minutes. I scan the flight boards. Where is the next flight from San Diego? I don't see it. Wait, wait, wait.

It landed early. Five minutes ahead of schedule, and it's not at terminal one. It's in terminal two and I'm in terminal one and they're ten miles apart.

Okay, not ten miles. A lot less.

But still.

Then I pep-talk myself.

This is why you've been training for a triathlon. It's not to swim, it's not to bike, it's to run across the airport from terminal one to terminal two.

With my office supplies tucked under my arm, I pick

up the pace. I run past airline counter after airline counter.

"Excuse me," I mutter when I weave around a mother holding the hands of two small toddlers.

"Sorry," I say as I dart by a woman dragging two gigantic wheeled suitcases.

I race around a man pushing a cart full of luggage. I speed down the hall to terminal two, faster and farther, and I beam.

This is the airport chase.

This is the last road-trip trope.

This is the one that never happens anymore because we can't hurtle security gates and stop flights.

But I'm not running to stop him. I'm running to him, fleet-footing it, flip-flops slapping against the floor, office supplies tucked under my arm.

"Slow down," a woman in an official-looking airplane uniform shouts at me.

"Late for a flight."

"Well, be careful."

"I will."

But the time for careful is long gone. I'm not trying to be careful. I'm trying to be brave.

It's big-gesture time, and big gestures aren't for sissies.

They're for women who dare to take chances.

When I reach terminal two, I rush to the security lines, checking the time.

His flight is here. Right next to the security exit is a small waiting area where passengers congregate to meet their loved ones. A glass wall runs from floor to ceiling with a view of the passengers as they walk to the exit.

I head over there, and I hope I haven't missed him. My heart beats jackrabbit-fast, and I'm bubbling with excitement.

Travelers on the other side stream toward the exit, weighed down with messenger bags and backpacks, with purses and garment bags, wheeling suitcases behind them and beside them. With every cell in my body, I wish upon a star that that's his flight.

I scan the crowd, hunting for him.

Brown floppy hair. Strong shoulders. A chiseled jaw. Panty-melting glasses. A bouquet of flowers in his hand.

My heart rises skyscraper high.

But he's staring at his phone. That won't do. I send him a text.

Finley: Look up!

32

TOM

I write back to my brothers, updating them as promised.

Me: The eagle has landed, and the fat man walks alone.
Also, I'm in San Francisco.

Nash: Get on it.

Ransom: No more dicking around.

Gannon: Report back. DO IT NOW.

Another text lands on the screen.
   A new one.
   A small firework ignites. When I see the message,
the firework shoots high: *Look up!*

I snap my gaze, and I wonder if my eyes are playing tricks on me.

Is that?

Her . . .?

Here . . .?

With poster boards?

Thirty feet away, Finley waves at me frantically. Her hair is wild, and her eyes are wide. A smile tugs at my lips as I pass a bookstore, speeding over to her. A white poster covers her from waist to neck. I can't make out what's on it till she slams it against the glass. Squinting, I peer at it, the words taking shape as I reach her.

You had me at . . .

She flips it.

The boom box.

I meet her blue eyes, and they're bright and twinkling. She drops the first board and switches to the next one.

I'm just a girl, standing in front of a boy, asking him to . . .

She turns it over.

. . .

Laugh with her.

My smile is too wide to be contained as she places the next one against the glass.

I wanted it to be you.

My heart thumps at the tweaked *You've Got Mail* line, along with the *Jerry Maguire* redo, and the *Notting Hill* adjustment. It continues on the other side.

I wanted it to be you so badly that . . . I'm big-gesturing.

The final poster is simple, with her nod to *Ghost*.

Ditto.

She slaps it over.

P.S. I love you.

. . .

I feel like the sun. My heart soars. This is the real thing. Heart, mind, and body. I mouth to her, *I love you so much.*

She's such a complete goofball, and she's a fantastically imperfect person, who's perfect for me. I'm tempted to put my fingers against the glass, but that would tip the level of cheese to blue, and I can't stand blue cheese. But I do love this woman.

Like the kind of love in the movies. Only better because it's real.

With the bouquet of flowers in my hand, I jog then run through the exit and into the terminal. She rushes out of the waiting area, and I scoop her up in my arms as she tosses the posters to the ground.

She wraps her legs around my hips, clasps her hands to my face and grins.

"I'm so in love with you," I tell her.

"I am so in love with you."

Then I kiss the girl.

Everything is real, and everything is extraordinary. This is the moment when the curtain falls, the music swells, and the credits roll.

It's like the movies, but it's better. We get to live the next part.

33

TOM

I hand her the flowers after I set her down. "I didn't want to come to you empty-handed. But you kinda beat me to it with your big gesture."

She smiles. "I know. But in my defense, we really needed an airport scene in our romance."

I drape an arm around her, keeping her close as we head to the exit. "We had to do one."

"When else will we have the opportunity to participate in an airport chase?"

"You better not do an airport chase with anybody but me."

"I don't want to do an airport chase with anybody but you."

"Also, have I mentioned I'm in love with you?"

She dusts a kiss to my cheek. "I think you did, but I feel like it's the kind of thing I can hear over and over."

"I'm in love with you," I tell her again, and soon we're making out in the back seat of our Uber.

Thirty minutes later, we arrive at my home. I drop my bags in the entryway. "Can I give you the tour?"

She shakes her head. "I don't want the tour."

"What do you want?"

"I want you . . ." Her voice trails off and her eyes drift down. "To take off your pants."

"Pants are dumb."

We don't make it to the bedroom. We barely make it to my living room, where I strip her naked and she climbs on top of me, straddling me. When I slide up into her, I groan, close my eyes, and let the sensations wash over me.

This woman came into my life in the most unexpected way, and I'm going to do everything I can to keep her for all my days. Fortunately, I've learned how to do that.

She likes to talk, and I finally learned how to listen.

* * *

Later, we lie on my couch watching clips from *Splash*. "See? That's the line I was saying earlier, you big dork. You totally missed it."

"Well, I was a little upset. Also, were you calling me a fish?"

"That is seriously one of the most romantic things ever. *'All my life, I've been waiting for someone, and when I find her, she's . . . she's a fish.'*"

"We might disagree on the romance of the fish line."

"Don't you get it? I'm madly in love with you even if you're a fish."

"Our love transcends species? You're a little crazy."

She kisses the tip of my nose. "But you're my kind of crazy."

"You're my kind of crazy too." I run my hand through her curls. "By the way, I saw Cassie and apologized to her. Thank you for encouraging me to do it. It was like a weight lifting, and I also told her all about you."

She smiles, like this intel delights her. "You did?"

I nod proudly. "Told her I met this girl I was crazy about. And I am." I kiss her forehead, whispering softly, making sure she feels 100 percent secure in us. "Completely crazy in love."

I'm kissing her again when her phone rings. "Ignore it," I tell her as I slide my hand up her belly.

She melts under my touch, but then her phone bleats one more time. "Let me check if it's my dad."

She reaches for it, and it's "Spam Likely" again. She rolls her eyes, then stops mid roll when a new text message pops up.

She gasps. "It's Bruce."

34

FINLEY

"You don't answer your phone anymore?" Bruce barks at me. He's always barked at me, and it's oddly reassuring.

"It was on Do Not Disturb."

"Am I a disturbance, Peaches?"

"I don't know," I say, laughing nervously, because I have no clue why he's calling.

"I called you last night," he says gruffly.

"I didn't see a missed call from you."

"It wasn't from my office line."

"Oh," I say, and I furrow my brow. "Maybe my phone thought it was spam."

"Maybe my phone thought it was spam," he says imitating me in a high-pitched tone.

"Look, Bruce, I appreciate that you tried to call to give me a heads-up about the Douche Twins, but I went in like a big girl, and I took my medicine."

"And how did it taste?"

"Bitter, awful, like failure, but such is life, and I'll move on. I'm grateful for everything you've done."

"If you'd checked your messages, it'd have tasted like sugar, Sweet Cheeks."

I sit up, curiosity piqued. "What are you talking about?"

"I've left you messages all day. Do you think after all we've been through, after I fought for your show, that I'd leave you high and dry?"

"They said you were let go," I say, trying to piece together the details.

He scoffs. "Don't trust those cats as far as you can pet them. I wasn't fired. I left."

"I'm glad it was your decision. Thank you for caring enough about me to call."

"I'm not that caring. I called because I'm strategic and cunning. And because I didn't toss you out with the trash. Want to know why I made you write those scripts solo? Without any help from the network's assistant writers? Why I pushed you to deliver them to me in a week?"

"Why?" My interest climbs to Mount Everest levels.

Tom watches me, wiggling his eyebrows in a question.

"One word."

I wait.

"*Netflix.*"

I suck in a breath. "Does that mean . . . ?"

"Sweet Cheeks, I took a job at Netflix. Network TV is for the history books. Netflix is the future. We're blowing this popsicle stand. I sold *Mars and Venus* to Netflix. They bought the rights to the first season, and they made you an offer on a thirteen-episode renewal for season two."

I scream like I'm falling at sixty-six miles an hour on a roller coaster.

"I think you pierced my eardrums. Also, they don't fuck around. They love the episodes, and they want the rest of them in a month. It'll go into production this summer. Premiere in the fall. You're welcome."

"Thank you," I say, overjoyed.

"Also, why don't you make sure my personal cell isn't in your spam folder anymore? Do me that solid. I don't like it when I can't reach my star."

He hangs up and I turn to Tom. "He called me his star," I whisper in wonder, then I tell him the news.

"I always believed in you."

I slide my hands into his hair. "Thank you for being my muse, and for being everything else too."

When he kisses me once more, I know.

This is no rebound. I'm his everything girl.

35

FINLEY

A few weeks later

My dad tosses a tennis ball across the dog park. Mister Dog fetches it in seconds and brings it back stat.

He drops it at my dad's feet and stares pointedly at it, panting.

"This dog knows what he wants," I remark.

"He sure does." My dad picks up the ball and tosses it again, Mister Dog scampering happily to the green object of his affection. "Hey, do you think you could write him into your new show? He asked me when you're going to have a dog character."

Laughing, I grab the ball this time when the faithful pooch returns it. "Now that's an excellent idea. You know that line from *Shakespeare in Love*, after all?"

My dad lifts a brow in question. "Can't say I do."

"'*Comedy, love, and a bit with a dog. That's what they want,*'" I say, quoting from the Oscar winner.

He nods sagely. "Sounds about right."

Yes, I'd say it sure does, and I make a mental note as I say goodbye and hop on my bike to talk to Tom about adopting a dog someday.

I'm going to see him later, since he's driving up here tonight. First, though, I want to get him a gift. I ride over to Lucky Falls, stopping at A New Chapter. Once inside, I say hello to Arden, who's at the register, her blonde hair in a pretty French twist.

"Hey, sexy thing," I say.

"Oh, please."

"The hair looks good. Also, I'm looking for a cool new book on astrophysics. Something for the hot nerd in my life who's already read all the big, popular science books."

"I know exactly what you'll want, then, for the science *lover* in your life," she says with a wink and a definite emphasis on "lover." She knows about Tom, and knows we're together now.

She recommends a book that Stephen Hawking fans are loving, so I snag a copy and plop it on the counter. I tap my chin. "But maybe I should get something for myself too. What's the best story that you've read lately?"

Arden casts her gaze down, then glances around. The coast is clear. "I've been reading up on all sorts of naughty things."

My eyes widen. "You have? Spill the deets."

She brings me closer, waving her fingers towards me. Her cheeks go the slightest tinge of pink. "Confession. My reading last night consisted of *Fifty Ways to Spice Up Your Love Life*."

"Whoa. You're not just a sexy thing. You're a naughty girl." I lower my voice to a whisper. "Tell me everything. What did you learn?"

"I even made a list of all the naughty things that I want to do."

I'm salivating for details. "Who is this man that you're going to try these things with? Do you have a new guy?"

She shakes her head. "No. I'm not with anyone. But I do have somebody I want to ask to help me explore these things."

"Oh, like a Lessons in Seduction trope?" I ask, digging into my basket of tropes and bringing out one of my favorites. "Because that's a kick-ass one. You can do so much with it."

Arden laughs. "Yes, I suppose that's what it would be."

"And who is this somebody?"

"My good friend Gabe. We talk about everything, so I think he'll be willing, but the most important part is that I figured out a way that we can do this to preserve our friendship. They're going to be unconventional lessons."

"What makes them so unconventional?"

She lowers her voice another notch. "They're going to be hypothetical."

That piques my interest even more. "That's intriguing. How will you manage that? Is it like a workshop? A class?"

Laughing, she answers, "Sort of. But it sounds like the perfect way to preserve a friendship while still learning all the things I want to learn about the opposite sex, right? Sure, Gabe is gorgeous and sexy and fun, and we're great friends, but I don't see why it should be a problem at all to have hypothetical, hands-off lessons."

I don't tell her that sounds like she'll be facing all sorts of temptations. I'll let her figure that out for herself. "I can't wait to hear how it turns out."

That night, after I greet Tom at the door, there's nothing hypothetical about what we do on the couch, on the kitchen counter, and later, much later, after an evening of delicious conversation, discussions about dogs, and lots of laughter . . . in my bed.

EPILOGUE

Tom

One Year Later

We're in Singapore. It's opening day for my client, the billionaire real estate investor who bought a theme park and commissioned a new roller coaster, The Big Fall.

I introduce Finley to Keith at the ribbon cutting.

"It's a pleasure to meet you," the polished and poised Keith says to her, kissing the top of her hand.

"And you, as well."

"Mr. Sutcliffe talks about you so much, and it is an honor to meet the woman who has captured his heart. I hope you enjoy your first ride on the roller coaster."

"I know we will," she says.

After a photo shoot before the ride, it's our turn to get in line. "This time we don't have to ride it like civilians," she says.

We're at the head of the line, and I take her hand.

The last year with her has been a whirlwind. We did the drive-back-and-forth thing for about a month between her town and San Francisco. We both have flexible jobs, so I moved to Hope Falls, and we bought a bigger home.

It's right off Main Street, and near her dad too—who, for the record, is one of the coolest guys I've ever met. I like living here. It's close to Lucky Falls, so we pop over there often, where Finley visits her favorite bookstore to see her friend Arden, and I get to hang out with Gabe. It seems Arden has something going on with my cousin. Finley likes to whisper ideas and possibilities about what's up between them, speculating on whether they are dating or not. I have a hunch she's using them for inspiration for another show.

But that's a story for another time.

I also like living in Hope Falls, because I can see Nash at his nearby restaurant and give him hell for everything and anything. Plus, I have plenty of time and space to do my work. Much of it takes me on the road, but when I come home, I come home to Finley.

That is, when she's in town.

Her show has taken off. Turned out, all she needed was a company that believed in her, and she found that in Netflix. It's been a huge hit and was recently nominated for an Emmy for Best Comedy Series.

Mars and Venus is pretty fucking funny, if I do say so myself, especially that episode when they take off on the road trip. But I'd change a few things. After all, Amanda and Lane still aren't together. I guess it's true that romantic tension sells. The longer they stay apart, the more the audience wants them to fall into each other's arms.

In fact, the audience likes it so much that Netflix signed her to write another show.

I couldn't be prouder of her, and she couldn't be happier. The woman lives and loves to tell jokes and to make audiences feel all the things.

But today isn't the time for jokes. It's our turn to ride one of the badass-est of badass coasters I've designed.

Finley and I take our seats, and the shoulder bars secure us in place.

The car chugs out of the station, the clanking begins, and she smiles at me. A few seconds later, we drop, and it's a hell of a fall. A stomach-in-your-throat, blood-curdling spill that turns into a wild loop the loop.

It's terrifying and thrilling at the same time.

Sort of like falling in love.

When the ride rolls into the station two minutes later, she's breathing hard and smiling as wide as the sky.

"Did you like it?"

"I loved it."

"Did I ever tell you the best part of the ride?'

She shakes her head. "No, tell me."

"Keith didn't know what to call it, so he let me name it."

"You named it? That's amazing."

"I named it for you," I add as Keith walks past the car as it slows, tucking something important into my hand, as we planned.

"You did?"

"You once said it would be a good idea to name a

roller coaster after the woman you love. I picked the Big Fall because that's how I feel about you and about us."

The nerves dissipate as I reach for her hand once the car stops fully and the shoulder straps rise. I'm not worried. I'm only hopeful as I turn to her. "That's how I'll always feel about you. I love you more than a boom box outside a window, more than a man loves a mermaid, and more than I ever thought I would love anyone. Will you marry me?"

I open the box, showing her a bright, shining solitaire.

She clasps her hand to her mouth, crying and nodding. Twisting in the roller-coaster seat, she throws her arms around my neck. "Yes. I will marry you, and can we go bungee jumping too?"

"I dare you to," I whisper.

"And I accept."

THE END

Want more Tom and Finley? Sign up here to receive a bonus scene sent straight to your inbox! If you've already signed up for my list, be sure to sign up again! It's the only way to receive the bonus scene, but rest assured you won't be double subscribed to the list!

Also, if you're eager to dive into Gabe and Arden's love story, grab BEST LAID PLANS!! And escape into a sexy, witty, lessons-in-seduction rom-com with a twist!

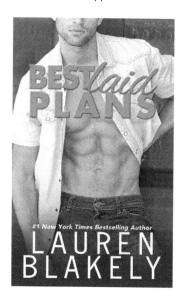

Next up is a fabulous standalone called BIRTHDAY SUIT!

There's only one rule a man should never break: Absolutely, no matter how beautiful, smart, clever and witty she is, do not–under any circumstances–fall in love with your best friend's woman.

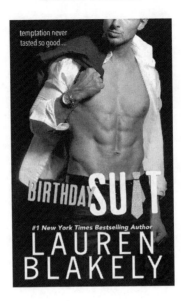

ALSO BY LAUREN BLAKELY

FULL PACKAGE, the #1 New York Times Bestselling romantic comedy!

BIG ROCK, the hit New York Times Bestselling standalone romantic comedy!

MISTER O, also a New York Times Bestselling standalone romantic comedy!

WELL HUNG, a New York Times Bestselling standalone romantic comedy!

JOY RIDE, a USA Today Bestselling standalone romantic comedy!

HARD WOOD, a USA Today Bestselling standalone romantic comedy!

THE SEXY ONE, a New York Times Bestselling bestselling standalone romance!

THE HOT ONE, a USA Today Bestselling bestselling standalone romance!

THE KNOCKED UP PLAN, a multi-week USA Today and Amazon Charts Bestselling bestselling standalone romance!

MOST VALUABLE PLAYBOY, a sexy multi-week USA Today

Bestselling sports romance! And its companion sports romance, MOST LIKELY TO SCORE!

THE V CARD, a USA Today Bestselling sinfully sexy romantic comedy!

WANDERLUST, a USA Today Bestselling contemporary romance!

COME AS YOU ARE, a Wall Street Journal and multi-week USA Today Bestselling contemporary romance!

PART-TIME LOVER, a multi-week USA Today Bestselling contemporary romance!

UNBREAK MY HEART, an emotional second chance contemporary romance!

The Heartbreakers! The USA Today and WSJ Bestselling rock star series of standalone!

The New York Times and USA Today Bestselling Seductive Nights series including *Night After Night*, *After This Night*, and *One More Night*

And the two standalone romance novels in the Joy Delivered Duet, *Nights With Him* and Forbidden Nights, both New York Times and USA Today Bestsellers!

Sweet Sinful Nights, Sinful Desire, Sinful Longing and Sinful Love, the complete New York Times Bestselling high-heat romantic suspense series that spins off from Seductive Nights!

Playing With Her Heart, a USA Today bestseller, and a sexy

Seductive Nights spin-off standalone! (Davis and Jill's romance)

21 Stolen Kisses, the USA Today Bestselling forbidden new adult romance!

Caught Up In Us, a New York Times and USA Today Bestseller! (Kat and Bryan's romance!)

Pretending He's Mine, a Barnes & Noble and iBooks Bestseller! (Reeve & Sutton's romance)

Trophy Husband, a New York Times and USA Today Bestseller! (Chris & McKenna's romance)

Far Too Tempting, the USA Today Bestselling standalone romance! (Matthew and Jane's romance)

Stars in Their Eyes, an iBooks bestseller! (William and Jess' romance)

My USA Today bestselling No Regrets series that includes

The Thrill of It (Meet Harley and Trey)

and its sequel

Every Second With You

My New York Times and USA Today Bestselling Fighting Fire series that includes

Burn For Me (Smith and Jamie's romance!)

Melt for Him (Megan and Becker's romance!)

and *Consumed by You* (Travis and Cara's romance!)

The Sapphire Affair series...

The Sapphire Affair

The Sapphire Heist

Out of Bounds

A New York Times Bestselling sexy sports romance

The Only One

A second chance love story!

Stud Finder

A sexy, flirty romance!

.

CONTACT

I love hearing from readers! You can find me on Twitter at LaurenBlakely3, Instagram at LaurenBlakelyBooks, Facebook at LaurenBlakelyBooks, or online at LaurenBlakely.com. You can also email me at laurenblakelybooks@gmail.com

Made in the USA
Lexington, KY
30 January 2019